WH[ ]
THE
THRILL
IS
GONE

ALSO BY WALTER MOSLEY

WHEN THE THRILL IS GONE

WALTER MOSLEY

RIVERHEAD BOOKS
A MEMBER OF
PENGUIN GROUP (USA) INC.
NEW YORK
2011

RIVERHEAD BOOKS
Published by the Penguin Group
Penguin Group (USA) Inc., 375 Hudson Street, New York, New York 10014, USA •
Penguin Group (Canada), 90 Eglinton Avenue East, Suite 700, Toronto, Ontario M4P 2Y3,
Canada (a division of Pearson Penguin Canada Inc.) • Penguin Books Ltd, 80 Strand,
London WC2R 0RL, England • Penguin Ireland, 25 St Stephen's Green, Dublin 2,
Ireland (a division of Penguin Books Ltd) • Penguin Group (Australia), 250 Camberwell
Road, Camberwell, Victoria 3124, Australia (a division of Pearson Australia Group Pty
Ltd) • Penguin Books India Pvt Ltd, 11 Community Centre, Panchsheel Park, New Delhi–
110 017, India • Penguin Group (NZ), 67 Apollo Drive, Rosedale, North Shore 0632,
New Zealand (a division of Pearson New Zealand Ltd) • Penguin Books (South Africa)
(Pty) Ltd, 24 Sturdee Avenue, Rosebank, Johannesburg 2196, South Africa

Penguin Books Ltd, Registered Offices: 80 Strand, London WC2R 0RL, England

Library of Congress Cataloging-in-Publication Data

Mosley, Walter.
When the thrill is gone/ Walter Mosley.
p.   cm.
ISBN 978-1-59448-781-1
1. McGill, Leonid (Fictitious character)—Fiction.   2. Private investigators—
New York (State)—New York—Fiction.   3. Murder—Investigation—Fiction.
4. New York (N.Y.)—Fiction.   I. Title.
PS3563. O88456W45   2011   2010039098
813'.54—dc22

Printed in the United States of America
1   3   5   7   9   10   8   6   4   2

Book design by Stephanie Huntwork

This is a work of fiction. Names, characters, places, and incidents either are the product of
the author's imagination or are used fictitiously, and any resemblance to actual persons,
living or dead, businesses, companies, events, or locales is entirely coincidental.

While the author has made every effort to provide accurate telephone numbers and Internet
addresses at the time of publication, neither the publisher nor the author assumes any
responsibility for errors, or for changes that occur after publication. Further, the publisher
does not have any control over and does not assume any responsibility for author or third-
party websites or their content.

To Gary Phillips

The tenor sax of the noir genre

1

SOMEWHERE BEYOND my line of sight a man groaned, pathetically. It sounded as if he had reached the end of his reserves and was now about to die.

But I couldn't stop to see what the problem was. I was too deep into the rhythm of working the hard belly of the speed bag. That air-filled leather bladder was hitting its suspension plate faster than any basketball the NBA could imagine. Nothing in the world is more harmonizing than hitting the speed bag at three in the afternoon when most other workers are sitting in cubicles, dreaming of retirement, praying for Saturday, or finding themselves crammed-in down underground on subway cars, hurtling toward destinations they never bargained for.

Battling the speed bag, first with the heels of your gloved fists and then with a straight punch peppered in for variety, you hone the ability to go all the way, as far as you can; getting in close but never allowing the bag to slap you in the face. Then, after that hard leather sack is moving more rapidly than the eye can follow, your hips and thighs, neck and head begin to move quickly, unexpectedly, like water, unerring in its headlong rush over and around any obstacle, wearing down your imagined opponent with the inevitability of time.

And, as any boxer can tell you, time is always running out.

Anybody you get in the ring with you is bigger and stronger, the worst problem you evah had in your lazy life, Gordo would say when I was a young man, sweating hard and thinking that I might be a professional boxer one day. *The only chance you got is to wear him down, them fists like pistons and your head a movin' target. You use your skull and shoulders, stomach and spit, anything you can to keep him off balance. And the whole time your fists is at him, they don't even know how to stop.*

"Give me four more." The words came, and then a whining groan of agony.

"I can't," the bodiless voice pleaded.

"Four more!"

The strain audible in the ensuing grunt sounded like a man vomiting up his guts.

"My chest!" he cried. "It hurts!"

"You won't die," the torturer promised. It was more like a pledge of vengeance than any assurance of survival.

Without looking in their direction, I lowered my shuddering arms and headed for the showers. Pain is of no consequence in a gladiatorial gym; neither is blood or bruises, broken noses or concussions, unconsciousness, or even, now and then—death.

OF LATE I had been taking three ice-cold showers a day. Only that restorative chill, along with working the speed bag and a daily counting of breaths, kept me from going crazy. At fifty-five, I found that as life went on, the problems mounted and their solutions only served to make things worse.

I didn't have a case at that moment, which meant that no money was coming in. When I did get a job, that just meant somebody was going to come to harm, one way or the other—maybe both. And even then I might not collect my detective's fee.

A good friend was dying in my eleventh-floor apartment. My wife was having an affair with a man half her age. And those were just the devils I knew.

AFTER THE SHOWER I was so spent that it was all I could do to sit upright and naked on the little oak stool that had somehow made its way into the locker room. The groaning from the gym was constant as my muscles still quivered from the exertions of the midday workout session.

Rising to my feet was an act of faith. I had the feeling of being the last man left standing after a lifelong battle in a meaningless war.

THE CHUBBY, café au lait–colored young man was in the middle of failing at executing a sit-up. He looked like a giant drunken grub that had lost its sense of balance, writhing and then falling back with the impact of a heavy mattress on the concrete floor.

"Three more and you're through," Iran Shelfly said.

Tiny Bateman, dressed in a gray T-shirt and shiny aqua trunks, let his arms fall to the side looking to the world like a fat drunk lowered to the ground on the curb in front of his favorite bar. Above him stood a well-built copper-skinned young man with a shaved head and a perpetual grin on his lips. His mirth seemed more predatory than happy, but Iran was really trying to help Tiny out.

"Three more," Iran commanded.

"That's enough," I said.

Tiny sighed in relief.

"He only been at it a half-hour, boss," Iran complained.

"Tomorrow he'll make thirty-one minutes," I said. "Isn't that right, Bug?"

I held out a hand and Tiny "Bug" Bateman grabbed for it twice before making contact. I pulled him to his feet and he genuflected, putting his hands on his knees, blowing hard.

"Hit the showers, young man," I said to him but it was all he could do to keep upright and gasp.

So I turned to Iran.

The thirty-two-year-old had on navy sweatpants and a white T-shirt that molded his well-defined physique like melted wax. This was the body that a stint in prison sculpted for you: either you were ready to kick ass or you got it kicked. He was five ten—four and half inches over me—and tense in spite of his lying grin.

"How's it goin', Eye Ran," I said, pronouncing the name as he did.

"It'll be eleven years before I put him in the ring," the bright-skinned young thief opined, "with a girl half his weight."

"I mean you. How you doin'?"

"Gym's goin' great," he said evasively. "Everybody's paid up and keepin' to Gordo's routines. Somebody gimme shit, I pretend to call you. And me, personally, I'm keepin' my head down like you said."

"Tell me if you have a problem," I said, "in or out of the gym."

He gave me a quizzical look, crinkling his nose like a wolf wondering at the hint of a scent of something strange.

"What?" I asked him.

"Why you wanna be helpin' me, Mr. McGill?" Iran asked. He had to. Suspicion was the primary lesson that any halfway intelligent convict learned.

A DECADE BEFORE, a man named Andrew Lodsman put on a ski mask and robbed a jewelry courier in Midtown at midday. The problem was Amy, an ex-girlfriend who hadn't been an ex when he planned the rip-off. Amy talked to the cops and they were after Andy. The gems were marked with a laser imprint, invisible to the naked eye. And so Andy gave me a small one that I dropped into Iran's sock drawer when he was down in Philly committing a robbery of his own.

Someone made an anonymous call about the Philadelphia robbery and the cops found the three-caret diamond mixed in with the socks—among other things. Doubt was thrown on Andy's involvement in the robbery and Iran was put away for two crimes—one which he did and the other he didn't.

That was a long time ago and I am no longer that kind of man. I was trying to make amends for my misdeeds by helping young Mr. Shelfly out. He was just one of a dozen private projects that I'd taken on.

He didn't know that I was the cause of his six-year incarceration. He didn't need to know.

The cell phone in my pocket vibrated and so I took it out rather than answer Iran's question.

? Client IO was printed across the screen of my phone: possible client in office.

I texted back *20*, meaning that I'd make it there in that many minutes.

"Just workin' on my karma," I said to Iran, feeling the pain of those words.

He didn't understand what I meant but he was superstitious enough to accept the words. In prison men learned first to be suspicious, then fearful, and finally respectful of a higher power.

I STUCK MY HEAD in the showers before heading down to the street. Bug was standing under the water with one hand holding on to the nozzle above his head.

"Is Zephyra worth all this pain?" I asked from far enough away not to get splashed.

It took him half a minute to gather enough wind to say, "Anything."

THE BIGGEST ENEMY of the revolution, my crackpot Communist father used to say, *is a man's love for a woman. He will turn his back on his comrades in a heartbeat if that heart beats for some señorita with dark eyes and a sway to her butt.*

I chuckled all the way down the stairs to the street and then half the way to my office, headed for the question mark of a client waiting therein.

2

I PRESSED THE buzzer to my office on the seventy-second floor of the Tesla Building, the most exquisite example of Art Deco architecture in all New York. A loud click sounded and I pushed the door open, entering the reception area of the large suite.

Mardi stood up from behind the big ash receptionist's desk that had gone untenanted for most of my professional life. She usually stood when I came into the room, her way of showing deference and gratitude. Pale and slender, blue-eyed with ash-blond hair, Mardi Bitterman was born to be my Passepartout. Her coral dress had a lot of gray to it, to tamp down the passionate under-layer of red. She wore no jewelry or makeup. What you saw was what you got.

"Mr. McGill," she said, "Mrs. Chrystal Tyler."

To my left, rising as I turned, was another, not quite so young, woman. This lady was brown like a shiny pecan and curvy, not to say voluptuous. Her hair was set in gaudy ringlets and the cheap silk of her dress was a carnival of blues and reds sprinkled over with flecks of confetti yellow. Her makeup was heavy but somehow not overdone. Her high heels and glossy leather purse were the same yellow as those flecks.

In those heels she equaled my height. Our skins were the

same hue, if not tone. She smiled, recognizing something in me, and held out her hand, knuckles up as if she expected me to kiss them.

"So glad," she said.

I knew instantly that this was a lie.

But I took that hand and shook it, saying, "Come on back into my office and we'll talk."

As I ushered my potential client through the door, Mardi and I made eye contact. Her brows rose and she shrugged slightly. I smiled and gave her a wan wave of my hand.

THE YOUNG WOMAN and I strolled down the long aisle of open and empty cubicles toward the door of my sanctum. I steered her in and got her settled into one of the two blue-and-chrome visitor's chairs that sat before my extra wide ebony desk.

I sat and fixed my eyes upon her.

Chrystal Tyler was a handsome specimen—very much so. Her eyes had a delicate, almost Asiatic, slant to them, and her nostrils flared when she looked out of the broad window at my back.

From that vantage point I knew that she was looking down the Hudson, all the way to where the World Trade Center used to stand.

We both took a moment to appreciate our different views.

"I need help, Mr. McGill."

"In what way, Mrs. Tyler?"

She held up her left hand and twisted it at the wrist—a gesture of speculation or, maybe, pretend hesitation. I noticed that her nails were painted in three colors: blue at the base and red at the tip with slanting lines of gold separating the two.

"It's my husband," she said. "Cyril."

She wore no wedding ring.

"What about him?" I asked.

She looked me in the eye and held my gaze long enough to make a normal man uncomfortable or maybe excited.

"He's havin' an affair."

"How did you end up coming to me?" I asked. It was an honest question. Her clothes and makeup, nails and elocution presented a mystery in themselves.

"I heard about you from a man named Norman Close," she said.

They called him No Man because of the way he'd introduce himself, swallowing the "r" when he spoke. No'man Close was a muscleman who rented out his fists and biceps for a daily rate. He would pummel and batter, intimidate and possibly even decimate for anyone who made his three-hundred-dollar nut. He was very good at what he did—until the day he ran into somebody better.

"Norman Close is dead," I said.

"He wasn't when he told me about you."

Chrystal might have been street, but she wasn't stupid.

"What is it you need from me?"

"I already told you," she said. "My husband's havin' an affair."

"What does this husband do?"

"He's rich," she said with a disdainful sneer. "And not just your everyday millionaire kinda rich. Cyril's a billionaire. His family built half the buildin's over there in New Jersey."

"His name is Cyril Tyler?"

"Uh-huh."

"If he's so rich why haven't I ever heard of him?"

"He likes to keep things quiet. If you don't need to know about him, you don't."

"And you?" I asked.

"What about me?"

"What do you do?"

She speculated a moment too long before answering.

"I paint," she said, "on steel."

"Steel?"

"Uh-huh. Big steel plates. That's what I do. That's how I met my husband. Cyril bought five big ones. They weighed more than a ton." Her sneer was a work of art in itself.

"And you two made a connection."

"You could call it that."

"And now he's having an affair and you need ammunition for the divorce."

"What I need is to not get murdered."

Almost everything you know or ever hear is a lie. Advertisements, politicians' promises, children's claims of accomplishments and innocence . . . your own memory. Most of us know it's so but still cannot live our lives according to this solitary truth. We have to believe in something every moment of our lives. Losing this illusion invites insanity.

I knew that the woman sitting in front of me was lying. Maybe everything about her was a falsehood, but under that subterfuge there was something true. The fact that I wondered about this underlying reality is what makes me a good detective.

The intercom buzzer sounded just then.

I pressed a button on my desk phone and said, "Yes, Mardi?" to the air.

"Harris Vartan on line five, sir."

That's when I knew it was going to be one of those weeks.

I held up a finger to hold the place of murder, picked up the phone, and pressed line five.

"Yes?"

"Hello, Leonid."

"I'm with a client."

"I'll be dropping by at around five."

The phone clicked in my ear but I didn't lower the receiver immediately. I sat there, listening to my own counsel. Like Iran, I was superstitious. There was something wrong with Chrystal Tyler. If I needed proof of this fact it was that one of the most dangerous men in organized crime had just warned me of his approach. I should have excused myself, given Mardi the week off, and taken a fast jet to the Bahamas.

At the very least I should have sent the handsome young woman away, but I was distracted by the mystery of time.

Many and most moments go by with us hardly aware of their passage. But love and hate and fear cause time to snag you, to drag you down like a spider's web holding fast to a doomed fly's wings. And when you're caught like that you're aware of every moment and movement and nuance.

I couldn't tell who was caught, me or Chrystal, but Vartan's call, rather than warning me off, only pushed me in deeper.

3

"IT'S A BIG jump from an affair to murder," I said after hanging up the dead line, "even for a billionaire recluse. Has he threatened you?"

"That's not how Cyril do things."

"Then why do you think he might kill you?"

"Allondra North and Pinky Todd," she said, as if this should mean something to me.

"And they are?" I asked, jotting down the names on my thick gray paper blotter.

"They were both his wives and now they're dead."

The young woman fixed me with a stare that laid claim to a truth that even an old cynic like me would have a hard time denying.

"Murdered?"

She looked to her left as if maybe there was someone there next to her, urging her on with the story.

"Can I smoke in here?" she asked, turning back to me.

"Sure."

She had a ritual approach to opening the bag, producing the red package, and teasing out the cigarette, then the unhooking of a bullet-shaped lighter from a chain, hitherto hidden by the thin silk of her dress. When she lit up I hoped she didn't notice the widening of my nostrils. Tobacco smoke brought out desire in me. Desire is an emotion that any good detective needs to hide.

"Murder?" I said to keep our minds on the subject.

"One night about two years ago I made some sangria spiked with a little red wine but mostly vodka. It was strong and tasted sweet so Cyril drank more than he usually does. That's what got him talkin'.

"He told me that him and Allondra would drink and then fight like cats and dogs, that one time they was on his yacht and had a fight. When he woke up in the mornin' the boat was far away from shore. He had a cut on his head and she was gone. They never fount her body."

"He admitted to killing her?"

"No. He said that he didn't remember nuthin'. A year later he married Pinky Todd. They didn't drink or fight, so he thought everything would be fine, but then one day she told him that she wanted a divorce and she needed fifty million dollars or she was gonna tell about how him and his friends was doin' insider tradin' on Wall Street."

"And he killed her?"

"He agreed to give her fifteen million, had it set up and everything, and then one day, just a few weeks later, she was walkin' down Fifth Avenue after shoppin' and a crazy homeless man hit her in the head with a chunk'a concrete from a construction site. She died right there on the sidewalk."

"What happened to the killer?" I asked. The word "killer" brought to mind Harris Vartan. I realized that I was more with him than with Chrystal Tyler.

"He got away."

"Was it nighttime?"

"Uh-uh. It was the middle'a the day, and the streets were crowded."

"That sounds bad, but a murder like that would be very hard to orchestrate."

"Cyril believes that he did it."

"He *believes* he did," I said. "How does that work?"

"He says that he thinks that his mind makes these people die, that if he starts to hate somebody they just perish."

Again I thought about Harris Vartan. His was the kind of mind that could feel an anger that brought about death. It would be, one day, a man like him thinking ill of me that would put me in an early, and possibly unmarked, grave.

The anticipation of Vartan was making me lose interest in Chrystal. I decided to ease her out of the office to face whatever fantasy her husband was entertaining.

That's when she reached into the yellow bag and pulled out an impressive stack of hundred-dollar bills. She leaned over, placing the pile upon the desktop, within my reach.

"Twelve thousand, six hundred dollars," she said, exhaling smoke. "It's all I can afford. I got more but I need that in case I have to go somewhere fast."

My nostrils flared freely and my eyebrows, I'm sure, raised.

"I had a necklace of rubies and emeralds that Cyril's mother gave me," she said. "I sold it to Sophia Nunn of the Indiana Nunns."

I had two kids in college and one who had just dropped out of high school. My rent was low but still needed paying. And Harris

Vartan was coming to make me an offer. With Chrystal's money in my pocket I might be able to turn him down.

The skin between my fingers actually began to perspire.

But still I did not reach for the money.

"You say it's been two years since you and Cyril had that sangria?" I asked.

She shrugged.

"Why didn't you come to me back then?"

The blankness of her expression was a wonder to behold. It portended a shift in our communication.

"I've had some hard things happen in my life, Mr. McGill," she said. "Very hard. People fight. Sometimes they kill. Where I come from you look after yourself first. Cyril and me had it okay. There was a prenuptial agreement, and I didn't know nuthin' about his business. We never fight. Why would he wanna start havin' bad thoughts about me?"

"And so what changed?"

"Cyril's always been kinda portly," she said. "But lately he been losin' weight and sleepin' in another bedroom. Late one night, a few weeks ago, I went down the hall to visit and heard him talkin' on the phone in there. I couldn't make out what he was sayin' through the door but it was definitely him bein' intimate."

"And you think it's a woman."

"Yeah."

"And because of that you're worried that he might kill you."

"He says that he's the reason his two past wives is dead," she said. "Wouldn't you be scared?"

"Has he acted differently?"

"He's sleepin' in another room," she repeated, allowing

exasperation to spice the words. "He's losin' weight and on the phone almost all night long, almost every night."

I couldn't argue with her logic, or the money on the desk.

"This is a lot of money," I said. She knew what I meant.

"I pay for what I need," she said. "That's all."

"What do you need me to do?" I asked.

"No'man said that you were the kinda guy could make things happen," she said.

"I used to be. Nowadays I've changed my spots. Somewhat. What kind of things do you want to happen?"

"I don't know. I mean, I don't want him to kill me. So maybe you could figure out what I could do to make him back off."

"But he hasn't threatened you."

"I already told you—that's not how he do. Maybe, maybe if you go and talk to him, tell him that you're lookin' out for me."

"I do that and maybe he'll start having bad thoughts about me," I suggested.

"Are you scared?"

Her question caused me to smile. My smile brought forth a grin from her lips. We might not have been two peas in a pod, but we were definitely cut from the same bush.

"I charge a hundred dollars an hour," I said, reaching for the siren stack of bills. "I'll hold on to this money as a retainer."

"A hundred dollars?"

"Yes."

"That's too much."

"Your life isn't worth that?"

"Ain't nobody do this kinda work worth a hundred dollars a hour. No'man only charged three hundred a *day*."

"No'man is dead," I said.

"I just cain't agree to no hundred dollars a hour," Chrystal Tyler said.

"How about ninety-nine?" I offered. "For every hour I work I'll take away a hundred-dollar bill and put a single back in the stack."

"That's still a lot, but at least it's not no hundred dollars a hour. I could hire ten men down from where I used to live for that kinda money."

"And not one of them would make it past Cyril Tyler's door."

"Okay," she said, reluctantly. "Ninety-nine. But I expect you to be able to prove what you worked for."

"Do you have a picture of your husband?"

That yellow purse was like Felix the Cat's bag of tricks; all kinds of things came out of it. Chrystal produced a creased five-by-eight photograph that looked like it had been taped into a frame until recently. It was her, in bright red, arm in arm with a chubby man who wore tan trousers and a cream-colored sweater. She was leaning forward and laughing with abandon while he hung back shyly.

"That was before he started his diet. Some people look better skinny, but you know, sometimes it ain't no improvement when they lose weight," she said with that telltale sneer. "Some people born to be fat."

It was the only unqualifiedly honest thing she ever said to me.

4

Tiny "Bug" Bateman was not only seriously out of shape, he was also one of the world's great minds when it came to computer technology and technique. He had created tools for me that I'm sure generals in the Pentagon would have drooled over.

All I had to do was set up search templates that he'd developed to interface with his private Internet access system. After seeing Chrystal to the front door, I filled in the names and relationships of the people I was looking for and the system did an in-depth search using logic that Bug had culled and stolen from a thousand different systems.

I set up queries for Cyril Tyler, Chrystal Chambers-Tyler (she'd left me with her husband's contact information and the correct spelling of her name), Allondra North, and Pinky Todd.

Chrystal had refused to give me her address or phone number because "Cyril got pockets so deep he could hide the state of Georgia in 'em. So I know he could buy a couple'a numbers. I'll call you tomorrow at about four."

The search system was thorough and so never took less than fifteen minutes to work. To fill the time I decided to log on to the shadow account that Bug had fitted for me to eavesdrop on my youngest, and favorite, son—Twill.

Since his juvenile authority social worker, Melinda Tarris, had signed his release from probation, Twill had dropped out of high school and become quite busy.

"School just not for me, Pops," he'd said when informing me of his decision. "I know how to read and write, think and do push-ups already, man."

"You know one other thing," I said.

"What's that?"

"How to get in trouble."

Not quite eighteen, Twill was slender and dark, handsome like a minor demon on a day pass from hell. When he smiled, you smiled; you had to.

"Don't worry, Pops. I learned my lessons."

He had dropped out of school, but his education—and my trials—were just beginning.

Among other things I had gleaned, through Bug's shadow-Net, was that Twill now had an account with an online Panamanian bank owned by an Eastern European concern. He started the account with a two-hundred-fifty-dollar check that Gordo had given him for doing work in the gym. This sum hadn't changed for three months. But that afternoon Twill's online account showed a balance of $86,321.44.

Going into his Twitter account, I found that he'd received, in the past week, 1,216 messages. Each message had a dozen or more return addresses to them. Each address deposited eleven dollars into Twill's online money-receiving account.

Twill's problem had always been that he's too fast, too good, too smart. Without limitations set on him, a man like that can get deeply into trouble before there's ever any warning. Men need trouble to gauge their success and temper the extent of their actions.

I was Twill's only real problem.

I WAS WONDERING how to figure out the nature of my son's latest scam when a chime sounded. The Internet search was over.

I was presented with a variety of online reports and images for each search. Allondra North's death had been ruled an accident by a Florida judge, while a distraught Cyril Tyler was exonerated of any foul play.

"This is a tragedy, not a crime," Lon Fledheim, Tyler's attorney, said to the *Miami Herald*. "It is a private heartbreak."

The photograph of Allondra proved that she was biracial, but I couldn't tell her specific ancestry. There was some white and brown in there, maybe some Asian and black.

Pinky Todd, a white woman, was killed by a berserker homeless man who all of a sudden went crazy on Fifth Avenue and hit her in the head with a chunk of concrete. The bearded homeless man fled, lashing out at anyone who tried to stop him, and disappeared in the crowd. He was never found.

Odd.

Things really got tricky when Bug's program presented me with an image and a bio of Chrystal Chambers-Tyler. She was indeed an up-and-coming artist who had attended Pratt Institute and produced paintings on highly polished steel canvases. She had reviews from all over the country and her work hung in a few of the smaller museums. Her marriage to Cyril was covered on the society page, and no one criticized her diction or ghetto sense of style.

Actually it was the lack of this latter style that made me take a second look at the digital likeness of her. At first it looked fine, but then, on closer examination, I was left wondering at the shape of her eyes and their slant toward the bridge of her nose. It was as if my streetwise client had had plastic surgery in order to look . . . a little different.

I tapped into the photo system that engaged automatically when someone came in the front door of the reception area. For a period of eight seconds three cameras took a dozen photos each of the new guest.

The images of the Chrystal Chambers who had come to my office were very close to that of the woman Bug's program presented to me—but not quite a match. The woman who came to my office was shorter, for starters. On the Net there was an image of Mrs. Chrystal Tyler standing next to her husband in shoes that didn't have heels. They were equal in height, whereas the photograph on my desk clearly showed that the woman who came to my office was the shorter of the two; not much shorter, no more than an inch.

Owing to my own stature, nearly five six, I'm oversensitive to height.

Both women had posed with Cyril. They were definitely related but were not identical twins. Sisters, half sisters, first cousins maybe. But why would one come to my office posing as the other? Especially with such a wild claim.

There was also a little article on an eight-hundred-thousand-dollar necklace that Cyril's mother had given to Chrystal. The piece was old and had a name—Indian Christmas. This referred to the country, a source of fine rubies and emeralds for centuries.

The case was beginning to interest me. Much of what the woman who came to my office said was true. She knew Cyril Tyler, and well, according to the photograph. She knew intimate details about the real Chrystal Tyler's life and the deaths of Cyril's previous wives.

If all this was true, then maybe someone's life *was* in jeopardy. The question was—whose?

FOR NEARLY AN hour I sat in front of that screen, trying to come up with scenarios that might explain what had transpired in my office: the street girl with the pretend billion-dollar husband taking the place of another black woman who was the real article.

Common sense told me to turn away, but ninety-nine dollars an hour said differently.

Finally I picked up the phone and entered a number.

Somewhere deep in Queens a woman's voice answered, "Leonid McGill's line. Hello, Mr. McGill . . . or Mardi."

"It's me, Zephyra," I said to my TCPA, my self-defined Telephonic and Computer Personal Assistant.

"How can I help you, boss?"

"I just came from watching your boyfriend spill sweat on Gordo's floor."

"Charles Bateman is not my boyfriend."

"Charles?"

"That's his name. Didn't you know?" she said. "I hope you don't think that his mother and father christened him Tiny, or Bug."

"Charles thinks he's your boyfriend. Why else would he be working out in a grimy gym for the first time in his life?"

"Did you call for some other reason, Mr. McGill?"

"I need you to try to get me an appointment with a reclusive billionaire named Cyril Tyler."

"Okay. I'll get right on it."

"Don't you need any other information?"

"No, sir. One of my clients is a masseuse, very popular among the wealthy. She's willing to make house calls and travel. Three times she's been to see Mr. Tyler. Is there any special reason I should give for the visit?"

"Tell him that it's an Indian Christmas in July."

5

GETTING OFF THE PHONE with Zephyra, I turned back to the pictures and articles offered up by the Net. I liked the name—the Net—because it made me a fisherman on the shores of some great electronic sea. I'd throw in my meshlike web and pull out treasures such as a series of eleven six-by-four-foot canvases of what at first seemed to be rusted-out and discolored plates of steel. But, as I looked at them, these marred slabs slowly transformed into landscapes and life studies cobbled together by the judicious and crafty application of corrosives, intense heat, and specially made epoxy-based acrylics. There was a lot of stippling and pointillism, very few bold strokes or pools of color.

There was life in these pieces of art that matched the wildness of the woman who called herself Chrystal Tyler; matched but did not equal. The execution of these paintings was subtle and deft, defiant of the supposed European and Asian hegemony while replicating these forms' grace and even their sense of history. The woman I'd met had no notion of this subtle and violent challenge to the so-called civilized world's domination of aesthetics.

These arresting works were of junkyard landscapes, of yellow and brown streetwise nudes made from what only seemed like rot and decay. I found myself wondering at the woman I had not met. Was she in as much trouble as her imposter claimed?

And why would anyone come to me pretending to be another in distress? Were they working together, or was this a plot against the real Chrystal Tyler executed by a murderous husband and a jealous cousin? Tyler's first two wives were both dead—that was a fact. Was I being set up for a patsy in yet a third murder?

The smile on my lips did not bode well for anyone attempting to dupe me.

I was sitting there, contemplating the nature of my own perverted mirth when the direct line to my office rang.

"Yes, Zephyra."

"You have a seven p.m. appointment with Cyril Tyler," she said, adding an address I already knew.

"Did you talk to him?"

"No. It was some kind of assistant. I told him what you said and he asked me to hang on. A few minutes later he got back on the line and gave me the seven o'clock option. I took it."

"Thanks," I said.

"And Charles is not my boyfriend," she added.

"Maybe not, but you won't ever find another man take the kind of pain he's swallowing over you."

"Is there anything else?" she asked.

"A whole universe," I said, and then Bug's search program chimed again.

"Call me if you need anything work related," Zephyra said.

We both disconnected and I pressed the enter key.

An image filled my eighteen-inch screen, a close-up of the blood-streaked face of Pinky Todd. Bug's system must have found its way into some newspaper's files to come up with that graphic image. Her eyes were wide open and a deep gash in her temple had allowed a rivulet of blood to travel down between those unseeing orbs.

This photograph sharpened my attention to another level of intensity. Blood is the mainstay of my particular branch of the PI profession; hot blood, spilled blood, common blood with a grudge. There wasn't always violence attached to the cases I was drawn to, that were drawn to me, but there was always an underlying pulse and at least a predisposition toward a bloody outburst.

Somewhere in the back of my mind I had the half-aware insight that this was the life I had chosen, that not everyone was prone to this way of being. I wondered, half consciously, if I could change gears and be another kind of man.

Who knows how far I might have gone down that avenue of thought if the intercom buzzer hadn't shocked me back to awareness, Pinky Todd's picture still glowing brightly on my screen.

"Yes, Mardi?"

"Harris Vartan, sir."

I had almost forgotten him.

"Show him in."

I logged out of Bug's program, sat back in my worn office chair, and laced my already large hands into one big oversized fist. I could bash through a length of four-by-four hardwood with that cudgel, but that meant nothing next to the power wielded by the man coming down the hall.

I stood up when the door swung open and Mardi stepped in, leading the modern-day mobster in the pale pearl-gray suit. His shirt was a wan yellow cinched by a maroon tie with flowing sky-blue highlights. He had silver hair and olive skin with eyes that rendered black a watery second cousin. Standing five nine, he was seventy-three but could have passed for somewhere in his fifties. He did push-ups and sit-ups every morning and could hold his own with any man, or woman, half his age.

Mardi stopped at the door while Vartan advanced toward me and held out a hand. He didn't shake hands with everyone. You had to reach a certain level in the hierarchy of sin to even see Vartan, known as the Diplomat to law breakers and police officials alike.

Until I was fifteen I called him Uncle Harry because he had been a close aide to my father when my father was a union organizer and Vartan was, too. The unions brought Tolstoy McGill to revolution and the violent overthrow of the capitalist dogs, while Vartan took the organized-crime route that labor sometimes offered.

Though they had taken different paths to their damnations, both men had one overarching philosophy in common: they saw all men's deeds as acts of fate and therefore were never plagued by guilt or remorse.

A man's actions are defined by history, my father had told me a hundred times before he went off to be swallowed whole by the Struggle. *Men are bullets shot from an unpredictable and inexhaustible Gatling gun. You may not be able to foresee where they'll end up, but they are always on their way there.*

"You're looking fit, Leonid," Vartan said with half a smile, the most he ever gave.

"Have a seat," I replied.

Mardi exited and Vartan sat, crossing his legs and sitting back like a southern European on a New York vacation.

In actuality Harris lived in Chicago. From there he ran a syndicate the size of which Al Capone couldn't have even imagined.

"How's business?" he asked.

"Just took on a new client."

"Still on the up-and-up?"

"More like the up-and-down," I said, "but, yeah, I'm trying to keep it legal."

"Really? It has been mentioned that you have developed a relationship with a man named Hush."

"What is it you want, Mr. Vartan?"

"You used to call me Uncle."

I shrugged.

Vartan waited a moment, to see if I'd show some heart—but he knew better.

"I came here to ask you to find a man for me," he said. "A man named William Williams, a former associate."

"Why me?"

"New York was his last address, and you're known to me."

I took a moment to pretend to consider his request. Then I said, "I will not, under any circumstances, work for you, Mr. Vartan. Not for any amount of money."

"I wasn't intending to pay you," he said. "I thought that you would do it as a favor for an old friend of the family."

"No reason for us to mince words here," I said. "I'm out of the

life, and that means I won't go back even if someone as dangerous and powerful as you tries to make me."

Vartan sat back so comfortably you might have thought he
was at home in his den, sitting in his favorite chair. He held his
hands palms up and raised his eyebrows.

"I respect your decision, Lenny," he said, using a nickname
that only he dared use. "But this request has nothing to do with
my business or anything illegal that I am aware of. This man is
an old friend from my youth. I promised someone that I'd find
him—for friendship, not business."

I had never known Vartan to out-and-out lie. His trade was
solving problems, not deception.

"And if you do me this service I will be in your debt," he added.

I'd burned quite a few bridges in the past few months. A
friend of Vartan's stature would certainly come in handy.

"This doesn't have anything to do with your business?" I said.

"Nothing."

"There's no crime, no vengeance involved?"

"Correct."

"Your word?"

"If you need it, it's yours."

"I'll think about it and call you tomorrow. Just give me a
number."

"I'll call you."

I gave him as hard a stare as a gnat can give a lion and then
nodded, accepting his terms.

"Have you been up to your mother's grave lately?" he asked.

"Why?"

"It's just a question, Lenny."

"There's questions I could ask you, too, Uncle Harry," I said. "Questions just as tough."

Instead of continuing, the Diplomat stood up and went to the door.

"I can see myself out," he said.

That was fine by me.

6

THE NUMBER 1 TRAIN at rush hour is a fast-moving mob. Commuting workers and others are piled on top of each other, using anything they can to escape the feeling of melee. Young people form into circles and talk loudly enough to drown out the shrieking of steel on steel. Families huddle, blue-collar workers nap, and almost everybody else is plugged into loud music, last night's missed TV show, or any game from sudoku to *Grand Theft Auto*. There are readers, too, concentrating on sensational magazines, nineteenth-century novels, and comic books.

I usually gravitate toward the end of the platform—the last car is most often the least populous. But I don't get distracted. I like watching people, seeing how they turn inward and turn away when finding themselves in a throng. You'd think that anyone who'd decided to live in a city like New York, to travel by underground train, would revel in the closely packed company of others—but no.

One day it came to me that the isolation and alienation of rush hour is like so many marriages I've investigated—a lifetime spent together in the same bed and still managing to keep separate and remote.

In the majority of my marital cases, I got the definite

impression that I knew more about the private lives of the couple than either of them did.

Those three monkeys, my father used to say, *Hear No, See No,
Speak No . . . Just drop the Evil and you have a civilized prole.*

I CLIMBED OUT of the Ninety-sixth Street station behind an old
white man who had to take the steps one at a time. His baggy
green trousers were held up by bright red-and-blue suspend-
ers worn over a gray woolen sweater. There were people coming
down the other side, so I couldn't go around.

"Hurry it up, will ya, man?" a voice behind me said but I had
no intention of interfering with the oldster's pace.

"Hey!" the voice insisted.

I stopped and turned to face a thirtyish young man dressed in
a style of someone ten, or even twenty, years his junior: a blaring
red T-shirt with a writhing form drawn upon it and jeans that
hung down on his hips. He was white but that hardly mattered.
He could have been any race and still held the same misconcep-
tions as to his place in the world.

At first the young man thought he could bowl right over me.
After all, he did his exercises and watched kung-fu movies. So I
held up a hand like a steam shovel.

He stopped and gave me the look—that gaze of resentment
and threat that has yet to reach a physical aspect.

"If you're lucky," I said before he could announce his own
undoing, "you will one day get to be old enough and infirm
enough to have some young man yellin' at you to hurry it up. If
you're unlucky you'll lay hands upon me."

The young man took half a step back. He thought about attacking, and then thought better. I watched him for the appropriate amount of time and then resumed my climb.

I love the subway system and the people it brings together. It's better than any sitcom or pop song. The subway and its nerve centers are like a jazz sonata, bringing the past into the future— all the generations crammed together in dissonant and almost unbearably sharp focus.

OTHER THAN THE FACT that it was constructed from glazed white brick instead of dark red, the building was nondescript. Nineteen stories high and taking up nearly the whole block, it had two fire-escape systems that I could see—one in the front down the middle, and the other cascading down the side, leading into a fenced-in alleyway.

I look for fire escapes wherever I go. This because of a dream I used to have every night and that still recurs now and then. I'm in a burning building, on a high floor, and there's no escape . . .

THE DOORMAN WORE an immaculate red-and-blue-trimmed uniform. The costume itself didn't set him apart from others in his profession but the punctilious attention to detail spoke reams about his persona.

He was a coffee-and-cream-colored man and, of course, taller than me by half a foot or more. He moved into the doorway at the top of the stone stairs to block me. To him I might as well have been a young man in a garish red T-shirt and slouching jeans.

"Can I help you?" he asked.

He had a beautiful voice. If his mother had paid more attention, or had his father been more understanding, he might at that moment have been preparing to sing opera in Cleveland, or maybe Orlando. Instead he positioned his big gut in my face, a living shield for his betters.

"Leonid Trotter McGill for Cyril Tyler."

"Who?"

"Which 'who' do you wanna know about?"

"Say what?" He had a good scowl, but I had a great left hook and so was unimpressed.

"I mentioned two names," I said. "And in answer to my declaration you asked 'Who.' "

"I never heard of a Cyril Tyler."

"Then either this is your first day on the job or you're stupid."

He took one step down the granite stairs.

"Why spill blood and teeth when you could just pick up the phone, brother?" I asked.

A friendly voice is often the most threatening.

He looked at me and pointed. "Wait here." And then went to his little vestibule to make the inquiry.

I wondered if Cyril had a private exit; if he had ever walked in or out the front door.

I took a deep breath, and then another. Events had been tumbling down too fast and I was losing the grip on my temper. And, as any fighter can tell you, while you have to stay hot in a fight, you can't let yourself burn out of control.

"Take the elevator to floor nineteen," the doorman said,

breaking into my reverie. "Turn left when you get out, walk down the hall to the other car, and take that up one floor."

"That's one more floor than you got," I said.

Big Red's reply was to step aside and allow me entrée.

WHEN I GOT into the tiny vestibule-lift the button for nineteen was already lit. This gave me the impression that not just anyone was allowed access to the top floor. I rode up without interruption and emerged into a hallway of apartments with doorways but no doors; no furniture or ornaments or tenants either. It was a floor full of vacancies in a neighborhood where the rent on a one-bedroom ranged from three to five thousand dollars a month.

Fake-Chrystal wasn't lying when she sneered about Tyler's wealth.

The light-green paint on the second set of elevator doors was cracked and peeling in places. Underneath, the metal was beginning to rust. This reminded me of Real-Chrystal's steel canvases.

There was no button but the doors opened for me when I arrived and closed after I got in. The trip upward was little more than the distance between the floor and ceiling and when the doors came open I found myself standing at the edge of a broad, bright-green suburban lawn.

One the other side of this verdant expanse was an over-sized ranch-style house with a glassed-in porch and a red-brick chimney.

"Mr. McGill?" The voice came from my right.

The young man was slender and would only be called

African-American by an American with a fixation on race. His skin was lighter than many a Mediterranean and his hair was curly but light brown. His features marked him as one of my people: broad nose and generous lips. His expression told me, however, that we had nothing in common.

"My name is Phil," he said, somehow making even this bland statement condescending. "You're here to see Mr. Pelham?"

I took a moment before answering, my momentary silence a reply to his attitude.

Phil was wearing a pale lavender suit and gave off the scent of violets. I wondered what he might smell like if the suit was strawberry red.

"My appointment is with Mr. Tyler," I said at last.

"Come with me," Phil replied as he turned and made his way across the lush lawn.

Tyler's building was the tallest for quite a few blocks and so no one nearby could guess at what was up there. If you were in the middle of that lawn, reclining on a chaise lounge, you could easily believe that you were in Westchester or Beverly Hills. It was Dorothy's house dropped by some twister on that Manhattan rooftop.

Phil moved swiftly but I kept up with him. We got to the glass door of the veranda behind which was a perfectly proper office replete with a blond desk, dark-green filing cabinets, and a computer.

Next to the desk stood a man somewhere in his sixties who was defined in various shades of white: light-gray suit, off-white shirt, an opal ring on the baby finger of his left hand, and crystal-line eyes that barely hinted at blue.

The man raised his ringless right hand and gestured for me to enter. At this sign Phil opened the door and waved me in.

From up close I could see that there was a scar, whiter than his skin, just above the boss man's left cheekbone.

"Mr. McGill," the white-on-white man said as a greeting. "My name is Arthur Pelham."

"Interesting scar," I said.

"Fell out of a canoe in some unexpected rapids," he said. "That was back in my college days."

"Oh?" I feigned. "Where'd you go to school?"

"Cambridge," he said, and then, as an afterthought, "Massachusetts. Have a seat, Mr. McGill."

There was a simple wooden folding chair there in front of his desk. He used the same style seating for himself. There was something I liked about that. I guess it was a little, barely conscious lesson learned from my father about the equality and simplicity possible in a modern life so filled with pretense and hierarchy.

I took my seat and Pelham did his. Phil closed the door behind me. I was neither in the house nor outside it. This realization made me smile.

"What can I do for you, Mr. McGill?"

"Nothing."

"Why are you here?"

"To see Cyril Tyler."

"About what?"

"That's private."

"I'm his personal lawyer," Pelham assured me.

I had no answer to this statement.

"Mr. McGill."

"Yes, Mr. Pelham?"

"Why are you here?" His tone hardened just a bit.

"We've already completed that circuit of the merry-go-round," I said.

"I am Cyril's conduit to the world, Mr. McGill. Anyone wanting to speak to him has to go through me."

"And here I am."

"If you can't give me a compelling reason why you should see Mr. Tyler, I will have to turn down your request."

I stood up, reached into my back pocket, and produced my decades-old, fat, red-leather wallet. From this I took a business card that had my real name and number on it.

I placed the card on the edge of the white desk and smiled.

"You tell Mr. Tyler that if he ever wants to talk to me he can use the number on the card."

I turned and almost took the first step.

"Hold on, Mr. McGill."

"Yes?"

"We are not the kind of people that you can bully."

I turned around to see that Pelham had also risen to his feet.

"We?" I asked.

"What do you want?"

"If I have to turn around again I'm walking all the way out of here," I said. "If you want to stop me you're welcome to try."

My temper still needed tending.

Pelham tried to smile, failed at the attempt, and then said, "Take the door behind me. Walk down the hall in front of you until you get to a cream-colored door."

7

IT WAS LIKE any hallway in any suburban ranch house—nearly. The ceiling was too low and the walls too close, like most American dwellings, but the hall was longer than usual. The rugs seemed to be composed of some kind of pale fur, and the claustrophobic walls were hot pink in color, accented by a lime-green trim.

Now and again, to this searing background a huge steel painting was secured. Up close you could see both the subtlety and the brutality of the work. They were informed predominantly by earth tones, like great rotting swamps made into human subjects by some capricious, primitive god. I liked the paintings and felt a certain kinship to the artist. I didn't stop to appreciate Chrystal's work, however. There were other pressing concerns on my mind.

Because I was having anger issues I tried to bring my thoughts to a calmer place in preparation for my meeting with a man who might be a murderer. There wasn't time to do a walking meditation so I decided to think of someone who gave me the feeling of tranquility. I realized, or maybe re-realized, that there are few islands of serenity among my relations.

I thought of Twill, but was reminded of his bloated bank account lying there like a fat grub on dead flesh. There was

Katrina, my wife of twenty-four years, who was having an affair with my other son's school chum. Thinking of Katrina reminded me of my ex-girlfriend, Aura—I definitely didn't want to think about her. Finally I achieved my quest for equilibrium by considering Harris Vartan. At least he was clear and stable. He was my Uncle Harry, asking for a simple favor from the son of a good friend.

As I came to the promised cream-colored door I decided I would find William Williams, just because the gangster was the only one I could think of who didn't trouble me.

I knocked.

"Come on in," a rough voice called from the other side. There was no discernible accent, but the words seemed to yearn for one.

I pushed open the door and came upon what I can only say was a shit-brown room. The curved lines of the huge mahogany desk made it seem like a dark hippopotamus squatting on the stained oak floor. The bookshelves behind the desk were planed from ebony wood and the books upon them were each specially bound in dark-brown leather and fitted in a case of the same hide and hue.

The man behind the desk had once been very tan, now not so much. His hair and eyes and suit were brown. He was rotund in a muscular way and, like the woman who came to my office earlier that day, he strongly resembled another.

"How can I help you, Mr. McGill?" the man asked.

"May I sit?"

I indicated with a gesture of my head a large-bottomed pine chair that might have looked white against all those deep browns if it had not been burned by dozens of different cattle-brands.

These sigils and signs gave the chair a darker hue and made it seem almost alive.

"Suit yourself," the second imposter told me.

The chair had wide arms for the elbows. I used them.

"Well?" the man asked.

The only color divorced from the brunette family was the fading blue sky filling the window behind him and to the left. I considered the relief of the atmosphere and said, "Well what?"

"How can I help you?"

"I don't know. What do you suggest?"

"You're the one who asked for this meeting," he said, a slight twang making its way into the words.

"Not exactly," I replied, appreciating the accuracy of the hazy phrase.

"Are you not the private investigator—Leonid Trotter McGill?"

The fact that he knew my middle name meant either that I had been inquired about or that Phil made a report as soon as he was out of earshot.

"I am," I said.

"And did your secretary call to arrange a meeting with Cyril Tyler?"

"Zephyra, yes, she did." Maybe the TCPA had given my whole name.

"Then how can I help you?"

"You can bring out the real Mr. Tyler and hang up this sham."

The brown white man did not like me. His sudden glare was very clear on that fact.

I crossed my right leg over the left and sat back comfortably.

It was a relief to be with someone else who had problems with anger management.

He stood up and for a moment I wondered, idly, if he might have a gun somewhere on his person.

Instead of shooting me, the angry man with the subdued accent strode from the room, slamming the door behind him.

I remained seated, staring at the darkening blue sky. This was the respite I had needed. I took a deep breath and then let it go. I did that again and allowed my eyes to close. Solitude is a dear friend to anyone in my profession. Most people I meet I cannot trust, believe, or believe in. The only thing that separates the majority of the people I work for from the targets of my investigations is the fact that my clients pay for the privilege of my attention. There are few people I come across that I can bank on, or even feel friendly toward—and so, sitting alone, even in that unpleasant color scheme, was a balm for me.

After five or six minutes of breathing I got up to examine the odd books lined up like so many dominoes in their box. The first volume I cracked open was a pulp novel about some warrior woman named Zarra the Magnificent. The next book was one of the Tarzan series by Edgar Rice Burroughs. I must have looked into a dozen of those cheap novels in expensive bindings. There was *John Carter of Mars, Doc Savage,* a volume in the Fu Manchu series, *The Shadow,* and other, less memorable, characters.

It must have cost thousands of dollars to rebind and case those worthless fifties reprints of the adventure magazines from the thirties. But what did that mean to a man who could dream of someone's death and have it become reality?

There came a small sound like the sigh of a toy trumpet. I

turned to my left to see that the plain brown wall had concealed a door that was now open. In that doorway stood a slender white man who looked very much like the rotund imposter and maybe a bit more like the chubby man in the photograph posing with the woman who looked like his wife.

"Mr. Tyler?" I asked.

The man hung back, not passing through the secret doorway immediately.

"Mr. McGill?"

"That's right," I said brightly.

He rested a finger on the door frame.

"I've been looking through your books," I said. "I don't think there's another collection like this in the whole world."

He brought his hands together and came through into the brown-on-brown-on-brown room.

"Have a seat, Mr. McGill," he said. "Let's hear what you have to say."

8

I FELT AS if I were at an audition where a scene was being reen-
acted by successive thespians going out for the same role. The
new aspirant shook hands with me before going to the chair that
the previous actor sat in.

Cyril Tyler, if this was indeed Cyril Tyler, had a fleshy and
moist handshake. He went around the big brown hippopotamus
and sat, moving with exaggerated gestures as if he were a much
larger man. This more than anything inclined me toward believing that he was who he said.

I returned to my branded chair, put my elbows back on its
arms, and made that big fist with my hands.

"How can I help you, Mr. McGill?" he whispered.

I could barely hear him but resisted the temptation to lean
forward.

"Come again?" I said loudly.

He smiled and then gave a slight grin.

"How can I help you?" he repeated only slightly louder than
before.

I smiled and nodded, not for him but for myself. The reason
I was in this dissembling profession was that I lied as much as
my clients, not to mention the subjects of my investigations. I

couldn't trust them, but they couldn't trust me, either—whether they knew it or not.

And my lying was always the best. I could tell you something that was ninety-nine percent truth, but the way I told it would be completely misleading.

"A woman came to my office this afternoon, Mr. Tyler. She said her name was Chrystal Chambers-Tyler and—"

"Chrystal?" he said, at a perfectly normal volume.

I nodded and continued. "She said that she wanted me to work for her. It seems she's missing a valuable piece of jewelry and is afraid to tell you about it."

"Afraid? I don't understand," he said, his eyes darting around the room as if there was some strange sound coming from behind the brown walls.

"I didn't either," I said. "She was obviously a rich and successful woman, the wife of a very wealthy man. Why would she be worried over a necklace that cost less than a million dollars?"

Tyler stood up—unconsciously, I thought.

"Where is she, Mr. McGill? And what do you mean, 'afraid'? What did she say about me? About us? What was she wearing?"

There was nothing commanding or dominant about the billionaire. He wasn't far from fifty but looked younger. There was something boyish about him that the years had not worn away. Tyler was the classic milksop who happens to be a billionaire but reads adventure stories so that he can imagine himself a hero in a world where deeds and not money mattered.

I liked him.

"An off-white dress and a gold chain with a single pearl," I said, remembering the picture Bug's program showed me. "She said that the missing necklace could be the last straw on the back of an already strained relationship. That's a quote."

"What strain? There's nothing wrong between us."

My lie was gaining momentum.

Even though I liked the man, I had no desire to let him get ahead of me. I took in a breath through my nostrils and held it three times as long as normal. I did this because I was beginning to lose myself to a feeling more dangerous than anger. I was becoming distracted by the puzzle of the man and woman, and maybe the woman and man pretending to be them.

"You know women, Mr. Tyler," I said. "They get squirrelly at the strangest moments. Maybe she's worried about you kicking her out if she lost something so valuable . . ."

"Never."

"Or maybe," I surmised, "maybe she's knows what's happened to the necklace and is afraid of what will happen when you find out."

"I don't understand."

"There might be a lover involved."

"No. No. Never." He sat down again. "And even if there was, she could still come to me."

I gave him a skeptical look.

"You don't understand, Mr. McGill. Chrystal is my life. I'd be lost without her."

"That may well be," I conceded, "but life and love are often more complex than they at first seem."

"What are you talking about?"

"People often react to fears that are in their minds and not the real world around them. They are reacting to the ways that they were raised, and maybe . . . abused."

"Chrystal had a perfectly normal childhood," he said. "There's nothing wrong with her."

"I wasn't trying to imply that there was," I said. "But it is possible that she feels guilty and has put that guilt on you."

"That's ridiculous. I love her," he said, and I almost believed it. "I would never do anything to cause her pain."

"Be that as it may," I said quoting a phrase my father used again and again in my radical homeschooling. "This woman did come to me, and she told me what I'm telling you."

"Where is she?" he demanded. "I need to talk to her myself."

"She told me that you might ask that question. She said that you'd offer me money to reveal her whereabouts and therefore she would not tell me where she was staying or how to get in touch. She said that she'd call me to find out what I had learned."

"Why did she think you'd talk to me if you were hired to look for the necklace?" he asked. He might have been weak but he was not a stupid man.

"She was worried that I would come to you for a better paycheck. She said that keeping her location a secret would assure my . . . fidelity."

"But you *could* find her for me," he insinuated.

"Probably. But I won't."

"Then why come to me? Why don't you do what she hired you to do?"

"I believe that she hired me to save her marriage," I said. "I

also think that she's confused about the necklace. She gave me a
lead or two, but those seemed to be dead ends. The best way to
solve the problems, as I interpreted them, was to come here and
lay out the scenario for you."

"I don't understand what you mean," he said. "What use can
you be if she doesn't trust me?"

"I've met with you. I can tell her that. I can say that I con-
fronted you about the necklace. Maybe that will convince her to
come clean."

"You think that she's lying to you?"

"No one tells the whole truth," I said, "even to a stranger."

"I'll pay you a hundred thousand dollars to find her, Mr.
McGill."

For a few seconds there my mind went as pink as the hallway
walls outside the shit-brown door.

I had to clear my throat before saying, "No."

"Why not?"

"You aren't my client."

"Then what do you want from me?"

"Is her ruby and emerald necklace missing?"

"I don't keep track of her belongings."

"Is *she* missing?"

He paused before answering, "For six days now."

I unlaced my hands and used them against the chair's arms to
sit up straight.

"It would be a definite conflict of interest to allow you to pay
me to betray her whereabouts to you," I said. "But . . . but I would
take ten thousand to deliver a message."

"A message?"

"Anything you want me to tell her . . . or maybe a note."

Cyril Tyler's face hid nothing. He was confused and worried, hopeful, even though he suspected that I wasn't being completely honest.

"I need her, Mr. McGill," he said. "Things *have* been strained lately, but it has nothing to do with our relationship, with her."

"Maybe you're the one having the affair," I said. "Maybe that's what drove her to make her own mistakes."

"Me? An affair? Never."

"I want to help you but I'm working for your wife," I said, telling two lies in one sentence. "I'll deliver a note for ten thousand. Take it or leave it."

"Will you take a check?"

"No."

He sighed and stood, walked to the door I'd entered through, and passed out into the riotous gallery/hallway.

After he was gone, I let my eyes nearly close and counted breaths until he returned, maybe ten minutes later. He handed me a white envelope, sealed, and a stack of crisp one-hundred-dollar bills.

"I expect something from this," he said.

"I'll deliver the note. That's all I can promise. Do you have anything else to tell me?"

"Like what?"

"Like why she left? Maybe . . . what she might be afraid of?"

"It's not of me, if that's what you're saying. I love Chrystal."

"I love hamburger," I said. "But when lunch is over the sandwich is gone."

"Chrystal is not a plate of food."

We parted in the brown library. I walked past Chrystal's paintings and into the glass office, which was now empty. I ambled across the lawn to the private elevator, then down the empty floor to the other.

The light-brown doorman ignored me as I passed out into the street.

Two blocks away I tore open the envelope and read the poorly scrawled note. *Chrystal, I love you and would never be upset about anything having to do with your actions or oversights.*

I was amazed at the legal quality of the message, but that didn't matter. I'm not an editor or a life coach. My job is, has always been, to take money from people either to assuage their fears or to fan the flames of their rage.

And there are worse elements to my profession.

9

CYRIL TYLER'S HIDDEN MANSION was only nine blocks from my place. The fact that it wasn't the gossip of the neighborhood proved that he had extraordinary clout—and was willing to use it.

I made it to my building in nine or ten minutes and then climbed up the ten flights to the apartment at a good clip. A man in my line should at least be able to run up some stairs if the situation called for it. Somebody might be after me, or me after him—either way, I needed the edge.

I got to our big black door and stopped. The blood slamming through my veins had reminded me of something and I knew that once I was in the house that detail might fishtail away. Taking out my phone I entered and transmitted a text message: *Mardi, download pic of woman who came in today. Said she was Chrystal Tyler but wasn't. Look up last bug-search I did and see if you can identify her. Probably a relative, likely a sister. Thanx.*

I could have called Mardi. She would have answered and promised to do the job. But the best way to talk to young people is on the tiny screen. They remember, save, and pay closest attention to the texts of their lives. That's how they stay connected, coincidentally avoiding the overexcitement and the inherent inaccuracies of aural memory. Maybe one day all of our memories will be contained on little devices in our bags and back pockets. People like me will make their money looking for lost and stolen electronic recollections.

"Who was I, Mr. McGill?" the potential client would ask my descendant.

"I'll get right on that, Mr. Doe. Just transfer the dollars into my Panamanian account."

I USED the special electronic key on the lock, and two bolts—one at the knob and the other in the floor—slid open.

The place was deceptively quiet. You might have called it peaceful if you weren't aware of the problems festering therein.

I walked down the hall toward the sanatorium that once was my office. I opened the door to see my wife and my best friend in the bed.

He was bare-chested, lying back on three pillows, while she sat at his side, feeding him soup with an antique silver spoon she'd inherited from her least favorite aunt—Gertie.

Gordo, boxing trainer extraordinaire, was dying of stomach cancer, and my philandering wife was nursing him.

The room was spotlessly clean and my friend was as comfortable as a man can be when he's recovering from his third course of aggressive chemotherapy in a strange bed, on the eleventh floor, with nothing in his future except a hole in the ground.

On the other side of the bed sat the nurse, Elsa Koen, a forty-something red-haired, mild-mannered, German woman. She was speaking softly to Gordo. He swallowed hard, as if attempting to gulp down a spoonful of crushed glass.

They didn't notice me at first. The women were concentrating their full attention on Gordo as he was experiencing the pain of dying slowly.

I took a step in and he became aware of me. That was Gordo—he caught every movement, in and out of the ring. He leaned forward as if trying to genuflect. Elsa placed a hand on his chest and one behind his head to help him. Gordo was one of the most independent-minded men I knew but he accepted the German's help stoically, maybe even with a hint of gratitude.

Katrina turned her beautiful, only slightly worked-upon, face in my direction. She tried to smile, but she loved Gordo almost as much as I did. Our differences hadn't dimmed her compassion.

"Leonid," she said, rising from the rented hospital bed.

"Hey, Gordo," I said. "What I tell you 'bout gettin' in bed wit' my wife?"

Elsa smiled as she placed another pillow behind the old man's back.

"She told me you wouldn't mind," he rasped. His sandpaper voice wasn't caused by the disease, or its treatments, but simply a tone left over after fifty-plus years yelling for his boxers to shape up or fall down.

Elsa stood and both women walked toward me.

You couldn't see where Katrina had her face-lift, or even tell that her lustrous blond hair color wasn't completely natural. If someone had told you that she was fifty-one years old you would have been surprised, but these were the least of her secrets.

She kissed my cheek, bending down slightly because I'm only five five and a half. Elsa touched my shoulder as she went past.

The women didn't talk to me because the ritual was solidly

in place by then: I'd come home in the evening and Gordo and I would have our powwow. The women saw to his physical needs, while I reminded him of who he was and why he struggled when he could have given up.

I pulled up a chair that was always there in the corner, next to the window.

"How's it goin', old man?" I asked.

Gordo tried to sigh but merely let go of a breath. He had always been slender but now he was nearly emaciated, sallow skin sagging on clearly defined bone.

"Poison doin' its job all right," he said. "Now we got to see if I could do mines."

When I asked the oncologist, Dr. Ives, what were my friend's chances, the physician said, *Little to none.* That was seven months before.

"Savin' your strength for the later rounds, huh?" I said.

Gordo showed his teeth in a grimace that was meant to be a grin.

"How you doin', boy?" he asked.

I smiled and shook my head, saying without words that the weight was beyond my range. It was a truth I wouldn't have revealed to most people. I wouldn't have even told Gordo, but he needed to be needed, and I needed him to be—period.

"What is it?" he asked.

I told him about the woman pretending to be another, about the man feigning his identity, too. I told him about the hidden house on top of the building nine blocks away.

"Tricky," the dying man said. "That's the kinda boxer you got to worry about. He have you lookin' for left hook but he bankin' on a straight right. You think you got it figured and then—bang!—outta nowhere you crouch down right into a uppercut."

It was good advice from a master trainer. Here I thought I had the case all figured, but the facts I knew really only told me that I didn't know anything.

"And then there's this guy," I said. "Harris Vartan."

"Vartan? What you got to do with that mothahfuckah?"

Gordo didn't curse, hardly ever. He always told me that women and children come to boxing matches and it's bad enough that they have to see their loved ones bleeding and battered.

They don't need foul language to spice the bloody stew, he'd say.

"How do you know Vartan?" I asked.

"Thirty-seven, no no no, thirty-eight years ago he come into my gym and told me that he owned one'a my boxers, said that he had plans for him. I told him that if he was a slave master, that if he thought of men as chattel, then he could take his property and get his ass outta my place. I let that boxer know the same damn thing."

"What happened?" I asked.

"Nuthin'. Vartan looked at me and then he kinda half-smiled. He had a torpedo with him. That guy took a step at me but Vartan held him back. Lucky for the gunsel that he did, too. You know I was hot."

"He let the boxer alone?"

"Sure did. Kinda surprised me, too. You know, I asked around about him. They said that he knew where the bodies were buried 'cause he the one put 'em in the ground. What you got to do with him?"

"He was a friend of my father's," I said.

"Oh. I see."

·

Gordo was respectful of the memory of my dad. Whenever the subject of Tolstoy came up he held back any opinion.

"How about you, old man?" I said to cover his embarrassment.

"This morning I heard Kat arguin' with some guy," he said. "The kids was all gone and they was talkin' loud. I didn't hear what she was sayin' except when she told him to leave. I don't know what the man said but he sounded pretty angry."

I wondered but didn't worry about the argument. Katrina could take care of herself. From there the conversation drifted over to the latest boxing matches. Gordo wanted to give his opinion on a potential Mayweather-Paquiao match-up but he started to fade before we got too deep into it.

I left the dying man dozing. Our conversations tired him out but he seemed to like them. They were the least I could do for the man who was more of a father to me than Tolstoy had ever been.

ENTERING THE HALLWAY, I saw Elsa going toward the front door. She had taken off her nurse's uniform and wore a pink dress that showed off her form. She was maybe ten pounds over her ideal weight but that just made her look better.

I walked down to meet her at the door.

"I wanted to thank you for how you've taken care of Gordo," I said.

"He's a good man," she said, "with kind eyes that take in everything. I always make him my last visit in case he needs me."

"Would you like to stay and eat with us?" I asked, expecting her usual refusal.

"Yes," she said. "I would like that."

———

I WENT TO the kitchen to tell Katrina about our dinner guest.

"She's a sweet woman," my wife said. "We're lucky to have her."

"Gordo said he heard some arguing this morning."

"Really?" Katrina said and then, "Oh. He must mean about Carlos."

"The super?"

"He came up and said something about the boys throwing cigarettes from the windows. I told him that no one in this house smoked."

"Huh," I grunted, wondering what she was hiding.

10

AT THE BACK of the kitchen there's a smallish walk-in pantry lined with shelves on every wall—from floor to ceiling. It's there that Katrina keeps her spices, condiments, and the more arcane of her cooking devices. I put a three-legged mahogany stool back there so I could get some peace in my own house now that Gordo was dying in the den.

Hunkered down on that little boxer's seat, I tried to regain my balance.

Watching Gordo fade was a hard thing for me. He was just ten days off the last dose of the medicinal poison the doctors used on him.

Gordo was a fighter, and I was, too. Watching him wilt under the cancer was like seeing your champion being worn down to a bloody pulp one fight after his heyday.

If stomach cancer was a man I'd've slit his throat, tossed him in the Hudson, and then gone out for a rare steak and red, red wine.

A tapping came at the cupboard door.

"Yes?"

"It's me, Daddy," Katrina's blood-daughter said.

"Come on in, baby."

The door opened, letting in the light and clatter from Katrina's kitchen.

"Why are you sitting in the dark?" she asked, flipping the light switch.

Michelle's skin was dark olive and her eyes were a definite almond shape. It wasn't the gentle sloping of Chrystal and her pretender but the real Asian variety. Michelle was another man's daughter, a diamond dealer from Jakarta whom Katrina once thought she might marry—after ditching me. But instead he was killed in an earthquake and Shelly was presented as mine.

The slender child plopped down on my lap, put her arms around my nearly bald head, and kissed me just above the left ear.

"How are you, Daddy?"

"Just about normal," I said. "Head below the waterline, but at least that's better than six feet underground."

She squeezed my head tighter.

"You sad about Uncle Gordo?"

"I ever tell you that he used to let me sleep on a cot at the back of the gym when I'd be on the run from my foster homes?"

"Yeah, but you could tell me again."

"Dinner," Katrina called.

I stood up, cradling Shelly in my arms. She loved to be held like a child and I loved her even though we had nothing in common, from the blood in our veins to our outlooks on life.

I TOOK MY PLACE at the hickory dining room table. It was large enough to seat ten but lately only four of us sat down for a meal—Shelly and Twill, Katrina and me. Dimitri had stopped

WHEN THE THRILL IS GONE

eating with the family since his girlfriend, Tatyana Baranovich, had gone off to Russia with her new beau, Vassily Roman. While Katrina and Shelly brought out the covered platters Gordo showed up at the door, leaning on a bamboo walker and assisted by Elsa. Her eyes were on him like a proud mother watching her youngest taking his first steps. Gordo's head was glistening from the exertion but he pushed right through the strain and made it to a chair at the far end of the table.

"Hail, Lazarus!" I proclaimed.

He raised a hand to bless me and I smiled.

Elsa sat on Gordo's right and Shelly took the left-hand side.

"Twill!" Katrina called. "Dimitri!"

"Dimitri?" I said to my wife.

"He's part of this family, too."

"But . . ."

Before I could say more the brothers rumbled in. Squat Dimitri was dark, my color brown, while Twill was lean and charcoal with not even a hint of his mother's Nordic blood in his skin.

Broad, earthbound Dimitri sat across the table from me, while Twill sat at my side.

"What's up, Pops?" Twill asked. He was no blood relation, like his sister, but he had been my favorite since the first day I laid eyes on him.

"Up?" I said. "Man, I'm flat on my back and the ref started the count at nine."

Gordo heard the joke and grinned, nodding like one of those bobble-headed dolls people used to put in the back windows of their cars.

Katrina and Shelly took the lids off the platters, revealing a feast of fried pork chops, spinach and collards chopped and sautéed in butter, potatoes cooked with bacon, onions, and vinegar, and homemade applesauce. Katrina was a magician in the kitchen.

"Hey, boy," I said to my one true son.

"Dad," he said.

Since I had tried to help his girlfriend, Dimitri felt conflicted about me. Where once he expressed only disdain he now conversed with tepid deference. This was a definite improvement in our relationship, but we had a long way to go.

"How's school?" I asked him.

"I haven't been goin' lately."

"What you been doin', then?"

"Nuthin'."

He looked down at the plate his mother had put before him. That would be all he'd say that night. His pain tore at me, but what advice could I give? My heart had been broken the same way and I was just as lost.

I turned my attention to Twilliam. He was saying something to his sister and she was holding Gordo's thumb.

"What about you?" I asked Twill.

"Same," he almost sang.

"What kinda trouble you gettin' into?"

"Not me, Pops. Now I'm outta school I put in thirty hours a week at the D'Agostino's. Got to make some money so I can move out when you let up on me."

"You're only seventeen."

"Alexander was leadin' a legion at that age."

"What you know about Greek history?"

"Whatever Mardi Bitterman says. She reads her dry books and tells me the story."

"Is she your girlfriend now?" Katrina asked.

"She's my friend, but I can't say from firsthand if she's a girl or not."

"Twill," Katrina protested. "That's rude."

The conversation went on like that, Dimitri brooding while Twill danced around any question asked of him. Gordo was served a special soup that Katrina made, and he fought bravely against the gravity of fate as Shelly regaled him about a trip she planned to take to Senegal. Elsa anticipated Gordo's every need. Her care for him somehow soothed me.

We ate and after a while Katrina broke out a couple of bottles of decent Spanish red. The liquor seemed to revitalize Gordo. He started telling us stories about the old days and the boxers he saw hitchhiking from one bout in Cincinnati to another the next day in Cleveland.

"Back in those days," he declared, "a man was fightin' from sunup to sunup. The only way he knew he was in a ring was he got a break when the bell sounded."

THAT NIGHT KATRINA gave me a sloppy kiss before drifting into sleep. It didn't mean anything. She was having an affair with Dimitri's school chum Bertrand Arnold. Maybe she thought I didn't know. I didn't begrudge her the passion. She certainly wasn't getting it from me, and since she was sated physically she wasn't so anxious. She could even fall asleep without the TV crooning in the background.

I was wide awake with all my responsibilities and failures floating aimlessly through my mind. I turned on the TV and caught the beginning of *The Thin Man* with Powell and Loy. The dry wit between the two made me restless. Before the final scene I climbed out of bed and went back to the dining room.

Elsa had gone home at ten and the large apartment was quiet. It was two in the morning but I entered the number on my cell phone anyway.

She answered on the first ring.

"Hello."

"Hey, Aura."

There was a moment of appreciative silence before she said, "Leonid, what's wrong?"

"I miss you."

"And I you."

"What were you doing?" I asked.

"Reading," she said. "Thinking."

"Thinking about what?"

She didn't answer the question.

"Can I meet you tomorrow?" I asked. "Maybe for breakfast?"

"Of course."

"I love you," I said.

"I'll see you then," she answered. "I really should be getting to sleep."

I went back to bed, but sleep had settled in another room somewhere, down the hall with the children and the dying.

11

THERE'S A SMALL diner on Forty-sixth just east of Fifth called Winston's. It's got a red linoleum counter and yellow tables along the plate-glass front. I didn't need to tell Aura to meet me there—it was our place. When I arrived just shy of seven I could see through the window that she was already at our table, just being served her coffee.

I stopped at the entrance and allowed myself to be amazed yet again at how my heart began to pound when I saw her. From this sphere of wonder I proceeded to the booth.

We didn't kiss hello.

I meant to say good morning but uttered "I love you" instead.

She reached out to touch my hand and I felt a thrill of excitement. "Me too."

I sat, and the waitress, a strawberry blonde with pale skin and a ballerina's body, took my order.

In contrast to the server, Aura was the color of glittering dark gold. Her hair was blond but wavy. She came by this coloring naturally, seeing as her mother was Danish and her father from Togo. Her pale eyes were no color that I could name.

Less than a year before I had almost died and she sat by me whenever my family wasn't there. Twill kept tabs on the visits and called her when the coast was clear. Now and then the fever would abate and I'd slit my eyes to see her waiting for my recovery.

I blinked and found myself back in the diner with the woman who willed me back to life.

"You need to pay your rent," she said.

"I got an advance yesterday."

The moments passed.

Our breakfasts arrived. I had grits, pork patty sausage laced with sage, and four scrambled eggs. She had grapefruit, Special K, and skim milk.

"What did you want, Leonid?" she asked after the silence stretched halfway through the meal.

"I want you back."

"How's Gordo?"

"Dying. Doin' pretty well at it, too."

"I can't," she said. "Not yet."

"Why? I'll leave Katrina."

"I know. And maybe if you'd done it earlier . . . No. It's not your fault. It's just that I, I'm afraid of losing you."

"You won't lose anything. I will be there."

"When I saw you in that bed I knew that someday you'd die like that," she said, "bloody and beaten."

What could I say? I knew it, too.

"Yes, but we all die."

"Not like that."

"No," I agreed. "Not like that."

"I'll leave the Tesla Building if you want," she offered.

"They'll just hire somebody else to throw me out."

"How is everything?" the dancer-waitress asked. She was standing there, smiling hopefully.

"Fine," Aura said.

"I haven't seen you guys lately," the waitress added. "You been away?"

"Different schedules," Aura said.

When the girl was gone I put down a twenty and stood up.

"Where are you going?" Aura asked.

"I have to leave. You'll have the rent by three."

12

THE ART DECO wonder of New York, the Tesla Building, was eleven blocks from Winston's, its elegant foyer replete with Italian marble and frescoes of monumental naked and toga-clad men and women. I had to smile as I walked past the security desk to the elevators.

It was no surprise to find Mardi sitting at her desk, studying her computer screen. She was the overachieving gal Friday of the movies from back before even I was born. Mardi was so concentrated that she didn't stand up when I came in.

"You were right," she said, not even looking up. "It's her sister, Shawna Chambers-Campbell, divorced."

There was a victory smile on her face when she shifted her gaze to me—but that faded.

"Ms. Ullman?" she said.

Mardi had been working for me less than a year and already she had become my closest confidante. The thirty-six years that separated us were nothing. I was a New York sewer rat and she a basket-case savant, raped for years by a man calling himself her father and then set adrift in a world that neither cared about nor comprehended her pain. Our unlikely alliance was, in its own way, perfect.

"I'm supposed to be the detective here," I said.

"But you just look so sad." Her eyes invaded mine with their compassion; the empathy of a girl made wise by psychic defenses a Soviet spy would have marveled at.

I pulled up her aqua visitor's chair and said, "Teach."

She gave me a wan smile—the doorway to acres of feeling I could only guess at.

"Her brother's name is Theodore but everybody calls him Tally," Mardi said. "He's under arrest downtown. Her mother—"

"For what?" I asked. Shorthand was all we needed to communicate.

"Possession with the intent to distribute," she said after hitting a few buttons on the keyboard. "Seven joints and an as yet undefined red capsule. Her mother is named Azure. She has a history of mental illness and is now a resident of the Schmidt Home in Battery Park City . . ."

You could see New Jersey out of Mardi's window. From the seventy-second floor it looked like a scale model of Purgatory.

"What's her problem?" I asked.

"Like that red capsule," Mardi said, "undefined. The father's name is Nathan. He lives in a retirement community, also downtown. He was a welder in the Merchant Marines for forty-six years. There's no record of a divorce or separation."

Mardi stopped reading the screen and looked up, allowing me to see in the deep well of her eyes that my sorrow was falling away.

"Shawna is a mystery," she said.

"Go on."

"At the age of sixteen she married Private First Class Richard

Campbell. Three months later they divorced, citing irreconcilable differences. In the last seven years I could find records about three children she had but there might have been more."

"Why do you say that?"

"Her sister wrote her a recommendation to an infant daycare center six months ago. None of the three children would have been that young, and it wasn't an employment rec."

"Got it."

"Shawna's last known address was a women's shelter on Eighteenth Street. The last place she worked was Beatrice Hair Design on Flatbush in Brooklyn. But that was four years ago.

"Both sisters dropped out of high school. Tally too."

I leaned forward, lacing my fingers and resting my elbows on Mardi's desk.

Listening to the thumbnail sketches, I was aware of Aura slipping out of my consciousness like a small boat left untethered at the shore.

A man is defined by the work he does, my father told me over and over again. *If he works for the corporation, then he is the corporation. If he works for the people, then he is the people.*

Mardi was saying something about a small school in Rhode Island that Chrystal had attended. She'd gotten her GED and made it to college.

And don't you go thinking that you're unique, my father went on to say, time after time. *That you have defined yourself. It's the city that has made you. The streets and streetcars, the police and the bankers. You aren't anything more than an ant to them, and they are the kings and queens, tunnels and mounds that keep you from what you could be. They have made you into a hive dweller.*

"Mr. McGill?" Mardi was asking.

"Yeah, babe?"

She always smiled when I said those two words.

"You drifted off."

"What about Twill?" I asked.

"Huh? What about him?"

"If I asked you to give me a brief interpretation of him, what would you tell me?"

The wan girl frowned and pulled her head back a quarter inch.

"I'm not asking you for secrets," I said. "I don't want to get into his business, at least not through you. I want to know how you would describe him if somebody were to ask."

"Why?" She put the word up like a storm trooper's see-through shield.

"You know what the most important thing is that a PI has to know?" I asked.

"What?"

"That everybody knows things he doesn't. Everybody sees things that he's missed. Everybody. If he only relies on his own mind and memory and point of view he will never get a leg up."

"But what if they lie to you?" Mardi asked. "Like Shawna did?"

"The only complete lie is that which goes unsaid and unseen," I said. "Shawna spoke a lie, but what she showed me—her face and style—that was a truth I had to decipher. That's why not everybody can do what I do."

Mardi eyed me with a feeling akin to suspicion. I was telling her the truth, but there was something that she was missing. She knew this but nothing more.

Under that scrutinizing gaze I remembered that this girl was actually a woman who had decided to murder the man she thought was her father in order to save her sister from his predation.

"It's like Achilles," she said suddenly, the words leaping from her mouth.

"What is?"

"Twill," she said. "He's like an old-time hero. Beowulf and Achilles and Gilgamesh were just men, but they were so perfect that no one believed it. And Twill is even better."

"How's that?" I asked.

"Because he doesn't think that he's better than anyone."

"So you're saying that my son is perfect."

"No."

"Why not?"

"Because he doesn't have that connection that everyone else does," the astute child whispered. "He, he sees things like they really are. And he isn't afraid to do what he thinks is right or, no . . . not right but *best*."

Yes, I thought, Twill was my father's ideal revolutionary, a willing passenger on that dinghy I left without mooring.

I stood up, headed for my inner sanctum. It wasn't until some time later that I realized I hadn't thanked Mardi for her insights and labors.

13

By EARLY AFTERNOON I was standing in front of the municipal courthouse downtown, waiting. I had on one of my four dark-blue all-purpose suits and size twelve triple-E dullish, black leather shoes. My white shirt had grayed a bit after hundreds of washings at Lin Pao's French Cleaners, and one of my socks was black while the other was dark brown. I'd become the downtrodden workingman that my father always wanted me to be—but with a twist.

I was also a predator that lived on the invisible ether of personal information. Not digital bullshit, I stalked people's souls, took from them their most precious possessions, their secrets. And even though I performed this heinous job day in and day out, still I would have called myself rehabilitated—a simple wretch who had once been a monster.

What was I doing there, on the street, waiting? I wasn't sure. In the past forty-eight hours I'd collected twenty-two thousand dollars in advances to protect a woman I had not met from a man who might be in love with her. A working-class hero from my father's cracked pantheon would never work on such a project. Realizing this, I smiled, feeling that I'd dodged the revolutionary's bullet—at last.

At that very moment I looked up and saw a young milk-chocolate-brown man clad in a fancy suit of synthetic olive-green snakeskin coming down the broad concrete staircase. He was skipping happily, moving fast. He, like I did, felt that he was getting out of a bad situation. I wondered, as I moved to block his egress, if I was as misguided as he.

"Tally Chambers?" I said in a mild voice.

"Say what?" His grin disappeared like a small white rabbit down a deep dark hole.

"My name's Leonid McGill," I said quickly. "Your sister Shawna hired me. She gave me the money to pay your bail."

"Shawna?" he said, stopping in spite of all instinct.

"Your other sister, Chrystal, is missing and Shawna felt that you might be able to help finding her."

Tally Chambers' hair was close-cropped and his head was sleek, styled for speed. He eyed me, wanting to run, but worried about his sisters and, on top of that, wondering how money was traveling through their hands into mine.

"I don't understand," he said truthfully.

"Shawna came to my office and said that Chrystal had disappeared," I said in my most effective, matter-of-fact tone. "She, Shawna, said that she was worried that Chrystal's husband had either killed her or that she was so scared of him that she ran to ground."

"How much Shawna pay you?"

"She gave me twelve thousand. I used eleven hundred to pay ten percent of your bail."

"Shit." Tally swayed away from me, ready to walk on.

I touched his arm with a blunt finger and said, "Chrystal gave

Shawna a ruby and emerald necklace that she sold to a woman
named Nunn from Indiana."

That stopped him.

"No."

"Hey, man. I'm all up in your family business. I'm not trying to hurt you. Does anybody hate you enough to go into debt
eleven thousand dollars over your bond?"

For a few moments he took the question seriously. Was there
someone who'd pay good money to have him hurt or killed? Was
there?

"You know there isn't, Tally," I said to the unspoken question.

I was a mind reader, and he a true believer. We made a connection and now all I needed were his secrets.

"So what is it exactly you need with me?" Tally asked, giving
in, for the moment, to my superior, moneyed position.

"Shawna wanted me to get you out of jail," I began.

"How she even know I was there? I haven't seen her in days."

"How many days?"

"Four . . . maybe five."

"What did you guys talk about?"

Theodore Chambers clearly remembered the conversation.

"I don't remember," he said. "Just shootin' the shit is all."

The kid was going to be a puzzle. That was fine by me.

"When she couldn't find Chrystal, Shawna went looking for
you," I said. "When you were nowhere to be found, she came to
me. I did a citywide systems search and found that you'd been
arrested. I told her and she said to get you sprung."

"Why didn't she come herself?"

"With both brother and sister missing she went into hiding,"

I said. "*I* don't even know where she is. She calls me to get her updates."

While Tally wondered at my story I got a closer look at him. The whites of his eyes were darkening and encroached upon by blood vessels. There was an odor coming off him that was mildly organic and not at all healthy.

Seemingly to underscore my perceptions he emitted a mid-lung cough.

"So what do you want, man?" he asked when the hacking subsided.

"Shawna wants to help you," I said. "She told me to get you out of jail and then question you about your sister. If you cooperate, I'm supposed to supply a lawyer to get you outta this jam and give you twenty-five hundred dollars."

"Show me the money," he said, suddenly all ears and blood-shot eyes.

I took three fresh new hundred-dollar bills from my pocket and handed them over.

"This only three hundred," he said.

"Down payment on the talk we have."

Theodore "Tally" Chambers was twenty-nine years old. I knew that from Mardi's research. His state of health made him look older, while his state of mind was reminiscent of a much younger man. I had him on my hook, but this didn't offer me any comfort. Usually, when things went too easily something was bound to go wrong.

"I got to get to my house, man," he told me and then he coughed some more.

"In Vinegar Hill?" Mardi's research had been thorough.

"Yeah," he said behind big reddish-brown eyes.

I hailed a cab and we piled in. Tally gave the driver his address after we both closed our doors.

"I don't go to Brooklyn," the foreign white man told us.

I smiled, thinking that this trouble was just the speed bump I needed.

"We're not getting out of this car until you stop in front of the address my friend gave you."

"I don't know how to get there," the middle-aged driver said.

"You take the Brooklyn Bridge—" Tally started saying.

"I'm not going!"

"Oh yes you are, my friend," I said calmly. "Because if you don't we're gonna sit back here all day long."

The man turned around in his seat, showing us a white wood baton that was about two feet long. Tally reached for the door but I laid a hand on his forearm and smiled for our mustachioed driver.

"Listen to me, brother," I said in a modulated but still threatening voice. "I have been in the ring my whole fuckin' life. Hit me with that stick and I will beat you until your own brother will not know your face."

I meant what I said, the driver could tell. He turned around and shifted the car into drive.

"Which way?" he asked.

On the way over the bridge I began the interrogation.

"Have you ever heard that Cyril was violent or threatening toward Chrystal?" I asked.

"Naw, man. But, you know, I never had much to do with him. Only time we evah really spoke was at the weddin', an' even then it was like he wasn't even talkin' to me."

"What do you mean?"

"It was just a whole bunch'a words. He talked but didn't listen, then moved on like I didn't make no difference at all."

"So you didn't like him?"

"I'm not married to the mothahfuckah," he said, raising his voice.

The driver looked up nervously into the rearview mirror.

The bark got Tally coughing again.

"Was Shawna close to him?" I asked after he got his lungs under control.

"Shawna don't care 'bout nobody, man. That's why I wondered why she send you to me."

This brotherly revelation renewed my speculations about Shawna's motives.

"She told me she cared," I said. "She gave me the money for your bond."

"Yeah," he said. "I bet."

There was something behind this private wager but it would take longer than a taxi ride to tease it out.

WE MADE IT to Brooklyn and Tally guided our reluctant driver through a labyrinthine journey to a house in a run-down neighborhood.

When we got out I gave the driver a fifty and said, "Keep the change."

"Fuck you, nigger," he said to me before hitting the gas.

I grinned, watching the yellow cab fishtail down the street. The man was Eastern European and unschooled in the ways of American racism. He used that word to hurt me and express his fear and resentment. But in truth it was I who had oppressed him.

There is no balance between men unless everything around them is even. My father used to say those words to me. On that ramshackle street in Brooklyn I began to understand their meaning.

"Come on, Mr. McGill," Tally said at my back.

He was walking down a lane between two six-story apartment buildings. I followed until we got to a little cove where a small tarpaper dwelling was nestled like a dying rat.

"Hey, asshole!" a voice called.

I glanced to my left and saw two good-sized young black men moving toward us. They were both wearing black leather jackets and blue jeans—uniforms of the street. Tally took a step back.

"So here's the rub," I said out loud.

"What you say, mothahfuckah?" the fatter of the two thugs said.

I grinned broadly.

14

OVERCONFIDENCE KILLED THE CAT, dog, pouncing lion, and the entire global alliance of the Axis powers. That is to say, when two men who have the strength to stand upright get in your face you have to act fast and with certainty.

I took a step toward them, holding out my right hand as if I expected somebody to shake it. The gesture was meant to say that we were all brothers there in the rat's-nest cove behind the dirty brick buildings. The smaller of the two men was five inches taller and forty pounds heavier than I. That put him well over two hundred pounds. I could see that it wasn't all fat. He tried to stiff-arm me when I got close enough. I lowered down into a squat and hit him with a left hook to the gut that made him whimper. Instantly, with my right hand, now a fist, I slammed the jaw of Shorty's jumbo partner. He would have hit the ground if I hadn't followed up with six or seven punches that both debilitated him and kept him standing upright. Then I turned back to the whimperer and threw a long right hand.

That was a mistake.

Sometimes I forget that you are not compelled to follow the rules of boxing when in the street. The second man stood back and pushed against my shoulders. Already off balance, I fell to the ground. Even though he was probably suffering from a broken rib or two, the guy tried to kick me in the head. I rolled onto my left shoulder, grabbed his ankle, and yanked. Falling, he cried out again. I climbed up his prone body, throwing punches at anything flesh. I connected with half a dozen punches and got to my feet just in time to duck under a fist aimed at my head by Jumbo. The fact that he was still conscious meant that he would have made a good specimen for the sweet science. But he was raw, untrained.

We traded blows for all of ninety seconds, me landing and him not. When it was over he'd lost a few teeth, broken his right hand against a brick wall, and had blood streaming from three cracks in his face.

I stood back and gestured at the two men; the larger one was down on one knee and Shorty was lying on his side, wondering how to breathe right.

The gesture said that if they wanted more I had it for them.

Working together, they managed to get to their feet and stumble away.

To my surprise Tally had not fled. He hadn't helped in the fight, but he was standing in front of the shack with a fist-sized rock in either hand.

"You were waiting for me to soften them up?" I asked the frightened young man.

Tremors traveled from his shoulders down into his hands. He showed his teeth in a rictus that might have been anything from a laugh to the beginnings of a heart attack.

"Shall we go inside?" I said.

He looked back the way his attackers had gone.

"They'll need medical help before coming back here," I said. "You think they might send some friends?"

He shook his head and then gazed at me with those unhealthy orbs.

Dropping the stones, he said, "You know how to fight."

"Comes in handy in back alleys and jail pens."

Tally pulled a key from his pocket and turned toward the entrance. He went through the rough-hewn door into a dwelling that was most likely a temporary workman's shed when it was first thrown up.

It was a medium-sized room with no windows, a cot against one wall, and a huge plank table against another. There were clothes on the floor and comic books strewn around. Taped and tacked up on the walls were blue-lined sheets of notebook paper that had drawings of faces on them. Lots of native talent with little follow-through. The doodlings of a talented but hyperactive mind that the teachers never got through to—if they ever tried.

There was no bathroom that I could see but he had a chrome sink filled with dirty dishes. This was a poor, uneducated man's home, replete with the earmarks of poverty in the twenty-first century. There was a brand-new laptop computer and an Xbox on the desk amid the empty pizza cartons, *Avengers* comic books, and reams of lined paper, either scrawled upon or waiting their turn.

"Nice computer," I said.

"Chrystal gave me that stuff."

"That was nice of her."

"She just wants me to stay away, so she gives me stuff not to feel guilty."

"Who were those guys?" I asked.

"Big Boy an' Two Dog," he said. He pulled out a metal-and-vinyl folding chair from a corner and set it out for me.

He plopped down on the cot and said, "They give me some weed to sell but the cops busted me and took what I had left and all my money. But, you know, them two expect to get paid, or kick somebody ass."

I had yet to sit down. I was still wondering what I could hope to get out of this hopeless brother.

The shack smelled of Tally, that hint of rot that you might find in the wing of a hospital where they put the patients who can't pay.

I sat and asked, "What does Chrystal have against you? You're both artists."

"You like my drawings?" he asked.

"They have a lot of power. Portraits mainly, huh?"

"I like faces. Sometimes I ride the subway all day long and just draw one face after the other. They got every race in the world right down on the F train."

"That why you have problems with Chrystal?"

"What you mean?"

"Maybe she thinks you're competing with her," I suggested.

"The last time I went to her house some kind of silverware went missing," he said. "I didn't steal it. What I want with some old forks and spoons? Probably one of the servants did it, but they blamed me 'cause when I come around is the only time they check.

"But you right about that art, man. It was me who first asked Dad if maybe I could have a welding set to copy comic-book characters on steel. He got it for me but then, after a while, it was Chrystal doin' it all the time. She hogged it up and now she famous, married to some rich white man, and blamin' me for a thief."

To punctuate his dissatisfaction Tally took off his fake snake-skin jacket and dropped it on the splintery floor. His black T-shirt showed off arms that were thin and unencumbered by muscle. His milk-chocolate lips hung down in defeat.

"So you wouldn't know where she went or how I could get in touch with her," I said.

"We don't talk. Shawna said that Chris went on a vacation or somethin'."

"She tell you that four or five days ago?"

"I'ont know, man," he complained. "Neither one'a my sisters care about me. Shawna just wanna use you an', an', an' Chrystal don't wanna hear from ya."

"Chrystal gave you the computer and games."

"But she don't care. All she got to do is leave a note with that Mr. Pelham. She don't even have to go shoppin', just tell him what to buy an' where to bring it. And he don't come himself. They got that white niggah Phil to bring it out here. He just call on the cell phone and I got to run outside to pick it up from his limo."

I could see the kid's point. I understood his sister's position, too. The thing I didn't know was about my employer.

"What's your problem with Shawna?" I asked.

"Why?"

"She hired me and you said that she must not really care and is tryin' to do something I don't even know about," I said. "I don't wanna be used any more than you do."

"Shawna smile in your face, call you her best friend, and then, when you tell her sumpin', it be all ovah the street before you could sneeze. She jealous an' spiteful and won't even visit her own mother in the hospital. If she got hold of that green-and-red necklace she prob'ly stoled it. Prob'ly stoled that silverware, too, and then told Chrystal it was me. I bet she did."

I wondered. The words indicted Shawna but he delivered them in a way that seemed . . . insincere. I was sure he knew more but this was neither the time nor place for a full interrogation.

"You know you can't stay here, Ted."

"Why not?"

"Because Big Boy and Two Dog will be back."

Tally glanced at his one door and I suppressed a smile.

"Where I'ma go?"

"I got a friend in the Bronx got a pool hall needs cleanin' and a room for the janitor. I could get him to let you stay there for a week or two. In the meanwhile I got a lawyer that can represent your case."

"Why you wanna help me, man?"

"I was hired to do a job by a woman you say I shouldn't trust. Don't get me wrong, I'm not just taking your word on that, I have my own suspicions. So I might need you to help me later on. The only way I can be sure you will is if I help you now."

15

I CALLED MY LAWYER, Breland Lewis, and informed him about Tally.

"Have him get in touch tomorrow afternoon," he said. "Shirley will take down the information and make his appointment. I'm sorry, LT, but I'm due in court in a few hours and I still have notes to pull together."

Breland was in a rush but I didn't mind. I never like talking to lawyers—even when those lawyers are my friends.

"WHATEVER YOU SAY, LT," Luke Nye told me over the airwaves. "What's it with this kid?"

"Don't leave out your fancy silverware," I replied.

After that we put the Xbox and computer, some comics, and a ringed notebook of lined paper in a suitcase. Tally hauled his luggage four blocks to a limo service, where I paid the driver up front for the long drive to the Bronx.

As I watched the beat-up, dark-green Caddy drive off I wondered if Tally would be at Luke's when I needed him—*if* I needed him. He was a lost cause, even by my standards. I kinda liked the kid.

———

I STOOD OUT in front of the hole-in-the-wall limo service for a few minutes, thinking about the young man and his life, such as it was. America was tethered to its lineage by a frayed rope made up of millions of young men and women like him. It wasn't any wonder that so many of these youth had no notion of their history and no hope for a future except what they were told by the TV.

This notion felt very important at that time. I must have seemed a little cracked standing under the hot sun in a dark suit, sweating and staring at the empty street.

Finally I decided to walk to my next meeting. The task, I felt, would be some kind of penance for my abandonment of so many youngsters like Tally.

IT WAS A NICE DAY and so there were hundreds of people ambling and power-walking, running and biking across the Brooklyn Bridge. They spoke French and Mandarin, Spanish and Russian, with English accents and southern drawls. Bicycles whizzed by my right side as lovers holding hands unconsciously nudged me into the bike lane. Joggers weaved in between the tourists and lovers, and every sixth or seventh stroller was chatting on a cell phone. The sky bloomed with clouds over the dark, sinewy East River, and my dome was beaded with sweat.

The bridge always made me happy. Tally and Two Dog and Big Boy would live or die, but the bridge would still be standing, connecting the world with a history that cannot fade.

———

PRISTINE ENTERPRISES Retirement Community was on Rector Place, in the center of Battery Park City. It was a pink-and-clear-glass building that took up half a city block. The front desk was round with a raised floor that allowed the copper-skinned receptionist (whose nameplate read D. DIAZ) to sit in a swivel chair instead of standing on her feet, cultivating varicose veins and bad knees.

Ms. Diaz had a skinny frame and a pinched face. Behind her was a large circular area where there was a wide variety of chairs interspersed with uniform, dark-orange sofas. This furniture was populated by maybe half a dozen oldsters and their visiting kin. The ceilings were high, somehow putting the dread of death at a distance. The windows allowed in copious light.

I wiped my mostly bald head with a napkin left over from breakfast and said, "Nathan Chambers, please."

"And who are you?" Ms. Diaz asked with no discernible accent.

"Leonid McGill," I said. "I've come to discuss business with him, representing his daughter."

The copper woman smiled for the first time.

"Chrystal," she said.

"Shawna," I corrected.

The smile went away.

"And what is your business?"

"Shawna wanted me to ask her father about Chrystal and her brother Tally. She's been trying to get in touch with both of them but hasn't been able to make contact. She thought Mr. Chambers might have some idea where they are."

"Why didn't she come herself?"

"She's indisposed."

"Neither Chrystal or Tally have been here lately," the guardian said.

I was slightly surprised that she'd be so certain of this. There were obviously many residents of the home. Why would she know so much about one single man's guests?

"Is Mr. Chambers too busy to receive guests?" I asked.

"I've answered your question," Ms. Diaz said stolidly.

On a hunch, I asked, "Do you have a number for Cyril Tyler in your Rolodex?"

"What?"

"If you don't, I have it. Either way, I'd like you to give him a call. Tell him that you are refusing entrance to Leonid McGill."

A jolt went through the slender woman's angry face. She swiveled around in her chair and picked up a phone. I couldn't hear what she was saying or guess who she was talking to. After a minute or so she turned to face me again.

"Mr. Chambers will be down in a little bit. You can sit in the visitors' area."

I CHOSE AN empty orange couch near the southern window. The floor was a little higher than the street and so I could see only the heads and shoulders of pedestrians walking past. I thought that Tally would have a good time here, seeing faces by the hundreds march by.

I had a soft spot for lost young men. That was me back in the days after my father was killed in some South American revolution and my mother died of a broken heart. For the longest time I destroyed young men like Tally for a profit; now I tried to save them—but it was all the same.

"Excuse me," a voice said.

He wore pajamas that were so light blue someone might mistake them for white. The nightclothes were old, threadbare in spots. But they were clean and the man was sturdy. Five eight with maple-brown skin, Nathan Chambers was near seventy but had not yet crossed that border. He neither smiled nor frowned nor exhibited any other emotion beyond mild curiosity.

"Mr. Chambers?" I said, standing and extending a hand.

His handshake had some strength to it. He had more hair than I did. I'm sure to the casual observer we would have appeared similar in age.

"You look surprised," he said. "You expectin' somebody else?"

I sat back down, and he settled next to me.

"No, it's just, just that I'm surprised that such a healthy man would be in a place like this."

Chambers grinned, showing me a mouthful of dingy but otherwise strong-looking teeth.

"This is an elder community, young man, not a nursin' home. I'm here 'cause the retirement pays for it and there really ain't nowhere else to go. Your ship sink in a storm, you take the first island you see."

I could see Tally's features in the older man's face.

A gray mouse ran along the edge of the windowed wall, stopped a moment to regard us, then hurried off. Nathan noticed me noticing the rodent.

"Cute little things," he said. "On the cargo ships I worked, their relation, Brother Rat, always had a berth. The sail-ships of old colonized with both man and rat."

"I wanted to ask you some questions, Mr. Chambers."

"Call me Nate."

"Nate," I said. "I'm LT, Leonid McGill, a private detective."

"Oh?"

"I'm working for your daughter."

"Chrystal?"

"Shawna."

"Shawnie? Where she get the money to hire you?"

"I'm not sure," I said.

"That's a Russian name—Leonid."

"Yes sir, it is."

"You don't sound Russian."

"My father was a sharecropper turned Communist."

"Negroes do the craziest things," Nathan Chambers said. "Here you think you got 'em pegged in the slums and prisons and they turn around like that mouse, or Brother Rat, an' move to China an' open a pizza restaurant.

"What Shawnie want?"

"She came to my office and said that her sister was missing and that Cyril, her husband, was planning to kill her, Chrystal. Shawna wanted me to dissuade the husband, but when I went to him he said that he loved your daughter and wouldn't hurt a fly."

The retiree's conversational philosophy dried up for a moment. His face became sober and he wondered.

"I love Shawnie, but she's a mess," he said at last. "Six children by that many men and movin' from place to place. You just as likely to find her in a Catholic pew as an opium den. For a few years now she been livin' with this commune, drift from place to place. They like a wild tribe down in South America, think the whole continent is theirs—tax free."

"Your son Theodore thinks that she's probably lying about something," I said.

"We all lie about somethin'," the father told me. "The child who never lies don't make it past Sunday school."

"Why would Shawna lie about Chrystal?"

"Chrystal reached out for the brass ring an' come back with platinum," he said, looking directly in my eye. "Shawnie falled off the hobby horse. She been strugglin' since the day she was born. Don't ask me why. She love her sister, though. That's a fact. But what's not to love? Chrystal wanted to be a welder like her old man was in the Merchant Marines. I told her she couldn't and she told me that I was wrong. Damn if she wasn't right."

"Tally said that he was the one who asked you for the tools to draw on steel."

"Oh?" Nate said. "Well, maybe he did. But, you know, Teddy got restless hands. He needed to settle on one thing but never could. Football, baseball . . . drawin' on steel. He did it all, where Chrystal only cared about one."

"Have you heard from her?"

"Two weeks ago Monday she come by. Brought me some walnut fudge and a little square of steel. Said it was a blank canvas for me if I wanted to do a show with her. Hmm. She a good daughter. The best."

"You think her mother might know something about her?" I was fishing with the Merchant Marine.

"Azure," he said, making three syllables out of the word. "I'ont know. I haven't seen my wife in three years."

"She's only a few blocks from here, isn't she?" I asked. If Nate was a friend of mine I would have kept silent, but this was my job.

"I'd like to see her, I would, but she got nerves. You don't comport yourself just right and it makes her crazy for days. I bring her flowers every Tuesday, Tuesday. A Miss Rogers at the front desk takes 'em and tells me what she said the week before. I love my wife and my kids, Mr. McGill."

I believed him.

"I learned when I was at sea," he continued, "that a black man don't need to let his head hang down, he could have just as big dreams as any white man or Brahmin, Aztec princess or Gypsy king. I gave my children the kind of dreams they could live by, but dreams are like oceans, Mr. McGill. If they're worth a damn they're bigger than the dreamer, and sometimes, when the one dreaming wants to be as big as what they imagine, the wave pulls 'em down."

His words washed over me like the ocean they evoked. I ignored the impact for the time being because I had a job to do.

"Do you know where I can find Shawna?" I asked.

"No sir. No, sir, I don't. I never go lookin' for Shawnie. You know, a man lookin' for trouble is sure to find it."

16

ON THE STREET I felt like an adolescent again—on the run, back under the radar of the foster-care system. This was due to the broken family, missing sister, and words of Nathan Chambers.

. . . dreams are like oceans . . .

All the years I had spent hating my father for his laser-like attention and then abrupt abandonment, and it only took these few words to explain him in a way that the twelve-year-old in me could understand. Dreams are like oceans and sometimes they pull the dreamer down.

Just a few blocks from the Schmidt Home, Azure Freshstone-Chambers' residence, I came upon a desolate park. It was a patch of concrete, devoid of vegetation, with three benches set in a circle, looking out. One of these benches was occupied by a street denizen with a shopping cart, three suitcases, and at least eight neatly squared and piled blond nylon bags. I couldn't tell if the heavily clothed traveler was male or female, black or white. But these details hardly mattered. I sat down, facing the Hudson, though not looking there.

. . . dreams are like oceans . . .

Four words and my whole history had been turned on its head, like my father told me Marx had done to Hegel. Forgiveness for his inability was ripped from my chest by this slightly older man who blamed himself for shining a similar light in his own kids' eyes.

I could smell my neighbor. The odor was musty, dusty, and yet rich like loam. I wasn't thinking anything, not really. Nate left no room for conjecture. He told the truth, whether he believed it or not, and I was left with consequences that he'd never know he'd wrought.

I NEEDED TO go on with the case, but there wasn't room for it in my mind right then. I might have sat there in the company of that fragrant phantom for hours if my phone had not sounded.

It was the growling of a bear, a stranger—maybe.

"Hello."

"What's wrong, Lenny?" Harris Vartan asked. "You sound upset."

The tide of my thoughts receded. Vartan was another kind of force of nature.

"I'll look for the guy," I said.

"I appreciate that."

"Tell me something, Uncle Harry."

"What's that, Lenny?"

"Did you talk to my father before he left the country the last time?"

"Yes."

"What did he say?"

"That he didn't want to go but, knowing what he knew, he didn't know how to stay."

"Yeah," I said. "That's right. That's right."

"I begged him to stay," Harris said. "I told him what would happen if he died."

"So," I said, "what do you have for me?"

There was only a brief pause on the line, Harris paying deference to the pain he knew in me.

"Corinthia Mildred Highgate," he said.

"Who's that?"

"She knew Williams and last saw him somewhere between ten and twenty years ago. She lived in Manhattan then. Maybe she still does—if she's alive."

"Anything else?"

"Not really. Williams knew this Highgate. If you can locate her, and she's still alive, I'd like you to ask where he might be."

AFTER GETTING off the phone with the ghost of Christmases past, I called another number.

"Hello?" he said, panting like a fat dog after a young bitch in heat.

"What's up, Bug?" I asked the systems whiz kid.

"How many push-ups can you do, Mr. McGill?"

"Eighty or so—if I get warmed up first."

"Eighty?"

"Yeah. Why?"

"Straight out? I mean, not on your knees or an incline?"

"Straight out."

"I have to stop after three."

"Three months ago you'd have stopped before you started."

He took in a breath, tried to talk, inhaled again, and said, "What can I do for you?"

"You know those messages Twill's been getting on Twitter?"

"Yeah."

"I want you to send the eleven dollars to him and give that fake address Zephyra has for me in Queens."

"What's the address?"

"I don't remember. Call her and find out."

"Um . . ."

"What?"

"Uh . . . you want me call her?"

"I take it you want to do a lot more than talk with Zephyra."

"Yeah but . . . I mean, um, you know."

"Listen, kid, the girl wants *something* from you. There's no doubt about that. Maybe she just wants to be friends, but if that's so, why'd she say that you should get in shape?"

"We only saw each other alone that one time."

"I'm not askin' you to go see her. Just call."

I broke off the connection and glanced over at the resident of the adjacent bench.

What might have been a black man was in reality a middle-aged white woman rearranging her nylon bags to achieve some aesthetic effect that escaped me.

She looked up at me with her broad potato face and smiled.

Taking this as a good omen I waved, then set my feet back on the path to Azure.

17

Mrs. A. Rogers was in her middle fifties, like me, but she'd taken a very different path getting there. She was white with comfortable padding, delicate, and at ease with the insipid tranquility of her job. Her desk was a small maple table that had a green blotter, a tan phone with an array of buttons on it, and a solitary framed photograph of herself, ten years younger, standing with a friendly bearlike man, his arms circled around her and his smiling eyes peering into the lens.

Above Mrs. Rogers' head, a gray sign, stamped upon in blocky yellow letters, said ADMITTANCE. The reception room was little more than a vestibule. This was the wasp waist of the upscale mental institution through which visitors and professionals passed like grains of sand ticking off the monotonous microseconds that made up the infinity where Mrs. Rogers patiently waited.

She smiled in bland welcome.

"Leonid McGill for Azure Chambers," I said.

"Are you a relative?"

"Chrystal sent me with a message." I'd learned my lesson. Even though Shawna had hired me, I had to keep up her lie if I didn't want to be frowned upon and turned away.

"A message?" this middle-aged woman from the middle of Middle America said.

"Yes. I'm supposed to speak with her about something . . . private. I've been prepped on how to comport myself in her presence, and Mr. Tyler is aware of the visit."

The second key for entrée would certainly be Tyler. The milksop nerd was a god among citizens like A. Rogers.

The prisoner loves his warden, my father's words came back to me. *The slave fairly worships his master, and the worker deifies even the name of the rich man.*

Her gray eyes fixed on me, A. Rogers' smile dimmed.

"Mr. Chambers told me to tell you hello," I said, trying to keep the ember of that smile alive. "He told me how you always deliver his flowers."

A brief schism of mild pain passed through the otherwise plain woman's face.

"He's such a dear man," she said.

I nodded, ever so slightly.

"I hate doing that to him, but even flowers are too much for Azure," A. Rogers said to me, her temporary confessor. "I give them to other women residents. Those poor souls would love to have a husband like Nathan."

I tried to look understanding.

It was this tame expression that finally overcame the passive barrier, the infinite boredom of that room.

"Have a seat, Mr. McGill," Mrs. Rogers said.

I looked around and noticed a spindly rosewood chair that was, I thought, unlikely to hold my one hundred and eighty-three pounds. I took this offer as a challenge. Maybe Mrs. Rogers was testing me to see if I could manage not to break her furniture before she trusted me with Azure.

I sat delicately, tensing my thighs to lessen the burden on the chair. But as my weight tilted unerringly earthward I realized that there was a strength in that doelike seat that one wouldn't, one couldn't, have imagined.

I sat there while the mild-mannered woman went about reading and amending notes on tiny slips of pink paper. She hadn't made a call or sent any other message that I could discern.

I had begun to wonder if her offer of a seat was just a kindness and not an invitation when a door to her right opened.

The woman who came into the vestibule-office was Mrs. Rogers' spiritual twin. She was in her thirties, dressed in a nurse's uniform instead of civvies, caramel colored, and thin, with a severe cast to her face. But, still, Colette Martin had all the earmarks of bland resistance.

"Mr. McGill?" Nurse Martin said.

I never did figure out how she knew my name. I only knew hers because of the name tag over her tiny left breast.

"Yes?"

"Come with me."

I got to my feet and followed Nurse Martin into a long hallway where the walls, floors, and ceiling were the same nearly colorless gray hue. Every fifteen feet or so we passed a set of greenish-yellow elevator doors. Three elevator banks down, Colette stopped, pulled a keychain from her clamshell white pocket, and carefully chose a key that fit into a slot next to the lift. The doors slid open immediately and we entered into a surprisingly large space.

Choosing another key, Colette turned the lock for floor seventeen.

There was no further verbal communication between Nurse Martin and me. There was nothing to impart, nothing to gain by words. I simply stood, waiting to arrive, and then, when the doors slid open, she moved to the side, indicating to me by this gesture that I'd be getting off by myself.

THE SITTING ROOM I entered was a palette of pastel blues and grays. There was a window, but its light-gray shade was pulled, a diaphanous blue curtain drawn over that. The table in the corner was almost, but not quite, white, and the chairs (relations of the fawn downstairs) had considered green but gave up half the way there.

I don't think that I'd ever experienced such spatial peace. It was like the experience of a zazen breath exhaled into a room where it had become both real and ethereal.

"Hello."

She was what the old folks called *high yellow*, the color of a darkening lemon. Her gown was creamy blue with a hint of satin, somewhere. The gray-and-brown hair was coarse, combed back from a well-defined round face that was understated and yet deeply aware.

We might have shared the same birth year.

"Mrs. Chambers," I said.

"Azure," she replied, making it three syllables as her husband had.

It made me happy to think that even in their separation she and Nate were of the same mind.

She turned her head slightly and I understood that she was offering me a chair.

I also knew that I should leave my hands at my side, speak in a modulated tone, and keep my eyes focused on her while not staring her directly in the face. She was royalty and I a subject, but this distinction had nothing to do with hierarchy; it was more a system of shared duty.

It was as I lowered into my chair that I realized a piano sonata was playing softly, maybe in another room.

My host did not sit. She stood behind the chair across the table from me, resting her delicate hands on its back for support.

Behind Azure the wall was recessed. In this shallow alcove sat the only aberration in an otherwise perfect environment. It was a thin, coal-colored table against the wall supporting golden frames of the picture-portraits of her children and husband.

"And your name is?" she asked, giving me her full beneficent attention.

"McGill," I said, hoping that the word wasn't too pointy or sharp.

"You have a message for me from Chrystal?"

I glanced at the portraits behind her.

"Your daughters look very much alike."

"Very."

"Did people confuse them for each other from time to time?"

"When they got to be eleven and twelve they used to switch places. They never fooled me, but even their aunts and uncles were tricked sometimes."

"How could you tell the difference?" I asked.

"If they were standing you could always see that Shawnie was the shorter one. But when they were alone or sitting down you could tell by their eyes. Chrystal has the eyes of an ancient, and Shawnie has the look of a wild creature that stumbled into civilization and can't find her way back to the wilderness."

Hearing this analysis, I could imagine the long talks that she and Nate must have had. I felt the pain of his loss—and hers.

"Why are you here?" I asked.

"Where?"

"This, this place."

"Oh," she said, "yes. I have a condition, a mental condition."

"You seem very normal to me."

"In here I do. But the noise and mess outside drives me crazy. There's a science word for it but it's what our mothers would have called nerves. Doctors say that there's a medicine I could take but I'd rather just keep everything around me quiet and peaceful. That way I don't have to feel like I'm sick.

"You're smiling, Mr. McGill."

"Oh? I hadn't realized. I guess it's because what you're saying is that you are only emotionally disturbed when there's someone else in the room."

Azure laughed. It was a very pleasant sound.

"Yes. And only a kindly gentleman like yourself, who keeps still, can know the real me."

"Who pays for all this?"

"That's a very blunt question, sir."

"I'm sorry, but I'm trying to understand who I'm dealing with. Not you, but your daughters and Mr. Tyler."

"Cyril owns the nursing facility. He bought it when Chrystal couldn't find a suitable place for me," she said, adding, "You said you had a message from her?"

"Indirectly," I said. "A woman who looks like Chrystal came to my office and asked me to help with a problem. But I'm beginning to believe that it was Shawna who approached me, and I'm trying to figure out why."

"Was she asking you to help Chrystal or herself?" Azure asked with no visible tension showing.

"Chrystal," I said. "But I'm not sure that Chrystal has a problem."

"That's very odd," Azure commented. "It's Chrystal who looks after her brother and sister. She was here visiting me only two days ago."

"Really? What did she say?"

"That she and Cyril were going on a cruise," Azure said. It was the first lie she told me. "Chrystal has always wanted to be a Merchant Marine like her father. She loves boats, and Cyril is not a very physical man. He lets her take care of everything when they go out on his yacht."

"Do you know where I can find Shawna, Ms. Chambers?"

"Azure. Call me Azure."

"Azure," I said as if speaking an incantation.

"There's a red-brick building north on D past First, that's what Chrystal told me. It has a stand of aspen on the roof."

For a moment Azure's mind traveled to the faraway tenement

inhabited by her wild creature daughter. Her lips twisted and she directed that gaze toward the reassurance of a blank blue wall.

"I should probably go," I said.

"My husband, Nathan, doesn't know how to talk like you," she said. "He needs to move around too much, and he, he touches me."

"I'm going to stand up now," I said.

"It was nice seeing you, Mr. McGill. You're a kind man."

18

I T   W A S   L A T E in the afternoon but the summer sun was still up and luxuriant. I considered walking across town to the place where Shawna might live but gave up on that idea for the moment.

Age has taught me to take my time with some destinations.

That includes going home.

I started walking north on Greenwich Street, realizing as I went that I was probably going to walk the eight miles to the Upper West Side and my broken family.

W A L K I N G   T H R O U G H the borough of Manhattan is another supplementary exercise for me; I feel my whole history passing down the blocks of my delinquent adolescence and criminal maturity. The bricks and concrete, stoplights and police cruisers were my indictment for a thousand crimes committed without remorse, or even much awareness. I'd never been caught or convicted, not so much as indicted for the lives I'd shattered. But I remembered when walking who I'd been and why I paid penances like sitting patiently with innocents like Azure Freshstone-Chambers.

At Christopher I turned right, making my way over to

Hudson Street. Six or seven blocks north of there Hudson became Eighth Avenue, the artery toward Broadway and, ultimately, my home.

As I was crossing Thirty-second Street I pulled out my cell phone and called information.

"Say a city and state," a pleasant woman asked over the invisible waves of communication.

"New York, New York," I said.

"Say 'residence' or the name of the business you wish to call."

"Residence."

"All right. You said 'residence.' Is that correct?"

"Yes," I said, looking up toward the Thirty-third Street sign.

"Say the last name and the first."

"Highgate, Corinthia."

"Yes. Corinthia Highgate. Would you like me to connect you at no extra charge?"

"Yes."

The phone went dead for a moment, but I knew from experience that this was just part of the charade. The human voice without a soul returned to her electronic tomb and the system passed along the digital impulses of my request.

A phone rang. It did this seven times. I was prepared to leave a message. And then the eighth ring was cut off midway through its arc and a frail woman's voice said, "Hello?"

"Mrs. Highgate?"

"Miss Highgate. Who is this?"

"My name is Ambrose Thurman," I said, using the name of a man who might have been a friend if he had not died violently. "I'm a—I'm the nephew of a man named William Williams."

"Lee. Oh, I haven't heard that name for many years, many years. You're his nephew, you say?"

"Yes. Well, not actually. My father, John Laniman, died soon after I was born—"

"I'm sorry."

"That's okay. It was a long time ago, before I can remember. Anyway, my mother got remarried—to William's brother, Thomas."

I thought that it would be a nice, and convincing, touch to make me, a black man, legally related to the missing Williams.

"I never knew he had a brother."

"He was just a half brother, and the family was sort of estranged," I lied. "Anyway, my stepfather died recently and I decided that I should get in touch with old Bill."

I studied acting for the express purpose of being able to lie convincingly on the fly.

"Lee," she said, not as a correction but as a fond memory. "It's been a long time. More than fifteen years certainly. More than that. He was such a nice man, your uncle."

"I hardly remember."

"How did you come across my name?" the disembodied, elderly voice asked.

"I ran into an old friend of the family," I said. "Harris Vartan. He said that he remembered Uncle Bill mentioning your name."

I'd agreed to do this job for Uncle Harry. Usually when anyone worked for the Diplomat of Crime they never spoke his name. But I wasn't working for that man. I was doing a favor for an old family friend and so his name was not taboo or forbidden—at least it should not have been. If it was, then he was lying and Miss Highgate had the right to hang up in my ear.

"Vartan, you say?" she asked.

"Harris Vartan."

"I don't know that name. Did he say I knew him?"

"No, ma'am, not really. He just said that Uncle Bill knew you some time ago."

"It's been years. What ever happened to him?"

"I was hoping you could tell me that, Miss Highgate. Losing my mother three years ago, and now my stepfather, I felt like I should reach out to him."

"I wish I could help you, Mr. Thurman. I really do. Bill moved to New Jersey a long time ago and we lost touch. I don't even have his number anymore. Anyway, I'm sure he moved from that address. I remember calling one day and a woman, I forget her name, said that he had gone away."

"That's too bad," I said. "Can you tell me anything else that might help me find him?"

"No. All I know is how smart he was and that he'd laugh at the strangest things."

"Like what?"

"One day we were walking through Central Park and a young woman asked him to sign a petition against cruelty to animals. Lee looked at her like he was surprised and then started laughing out loud. He kept saying over and over, 'Cruelty . . . to animals,' like it was the punch line to a joke."

Odd, certainly, but no help.

"Thank you very much, Miss Highgate. Maybe I could give you my number—"

"Wait a minute," she said, cutting me off. "I remember something, Mr. Thurman."

"What's that, ma'am?"

"Lee left a box of books with me. He said that he was going to come get them but he never did. You know, he used to read and reread those books over and over. I think that they were very important to him."

"What kind of books are they?"

"I don't know. Books about real things. I tried to read one once and I didn't even know what it was saying."

"Is it in English?"

"Oh yes. I knew the words but I didn't know what they were saying."

"Would you like to sell me those books, Miss Highgate?" I suspected that she could use some cash.

"I suppose so. You know I held on to them for so long because they were all I had left of Lee. But I guess he's gone now . . . and you're family."

She gave me her address and I promised to drop by the next afternoon.

AFTER TALKING TO Miss Highgate I walked on, counting my breaths in Zen fashion. When my thoughts became tangible I found myself thinking about Shawna and her mother's description: *a wild creature lost in civilization.* This portrayal of the young woman, who looked so much like her sister, had a resemblance to me and my life, also to Twill and his. We were, the three of us, outsiders who found ourselves trapped in a world of conformity. We pretended to belong. We acted as if we accepted the laws and regulations, but really we ignored any rule of conduct that got in our way. We were why law-abiding citizens were uneasy about the notion of freedom; because true freedom brooks no interference and pays fealty only to desire.

AN HOUR OR so later I realized that I had walked eight blocks past my street. Something had thrown me off my game, but it wasn't clear, as yet, what that something was.

I looked at my watch and realized that the appointed hour, four P.M., had come and gone without Shawna calling in.

19

WHEN I GOT home I went straight to the dining room because I wanted to pull myself together before talking to Gordo. It was okay to ask him for advice, but I didn't want him worrying about me. And the thoughts in my mind were worrisome.

Usually the dining room was empty unless we were eating; and Katrina had gotten into the habit of delaying dinner until I got home. Even though she had reverted to her old cheating ways, she still showed me respect in my home—I liked that.

I walked in, expecting solitude, but instead I found Shelly sitting at the hickory dining table, looking perplexed.

"Hi, Dad," the dark-olive-skinned Asian girl said. She came over to me and kissed my cheek.

We had not one strand of DNA in common, going back over twenty thousand years, but she didn't know that and I didn't care. Blood may be thicker than water, but family has them both beat.

"Hey, babe," I said to Katrina's love child. "You look worried."

"Tatyana called," she said.

I turned a chair around and sat, heavily. "Oh? What did she say?"

"She just asked to speak to D," Shelly said, pulling her seat up to face me.

She reached out and took my right hand by the thumb and forefinger.

Shelly, Twill, and Dimitri were everything you could want in kids: nothing alike and deeply connected.

"What did he say?" I asked.

"He took the phone into his room," Shelly said, "talked for about twenty minutes, and then left."

"Did he pack a bag?"

She nodded and squeezed my fingers.

Tatyana was Dimitri's first real love. He was nearly twenty-two but that girl had him by the short hairs and he liked the pain.

"Does your mother know?" I asked.

"No. She was out when he left. I know how much she worries about D, so I thought I'd wait and tell you."

I patted her hand and took in a deep breath. My daughter's eyes met mine.

"What should we do?" she asked.

"Let's wait and see if D calls. We'll tell your mother that Taty-ana came back and D ran off on some holiday with her. She'll be so upset about that, that she won't worry about the worst."

The apprehension flowed away from Shelly's face. I was responsible now. That was why she waited for me in the dining room, to pass the torch of anxiety.

"Gordo in there with Elsa?" I asked to remove the last vestiges of her worry.

"He seems a lot better," she said, nodding.

"The chemo's over," I said. "He's bound to bounce back—for a little while."

"You don't think he's got a chance to get better?"

"In my experience," I said, "things only get worse."

I stood up and walked out.

I ENTERED GORDO'S studio sanitarium and found him leaning against a stack of pillows with Elsa sitting in a chair at his side. I wasn't sure, but it almost seemed as if they had been holding hands and let go when I walked in.

Gordo pushed himself up a bit and smiled at me.

"Hey there, young man," he said in a tone reminiscent of him before the cancer.

"Hey there, old man," I replied.

Elsa smiled and stood.

"Mr. McGill."

"Ms. Koen."

"He's doing much better today," the nurse said. "He asked me if I knew how to dance."

"He asks every boxer that," I said.

"If you can't dance then you sure can't box," Gordo and I said together.

We laughed and I felt a sense of unfamiliar lightness.

"I'll go into the other room," Elsa said, "and let you men talk."

She walked away with a sway to her gait that I hadn't noticed before.

"Fine-lookin' woman," Gordo said as the door closed behind her.

"I'm just seein' that," I said.

I eased into Elsa's seat and took my own appraisal of my oldest friend.

"You do look good," I said.

"Feel great," he replied. "I've taken enough of that poison. Shit. Even cancer feels better'n that. How you doin', son?"

"It's thirty seconds into the third round and the other guy, who everybody said couldn't punch, has knocked me on my can—and I'm not seein' double, but one and a half."

Gordo grinned.

I continued the metaphoric list. "I'm worried about the round, the fight, and my own two feet doin' what I tell 'em to."

"It don't get any better'n that," Gordo said.

"Did I tell ya that the referee was the other boxer's brother-in-law?"

"I heard Katrina fightin' with that voice again today," the ancient trainer intoned. "It was a young man, I'm pretty sure. I couldn't make out what they were sayin' but there was some threat in there."

"What time was that?"

"Between twelve and one. Before Elsa got here."

The phone rang in the hall. I wondered if it was Dimitri but pushed the thought out of my mind. Shelly would tell me if it was.

"You look good, old man," I said. I was tired of conflicts and mysteries.

"I feel good."

I decided to quit while we were ahead and rose to my feet.

"Your head'll clear by round five," Gordo told me.

"If I don't get knocked out in the fourth."

SHELLY AND ELSA were talking in the hallway.

"Who was that?" I asked my daughter.

"Mom. She said that she's going to the movies with Magda and that dinner's already made in the refrigerator. Elsa said she'll stay and look after Papa Gordo."

"Where's Twill?"

"He's out with some friends," Shelly said. "You know what that means."

"Either he'll be home by dawn or the police will be calling at three in the morning."

Shelly and I both smiled but Elsa looked perplexed.

"Don't worry, Ms. Koen," I said. "We love Twill."

"He seems like such a nice boy," the nurse offered.

"You won't find finer on four continents," I said. "But trouble sticks to him like white on rice."

THE MEAL KATRINA left us was magnificent. Glazed oxtails with red cabbage, saffron rice, and walnut pie for dessert.

When Gordo asked for seconds on the pie I began to wonder if Western medicine was something more than insurance scams and doctors' excuses.

ELSA AGREED TO spend the night in case Gordo had problems. Shelly said they could set the guest cot up in her room.

I WENT TO bed early, wondering what force it was that kept me moving forward with so much to do and most of it left undone.

Sometimes a soldier finds himself in a war so long that he forgets his goal, Tolstoy McGill had once said to me at bedtime. He should have been telling me the story of Little Red Riding Hood, but instead I was receiving an anarchist's indoctrination. *At a time like that all he has to do is remember his last order and keep moving toward that. Because, like everything else, life is just a reflex.*

I'd hated my father up until the moment Nate Chambers told me that dreams were oceans. And now, after forty-three years of spite, I went to bed with no hatred to give me solace, or to keep me going forward. My last orders had been nullified and there were no new instructions to replace them.

With these thoughts in mind I fell into a fitful sleep. Somewhere just after four I woke up to find Katrina there next to me. She was dreaming peacefully. A sigh escaped my lips but no one heard, and so no one cared.

20

By 5:09 I was out of bed. I took my clothes from the closet, picked up my shoes and socks from the floor, and made my way out of the bedroom, lumbering but silent—like a bear.

Twill and I approached the dining room door at the same moment. He was wearing black pants and shoes, scarlet socks and a light-gray linen shirt. His dark smile was welcome even if his hour of reentry was not.

"Where've you been?" were the first words from my mouth.

"Out with Ginko and his friends," he said. "You up early, Pops."

"Your mother worries," I answered.

"I'm sorry, man."

"You could call."

"I promise I will, from this day on," he said and I knew it was true. Twill didn't always tell the truth, but he used a certain tone when making commitments.

"What are you into, boy?"

"Nuthin'. Just havin' some fun."

He looked at me and I hunched my shoulders. He was the last fighter a slugger like me wanted to meet in the ring. Didn't have much of a punch but he could hit you all night long, and all you'd connect with was air.

I TOOK A cab down to Winston's Diner to get my breakfast—and, hopefully, a glimpse of Aura. I knew she dropped in there sometimes to get her coffee before work—usually about seven.

But that hour came and went and all I had was the *New York Times* to keep me company. A man in Queens was caught building a fertilizer bomb in his basement. He planned to blow up his entire block; would have succeeded, too, if the guy who logged gas usage hadn't noticed some of the telltale signs of bombmaking in the trash outside the garage.

The greatest natural disaster in the history of the world has been the human brain. Get rid of us and Eden will return unaided.

"Here you go," said the strawberry blond waitress from the day before.

I had ordered fried pork chops, a short stack of oat pancakes, two eggs over easy, and a patty of grated and fried potato.

I ate my poisonous meal with hot sauce, maple syrup, and black pepper—all the while watching her dancer's body move from counter to table, table to kitchen.

There was an emptiness in my chest that Nate Chambers had created by yanking the hatred out of there. No food or lust could fill that empty space.

"Anything else?" the waitress asked me.

"No," I said, clipping the word down to its shortest syllabic span.

I wanted to ask her to come have dinner with me that night. I needed something, but it wasn't her.

The check was $21.46. I left a twenty and a ten under it, hoping that maybe the next time I came she would ask me about my needs again.

THE RED-BRICK BUILDING took up the whole center part of the south block of D, north of First. I spied the rooftop stand of slender white tree trunks from the corner.

Approaching the eight-story building from across the street, I noticed a few things immediately. First, it was more like a fortress than the surrounding, gentrifying apartments and condos. The windows on the first and second floors were all blocked in different ways. There were grids and barbed wire, horizontal, vertical, and even slanted bars used.

Some of the upper windows were open. On the seventh floor a large woman was sitting on the sill, looking down at me looking up at her.

Crossing the street, I noted that the front door, actually a barricade, was fretted and strapped with forbidding green metal. There was no button or even a knocker to request entrée. The spray-paint red graffiti on the door read FREEDOM'S RESERVATION.

Why couldn't I catch a normal case, a woman who runs away from her bourgeois husband with the janitor, living in a Jersey motel and dreaming about coming home?

I knocked on the door. It sounded like a three-year-old pounding on a pillow.

No one answered, so I waited.

————

PATIENCE IS ONE of my best qualities. I have sat in my classic car for days on the slim hope of catching a quick look at a cheating wife or a bail jumper's yellow shirt. But patience is not my only virtue; I can also take a punch, or a hint, go for years without love or relief, and I can face Death in the eye and hardly flinch. Not only can I stand up under pain, but I can ignore the pain others feel. I always pay my debts but rarely act out of a desire for personal revenge.

Given all that talent, I could stand out in front of that red-brick arboretum for hours with no anxiety or rancor to get in the way.

A lonely seagull cried in my pocket.

"Hello, Aura," I said after three heartbreaking exclamations. "I was at Winston's this morning."

"I've been thinking about you."

I could face Death, but Aura made my chest quiver.

"Oh?" I said, fooling no one.

"I love you, Leonid."

Those few words created a fissure deep down in the soul my father declared did not exist.

I was searching for an answer when a youngish white man clad in varying shades of green walked up to the fortified door. I say young, but he might have been all of forty with the youth preserved in his eyes and skin. There was something mirthful about him—a demeanor fit for one of Robin Hood's merry men of legend.

"I got to go, Aura," I said.

I disconnected the call before she could respond. It wasn't a conscious act. Was this the warrior's reflex my father was talking about?

Even the newcomer's straw hat was green. His pants were olive and his T-shirt teal. His shoes and socks were crayon green.

His eyes were brown and they gauged me. If there was suspicion there I missed it, hidden behind a smile that was both practiced and natural.

He reminded me of the Artful Dodger. In my mind, that's what I dubbed him.

He nodded out of simple civility, removed a tiny green phone from his shirt pocket, and made the call.

We watched each other and waited five seconds.

"Fledermaus at the door," he said, "with someone who wants in, it seems."

"I knocked but no one answered," I said to the Dodger as he pocketed the cell phone.

"Fledermaus," he replied.

"That a name or a code word?"

"They never let anybody in."

"What are you waiting for, then?"

"I'm somebody."

"Doesn't a somebody have visitors now and then?"

"They have to be on guard for police spies," he told me. "The previous owner of the building died with no heirs. The current residents are pioneers who have claimed the property, but the cops work for the bosses and want to take their squat away."

There was my father again, this time lecturing me and my brother Nikita about the Paris Commune and what Engels did to free the workers.

"You say 'they,'" I said. "Aren't you one of them?"

"I'm a friend of a lot of people down around here," he said. "They ask me to do favors now and again."

"I have to speak to the woman who hired me," I said. "A Shawna Chambers. Her mother told me to look for her here."

"If you work for her why did her mother have to tell you where she lived?"

"Ask her, and send somebody down with an answer." I was turning serious, a natural reaction against that perpetual smile.

My phone chirped.

"Shawna?" the Dodger asked.

"That's all—and everything," I told him.

The door pulled inward. There were at least seven men standing in the entranceway.

Fledermaus nodded to me and winked before making it through the mob and into the building. I considered trying to bull my way in but nixed the notion.

"Tell her that it's Leonid McGill," I said before the heavy door slammed in my face.

On the glass face of my cell phone the words *These waters run deep* glared in black and gray. It was a message from Aura.

I stood there, wishing I still had a father to hate.

21

ALONE AGAIN, I wondered if the merry man called Fledermaus would deliver my message. Even if he did, Shawna might not appreciate me finding out who she wasn't. There was almost definitely a variety of other exits she could use to avoid me. But, I reasoned, a woman with six children couldn't run as easily as a woman alone—again, like me.

The phone now growled in my pocket.

"Hello?"

"Mr. McGill?"

"Ms. Koen," I said. "Anything you need?"

"He wants to talk to you."

"Put him on."

"Kid?" Gordo said in my ear.

"What's up, old man?"

"I got a call from Firpo. He said that Iran had some rough visitors up at the gym today. Lucky for Eye, he was out. They told Firpo to keep quiet about them bein' there, but he called me first thing."

Firpo was a jazz musician, a tuba player turned janitor. The tragedy of the human brain is that it is aware of what it has lost and where it's headed—both at the same time.

The barricade door swung inward and a solitary man blossomed forth.

"I got to go, Gord," I said. "I'll look into it right after I finish what I'm doin' now."

"Cool."

The forty-something man was white and extra-large with hard muscles that proudly exhibited their definition. Six foot even, he was completely bald, had a variety of facial scars, and the blue tattoo of curling barbed wire trailing off from the left corner of his mouth down past the collar of his incongruous pink T-shirt. The look on the big man's face was designed to instill fear.

I smiled for him.

"Who are you?" he asked in a guttural Muscovite accent.

"Leonid," I said, pronouncing the word as some Russians might.

It was his turn to smile. His teeth had been stained by coffee, cigarettes, and the bitter taste of state domination.

"Ivan," he said. "Ivan Beria."

"Any relation?"

"Ve are all brothers, are ve not, comrade?" he said, exaggerating his accent.

"I'm here to see Shawna Chambers."

"She is not here."

"But she lives here, right?" I asked. "Maybe I could wait till she gets back."

"Go away."

"Happy to, Comrade Beria, but I'll be back with the cops in under an hour unless I see Shawna in the next five minutes."

"I don't care about police."

"You should. Down in Philadelphia they blew up a house of squatters, mostly kids. You think you had it bad in the Old Country, but we have a saying here in America—wherever you go, there you are."

My tone, more than the information, worried the communal ex-Communist.

"Shawna is gone."

I didn't like the finality of his tone.

"What about her kids?" I asked.

"They are children."

"Either I talk to Shawna or her kids right now or the police with their helicopters and bombs will be at your doorstep for lunch."

From the threat in his eyes I could believe that this man was a descendant of the chief of Stalin's secret police. Luckily for me, the NKVD was no longer in power and we were on American soil.

"Come with me," the big man said.

He turned and walked past the vestibule and into the ground-floor hallway of the fortress.

I'm short but wide. My shoulders would easily fit on a man of Beria's height. His shoulders were sculpted for a giant. I followed him to a small elevator where we squeezed in and he tapped the button for the top floor.

It took a good deal of courage to keep my hands from fidgeting on the ride. I have severe claustrophobia issues, and small elevators in the company of men named after a mass murderer, serial killer, and rapist went to the top of my list of places to avoid. Heat radiated from Beria's pink chest as did an odor that reminded me of the barn my father, brother, and I slept in when we used to go to a private retreat in Appalachia for firearms practice with everything from .22-caliber long-barreled pistols to grenade launchers.

When the whiny door slid open I had to be mindful not to sigh.

The Russian led me down a long hall of apartments that ended at a door he pushed open.

This domicile was a surprisingly spacious room with high ceilings and many windows. A middle-aged woman from India was sitting at one of the windows, looking out. There were, I decided, many sentries at Freedom's Reservation. Around her was a group of six variously colored children—the oldest of whom was a girl of seven, or maybe eight. The youngest child, a boy, was whimpering on the oldest's lap.

All the kids were looking up at me and Beria with both fear and awe in their faces. All except the elder girl—a golden-skinned, copper-haired beauty—whose only defense against men like us was defiance.

"Do you recognize this man?" Beria asked the kids.

I thought the question was odd at first, but then, I thought, why wouldn't they know one of their mother's acquaintances?

At first the children didn't respond.

"Fatima," the Indian woman said.

"No," said the golden-skinned leader of the small tribe.

"Have you seen her sister—Chrystal?" I asked.

"Aunt Chris went on a cruise," Fatima replied, looking up at me.

"Your mom asked me to do Aunt Chris a favor," I said, "but I wasn't able to find her. So I came here to ask your mom what I should do next."

I was just talking. The agreement between myself and the child had already been struck. That look she gave me was one I'd seen many times in my client's chair.

Please help me, Mr. McGill.

The Indian babysitter and the Russian son of perdition stared down on the children, restraining them with their wills.

"Do you know where your mother is right now?" I asked Fatima.

The woman shook her head almost imperceptibly. Fatima cast a glance at her and then bowed, shaking her head at the floor.

"Can I speak to you outside for a moment?" I said to Beria.

He grunted and turned.

He was out the door first and I came just after. I allowed him to pull the unlocked portal shut before hitting him solidly in the gut. That right hook was executed just the way Rocky Marciano was teaching it in the Ph.D. program for pugilism up in heaven—or wherever. But I didn't rest on my laurels. I hit him three more times in the midsection, threw two uppercuts to his face, and then landed a straight right on the tip of his chin.

He was unconscious before the last blow, falling to the floor with a heaviness that was indicative of insensibility. I wasn't proud of myself. Hitting a man who is unaware of your intentions is the act of a coward, but as the referee of life says, *Protect yourself at all times.*

I turned my head to look down the hall. Fledermaus was standing there, three large steps out of reach. I thought about running toward him. A mind reader, he put up his hands in mock surrender. I looked back at Beria. He was going to be out for a while longer. So I opened the door to the apartment and walked in.

"Ivan wants to see you outside," I said to the Indian nursemaid.

She approached me suspiciously. I held the door for her and slammed it as soon as she cleared the threshold.

I could hear her muffled cry from the hallway but that was of no concern to me. It was a heavy door and there was a bolt, so I threw it. There was also a lock, which I turned.

The children had organized themselves behind Fatima. She was standing behind her stool, the dark-skinned two-year-old boy in her arms.

"Where's your mother, honey?" I asked the girl.

"Are you going to save us?" she asked.

"I'm gonna try my best."

"She's gone away to sleep."

"When did this happen?"

"Last night. I was asleep and then I woke up and saw the man . . . he was climbing out the window."

"Did he take her with him?"

She shook her head, holding back the tears with that motion.

"Then where is she?"

"Beria and them took her to the compost heap behind the People's Garden over at St. Matthew's. They put blindfolds on us to take us there but Boaz recognized it because the one time he ran away that's where he hid."

"But she was . . . asleep before then?"

Her nod had all the slow solemnity of a funeral march.

Somebody knocked on the door—with a battering ram.

22

"I HAVE TO ASK you a question, Fatima," I said to the head child.

She looked at me, hardly shuddering when the heavy object hit the door a second time.

"Do you want me to take you and your brothers and sisters out of here?"

She cocked her head and squinted as if trying to decipher a new slang.

"I'll take you out of here if you want to go, if you want to come with me."

She nodded and the children huddled closer around her.

THE DOOR TO their unit was the fireproof kind; plated with thin but durable metal and, most probably, reinforced on the inside. I propped a chair up against the doorknob. The heavy object shook the barricade hard enough for me to see the hinges move.

With Fatima's help I herded the kids to a fire escape that I'd located the moment I walked in. One little girl grabbed her favorite doll, and her brother, who was no more than ten months her senior, picked up a ray gun. I didn't try to stop them. Getting in the way of a child's imagination will almost always take more time than it's worth.

Fatima's toddler brother was crying. She handed him into my arms while urging her siblings through the window. The door shook again, causing the unfamiliar sensation of fear to blossom in my lungs.

The little boy stopped crying as soon as he could hide his face against my chest. We were the last two out on the fire escape. The others were scampering down, led by their courageous sister. She released the ladders and went from floor to floor, making sure that we were all safe. The second-floor landing was bolted and her hands weren't strong enough to throw the latch. I was about to bend down when she kicked the iron rod and the trapdoor fell through, allowing my newfound brood to clamber down to the sidewalk.

"Hey, you!" a voice shouted from above.

I didn't look up. Why would I? I knew that they'd be after us. Sometimes you just have to make the best of what you find.

I'm not superstitious as a rule, but when I saw the yellow cab trawling D for a fare I hoped that I hadn't used up my taxi-karma on the guy I forced to drive to Brooklyn.

"Cab!" I shouted in a voice I hadn't used in a long time.

He pulled to a stop.

"Get 'em all in," I said to Fatima.

A chorus of complaint roared out from the window and fire escape above.

"Goodbye!" I yelled up at our pursuers as Fatima hurried the kids along. "We'll see you when we get back from the zoo!"

I jumped in, gave the driver an address I knew well, and prayed for green lights.

IN THE CAR, with the toddler on my lap, I sighed. The fear I felt had nothing to do with my personal safety but with the jeopardy my actions may have placed the children in. I was pretty sure that my client was dead, and that the children were in greater danger in the fortress than they would be with me—but still . . .

I inhaled the various odors that cling to children. We were a few blocks away from the escape and I doubted that anyone would catch up to us.

If they did that would be their bad luck.

"Fatima," I said.

The child looked up at me. She was holding the hands of the four- and the five-year-old that separated her and her brother.

"Was your mother hurt?"

She nodded. The tears were behind her. I felt that she had swallowed the pain for all her brothers and sisters, that this child had already seen more hardship than I'd accrued in all my brutal fifty-five years.

"Was she scared about anything before that?"

"Mama was always scared about somethin'," she told me. "She said that there was a robber behind every door, even in the big house."

"The big house?"

"That's where Ivan lived with us all."

"Was Ivan your mom's boyfriend?"

"Sometimes."

"Did he hurt her?"

"Uh-uh. It was the man who climbed out the window."

"I'm going to take you to the house of a really nice lady and her daughter," I said, wanting to veer away from the underlying pain of loss.

"We want to go stay with our Aunt Chris," Fatima said.

"Yeah," one of her little sisters agreed.

"As soon as I find her I'll be happy to take you to her," I said. "But I have to get you someplace safe before that."

"What if we don't like it there?" the elder child asked.

"If you don't, then you don't have to stay."

She nodded once, and I had to remind myself that she was a child and not the woman she seemed to be.

AURA ULLMAN OWNED a very large top-floor apartment on Gramercy Park West. Her living room window looked down on the private square of green.

Aura's seventeen-year-old daughter buzzed us through the ground-floor entrance and opened the door once we'd climbed our way to the top. Theda was five ten, weighing no more than a hundred and five pounds with blue-black skin, gray eyes, and wavy brown hair that marked her complicated heritage.

"Hi, Uncle L," she said, smiling. "Who're your friends?"

She lowered to her haunches and Fatima's hard heart melted. The two hugged each other and the rest of the brood surged forward to get in on the action.

"Is your mother here?" I asked.

"You know she's at work," the teenager replied. And then she asked the kids, "Are you guys hungry?"

THEY HAD TOMATO soup, frosted flakes, peanut butter and jelly sandwiches, orange juice, milk, and three Cokes. Fatima made sure that all her brothers and sisters sat neatly around the kitchen table while she carried the youngest, Uriah, on her hip.

"Sure they can, Uncle L," Theda was saying to me. "Mama won't care if I say okay."

We had tried to call Aura but she wasn't answering any of her phones.

Because of her position in real estate, Aura was able to procure her ideal condo. I knew she had the space and the compassion to protect the kids. I would have taken them to my place if it wasn't for Gordo dying there.

"Tell her it's only until I find their aunt," I said.

"Don't worry," Theda assured me. "Mom likes kids."

I needed information but it was better to leave the brood under Fatima's care for a while before asking more questions.

I took out my phone, where I found a text from Mardi saying *K io. Wfu.* Kitteridge in office waiting for you.

23

"Do you mind if I borrow something from your mom?" I said to Theda. She and Fatima, and to a lesser degree Fatima's nearest sibling, Boaz, were organizing the children around the living room's plasma TV to watch the animated Disney film *Ponyo* on pay-per-view.

"'Course not, Uncle L," she said.

Aura's bedroom had the same sweet scent that I remembered from nearly two years before. I closed the door to the hall and then went to the wall-wide closet. Behind her clothes, underneath a silk scarf hanging, there was a wall safe. I knew the combination.

Inside there was an array of pistols and ammunition, among other things. One gun was a German Luger that had belonged to her father, a Togoan army officer who had gone rogue. He used that selfsame pistol to kill himself before he was to be tried for his crimes. There was a .22, a .32, and a .45 Aura had stockpiled from various offices and apartments that her crews cleaned out over the years. There was also a short-barreled .41-caliber six-shooter that belonged to me. I had left it with her one night when I was going out to meet with a man who had raped my client—Madeline Rutile.

His name was John Ball, and to most of the world he appeared to be an innocent. But when he got on the scent of a certain style of woman his gentility turned into regular intervals of bruising, biting, and humiliation that she would dread daily and carry with her for the rest of her life.

I had a meet set with John Ball one late evening—a job interview, you might say. It was the new, semi-rehabilitated me, pretending to be the old me. He was going to ask me to plant evidence on one of his victims. Her name was Jenna Rider. I had found out, from a weeklong investigation, that Jenna was another one of Ball's victims. John typically picked women who had something to lose if they went to the police. That way he could rape them with impunity. John was in possession of evidence that Jenna had been involved in an embezzlement scam at a previous job. I convinced Jenna to pretend to have filed a complaint against her tormenter—John. Then I had Randolph Peel, a dishonorably dismissed NYPD detective, get in touch with Ball to tell him of the impending indictment. For twenty-five hundred dollars he turned over the falsified records to the rapist. After that he threw my name at him, told him I was the kind of guy who could whack the girl and plant evidence in such a way as to gut the case against him.

This was business as usual for a guy like me. I have never, in my life, colored within the lines.

The night I was going to meet with John I was first at Aura's. My clothes and gun were on her pink-and-aqua chair. When I told her what I was going to do she made me leave my gun.

"You might lose your temper, Leonid," she said, "and kill him."

"He'd deserve it," I replied.

"But you do not."

I left the pistol and went to Ball's office. When he put out a hand in friendship, I coldcocked him.

I had expected to come away just with the information he kept on Jenna but instead I hit the jackpot. John kept a file cabinet with two drawers in his office. The top stack was the evidence he'd gathered on more than thirty women. The bottom held pictures, videos, and other remembrances of his predatory romps. Six of the files were still active—including my client's.

Aura was right. I would have killed him right there if I had kept my gun. Instead I relieved him of the contents of the top drawer.

I reported the attack on Ball to a cop named Willis Philby, whose specialty was sexual predation. I made my departure before the cops got there, leaving a couple of damning pictures out in plain view.

Charges were made and John, who has resources, is still on trial today. I returned the various files to their victims and bought Aura a single cabochon ruby depending on a slender 24-karat gold chain.

"MOM CALLED," Theda told me when I came out of the bedroom a couple of pounds heavier.

"What she say?"

"That we'd see when she got home. But I could tell that she's going to say okay."

ON THE STREET I felt safer with the pistol in my pocket. I had a carry license and reason to feel threatened. Beria might very well be looking for me. Maybe Shawna wasn't actually dead, but I had to play it like she was. The children needed time to calm down and feel safe before I could question them; Aura's presence would accomplish that end.

In the meantime I had to protect myself while roaming the streets of New York.

I'd been paid a lot of money, but for what purpose was not clear.

Shawna hired me to protect Chrystal, but now Shawna herself might be the victim. Cyril wouldn't be climbing through eighth-floor windows to murder women, but his money could hire a whole regiment of black-ops mercenaries to accomplish such a task.

This speculation was all fiction, pulp fiction, not worth the calories it consumed.

WARREN OH, the Afro-Sino-Jamaican, was at the front desk of the Tesla Building. He was a beautiful man: sixty but looking forty, with two children, half a dozen grandchildren, and a mother who was pushing the century mark.

"Hello, Mr. McGill," Warren said.

"Mr. Oh."

"Are you in for the afternoon?"

A solitary note tolled. It was the sound of the bell that started or ended a round. I looked at my phone.

"Maybe not," I told the security man. "Hello," I said into the phone.

"There's a couple'a guys here hasslin' Iran," the elderly Firpo said.

"I'll be right there."

GORDO'S GYM WAS six blocks from my office. A cab would have taken too long, so I ran. Really, full-out ran. I bumped into people, veered into traffic, ran against red lights, huffing heavily as I went. I didn't stop at the front door, either. I took the stairs two and three steps at a time until I was closing in on the fifth floor.

There I found two men dragging a slightly bloodied Iran Shelfly into the stairwell. The young ex-con wore the same clothes he'd been in the last time I saw him. The men were dressed in dark clothes that were not business attire or blue collar—more like thugland leisure wear. They were coming onto the landing while I was still two strides down. There was no time to get fancy or even try to fight. Iran was a good scrapper and they had obviously bested him.

So I reached into my pocket and came out with the revolver.

The two towering white men noticed the gun. They paid extra-close attention when I cocked the hammer.

Somewhere in the back of my mind I was thinking that I needed to get to my calm place, that my violence was escalating at an alarming rate.

But the gun was out, so I had to go with the script as it was being written.

"Do I have to say any more?" I asked the man who was right there in front of me.

The ugly white man smirked. He moved as if he were going to take a step down.

"Gorman," the other guy, who was standing behind Iran, said. "That's LT McGill."

Gorman's eyes shifted, reflecting the knowledge that he was far too close to death.

"This ain't none'a your business, McGill," he said.

"Get the fuck outta here or make your move, man." I've found that bad dialogue often accompanies stupid situations.

The standoff was no more than twenty seconds old, but it felt as if I had enough time to recite the Book of Genesis.

The guy behind Iran put up his hands and moved to the wall. I backed my way up around them, my gun leveled at Gorman's chest.

"This is a mistake," the headman said.

"Yours," I agreed.

The toady started down the stairs, leaving Gorman alone with Iran and me. Even without a gun we could hurt him.

Realizing his untenable situation, the one named Gorman took a step down, hesitated, and then took another.

"I'll be seeing you around, Iran," he said before turning his back and picking up speed.

24

"LEAN YOUR HEAD back, boy," Firpo—the tuba-playing, mop-wielding, sometimes cut man—commanded.

Iran was seated in Gordo's office chair while Firpo ministered to the wound over his left eye.

Firpo was small and wiry, with shiny black skin and eyes that see without looking. He had a full head of hair with less gray than one would have expected of his advanced years.

"I coulda taken 'em if I saw 'em comin'," the younger man complained.

I was standing guard over them, the .41 in my hand.

"If a man sees a club swingin' at 'im, he duck and run," Firpo said, dismissing the young man's bravado.

"I coulda taken 'em," Iran repeated.

"Put your head back."

In an odd way I appreciated this disruption of my case. The rough-and-tumble of brutish men and their misplaced confidence is just the kind of forum for my talents. Figuring out who's who among siblings and billionaires was challenging, if not out of my league completely. Lost children and their murdered mother set off an echo in my heart like a depth charge dropped on a submarine that ran silent but got found out anyway.

"Lay back, Iran," I said. "We got to get outta here before your friends decide to find some balls."

THERE WAS a back stairwell that led to a blocked-off alleyway. Across the alley was the door to an office building on Thirty-fifth Street. I had the only key to that door because I'd changed the lock for Gordo some months before; insurance policies aren't all paper and ink.

We made our way to the street and I gave Firpo a twenty to get home.

"I'll call you when we open the gym again," I told him.

"I need that job, LT," he said.

"You'll keep getting a check while this shit works out."

IRAN AND I headed toward my office from there.

"I coulda taken 'em," Iran said again as we entered the Tesla's elevator.

"So what?"

"Huh?"

"So what if you coulda? So what difference does that make? The fact is they got you. The fact is, if Firpo didn't call and I didn't come, your ass would be dumped in some alley and roaches would be crawlin' in your mouth."

"Say what?" Iran challenged. He needed to fight.

"Those men were gonna jack you up, Eye. There's no lie to that."

"But—"

"Tell me sumpin', boy."

"Wha?"

"If I was your trainer and sent you out against an opponent, a skinny little dude no one ever heard of before, and the first thing he does is throw a wild punch that sets you down for the ten count. If that happened, what would you say to me?"

The dawning of truth on the younger man's face was a comfort to me. Just the idea that someone, somewhere, could learn even just a single line of truth meant that there was hope.

"Yeah," he said. "I get you."

The doors slid open and we headed down toward what might very well have been a whole new set of problems.

CARSON KITTERIDGE was seated across the desk from Mardi, chatting happily, when Iran and I walked in. Carson stood up immediately because, in spite of any familiarity between us, we were, in the end, enemies—and you get on your feet when an enemy walks into the room.

We're the same height, more or less, both of us under five six, at any rate. He's balder than I am, and that's where the similarities end. Carson is a white man, pale. He's a featherweight where I'm a light-heavy. His eyes are the color of an overcast sky on a bright day. His suit and tie were machine washable, not the only indication that he was unmarried.

"Lieutenant," I said.

Mardi rose behind him.

"Mr. Shelfly," the cop said. "You been in a fight?"

"I work in a boxin' gym, man. Of course I been in a fight. You should see the other guy."

"Have a seat, Iran," I said. "Get him whatever he needs to keep up his strength, Mardi. Boxer gets hit that hard, might need some coffee or something.

"Lieutenant," I said then, "shall we go back into my office?"

WALKING DOWN the long aisle of empty cubicles, followed by the detective whose primary job it was to see me in the dock, charged with a raft of felonies, I felt at ease. Life is nothing without its challenges and only the dead are truly peaceful.

"I could tell that boy how he got convicted," Carson suggested before we'd gotten half the way to my office.

I stopped and turned to face his threat.

"That's the way you wanna play, we don't have to go any further than right here," I said.

"What?" he said. I think he was truly surprised at my anger.

"My father always told me that there's a line you need to have that people can't cross. I might one day be your prisoner, Lieutenant, but I will not be your bitch."

The policeman stared at me. It was the look that had broken down many a confident thug.

"What's with you, LT?"

"You want to drag me downtown? I can call my lawyer right now."

"Who's talkin' about arrest?"

"If you want to go tell Iran some fancy guesses you got, then get on with it."

Kitteridge put up his hands in false surrender. This reminded me of the man called Fledermaus: an emerald piece in an·otherwise black-and-white jigsaw puzzle.

"I'm sorry," the cop said. "Let's start over. I'm here to tell you something—something you want to know."

I turned back, leading the way to my office and wondering how long a man with my kind of temper could survive. By any sane reckoning I should already be dead and buried.

This realization in itself made me a survivor. Maybe I could start my own reality TV show. I smiled as we entered my office.

"Have a seat, Lieutenant."

I got behind my desk while he sat down and crossed one leg over the other. The lines between us had been drawn years before. We were no longer the same men we were when we met, but we were still fighting the same war.

"A complaint has come in on you, LT," my nemesis said, his hazy eyes reflecting a faraway, hidden sun.

"What kinda complaint?"

"Cyril Tyler says that you forced him to hire you by making accusations about his wife that he now knows are false."

He uncrossed his legs and leaned forward in the visitor's chair.

I just sat there, blinking like a suburban housewife whose insurance-salesman husband just brought home a two-hundred-pound dead stag and threw it down on the dining room table.

"So you just waltz in here and warn me about an active police investigation?"

"I owe you a favor," he said with a pout and a shrug.

"Uh-uh, no. You too much of a cop for that. You might tell the other cops I'm no good for this, but that wouldn't extend to you warnin' me. No. Not the Carson Kitteridge I know."

"Maybe I've changed," he said, unable to hide his smirk.

"More likely the pope became a Unitarian—and married his sister."

The cop squinted. This was a bad sign—for somebody. The good lieutenant was one of the smartest cops the NYPD had to offer. He was also honest to a fault. That was bad news to evildoers like myself. If Carson was on your tail, you were bound to go down, sooner or later—bound to.

"Look, LT," he said, all pretense and banter gone. "This Tyler has two dead wives in his wake. One, a New Yorker, fell off a boat in Florida, and the other was murdered by a crazed homeless man who somehow miraculously avoided capture. I was thinking that the information you had might get me closer to understanding these deaths."

"I did not extort the man," I said. "I told him that a woman claiming to be his wife had come to me afraid that he might intend her harm. He said he wanted me to bring him to her. I said that that would break client confidentiality. He offered me money to deliver a message. I took his money."

"What was the message?"

"You'll have to ask him that question."

"Did you deliver it?"

"Not as of yet."

"You need me on this, LT. I'm sure that this woman really is in danger."

"That might be true, but have you ever known me to take the easy road?" I stood up then. "I think it's time I got back to my business, Lieutenant. If I come across something that'll help you with these killings I promise I'll give you a ring."

He stayed in his chair another dozen seconds and then rose, slowly.

"Don't take too long," he said. "All Tyler has to do is raise his voice and you will be thrown down into a hole that even Alphonse Rinaldo can't dig you out of."

25

WHEN THE GOOD LIEUTENANT left I pulled open the bottom drawer of my desk and fiddled with the controls until the four monitors there showed him passing down the aisleway, and then through Mardi's office. I didn't have to watch him. Kitteridge was a straight arrow. He wouldn't perform an illegal search or plant any bugs on the premises. When he brought me down it would be on the strength of his police work, not the devious ways of people like me.

Iran jumped up when the cop entered. I liked that. The kid knew how to act. Mardi smiled sweetly and nodded at some blandishment Carson uttered.

When he was gone from the offices I closed the drawer.

The words "Alphonse Rinaldo" reverberated in the room as if Carson was saying them over and over. Rinaldo was the most powerful man I had ever met; the self-styled Special Assistant to the City of New York had helped many times when I found myself in the rarefied atmosphere of billionaires and high-end politicos. But the downtown ringmaster had cut me off for doing a private job too well. Losing Rinaldo's support was like blowing up the George Washington Bridge.

Oh well.

I got to my feet, a boxer to the end, and walked the same route that Kitteridge had just taken.

"Iran," I said and he stood up again. "There's a row of eight desks and cubicles in here. Pick one and stay there until I come back or call."

He stuck out his bottom lip and nodded.

"If Mardi needs anything, do what she asks," I continued. "And, Mardi."

"Yes, Mr. McGill?"

"If Iran wants to set himself up with a computer or something, you give him what you can."

"Where you going, sir?" she asked.

"To make a mistake most likely."

"What does that mean?"

"I'm going to do a favor for a friend."

Corinthia Highgate lived in the slums of the Upper East Side. It wasn't a ghetto, just a block of poorly maintained brownstones with tiny one-bedroom apartments and few running elevators. To the north and south, east and west there were fancy blocks where rich people traveled in upscale limos while on this street the denizens wore tattered sneakers and pulled rickety wheeled carts.

"Hello?" she said through the crackling building intercom.

"Miss Highgate?"

"Yes?"

"This is Ambrose Thurman."

"Who?"

"I called about William Williams."

The lady took a moment for recollection.

"Oh," she said. "Oh yes. You, you wanted his books."

"I wanted to buy them from you," I reminded her.

"Oh. How much were you willing to pay?"

"I'd have to see them first, ma'am."

"Who are you again?"

"Bill's nephew-in-law."

"Yes . . . that's right."

The buzzer sounded and I strode up to the fourth floor, to 4C, where the buzzer board told me that C. Highgate lived.

"Hello?" she said to my knock.

"It's Ambrose Thurman, ma'am."

If an inanimate object could hesitate, that's just what Miss Highgate's door did. At first it didn't move at all, then the knob wobbled, shook, turned. It came open maybe three inches and was stopped by a sudden jerk.

"Oh, damn," she whispered and the door closed again.

There came some clinking and the slither of the chain against the slot and jamb. The knob did its dance. The door slowly swayed until finally a small white woman with blue-gray hair was revealed, peering through thick-lensed round-frame glasses that magnified her eyes.

She was wearing a dark dress with white designs on it. I couldn't make out the nature of the print because of the loose-knit maroon shawl that covered it.

"Miss Highgate," I said with as kind a smile as a man like me can muster.

"Yes." The word had finality to it, as if I were the Grim Reaper and she understood she could no longer bar my entrance.

"Can I come in, ma'am?"

"I suppose."

She was in her seventies and just a little unsure on her pins. We waited a moment for her to move to one side. I walked into the living room of her apartment. It was a good-sized space and mostly bare. No carpeting on the floor, or even curtains in the small window. In the center of the room there was a dark table, maybe oak, and two folding metal chairs. There were some papers stacked on the floor under the window and a pillow next to a doorway that led further into her domicile.

"Spring cleaning?" I asked.

"What?"

"Where's all your stuff?"

"I hate clutter, Mr. Thurman," she said. "I had my grandniece throw out or sell everything I don't need."

"No TV? No radio?"

"There's a radio next to my bed, and TV is just a buncha junk."

I grinned and she said, "Have a seat."

She smiled down on me, giving the impression that we were old friends together again after many years of separation.

"Would you care for some port?" she asked.

"Sure."

She doddered out of the doorway next to the pillow and I sat, peacefully plotting my way back into Cyril Tyler's domain.

I didn't like it that he had turned me over to the police; that was a dirty trick, in my book. I wanted to ask him about it, but first I needed to look into the children's allegations about their mother—and I couldn't do that until the sun went down.

I smiled at the beam of sunlight on the hardwood floor, thinking, *the darkness is my friend.*

Miss Highgate came back into the room with a liquor bottle in her left hand and two tiny green liqueur glasses in her right. She set these down on the graceless table and took the opposite chair.

"Will you pour?" she asked me. "My hands shake sometimes and this is the good stuff."

Appreciating her choice of words, I pulled out the cork-lined stopper and poured out an ounce for each of us.

It *was* good stuff.

"Lee was your uncle, you say?" she asked at the onset of our second shots.

"My stepfather's brother," I said.

"I was going to say that you don't look much like him."

Her attempt at humor—I thought.

"Should we take a look at his books?" I suggested.

"Will you pour me another glass?"

I did so, happily.

"What do you do for a living, Mr. Thurman?"

"Elevator inspector," I said. "I'm the guy that signs those little forms that they keep under glass in every car."

"How interesting."

"Are you retired?"

"Yes. I worked at Blisscomb's Cosmetics for forty-four years. I had the same desk the whole time. When I got there it was brand new. By the time I left they called it an antique. That was ten years ago."

"How do you keep yourself occupied?" I asked, realizing that the biggest price I was going to pay for those books was time and conversation.

"Online poker."

"Come again."

"I gamble online. Gambling was one of the things Bill liked about me. He'd take me to Atlantic City and I'd win at the poker table until the pit boss would tell us it was time to go. I see all of the cards of the deck in order in my head. When a card is played it disappears from the array. That way I know what my opponents can and cannot have.

"I played until my hands start to ache. Lee loved to take me to Atlantic City. He used to say that gambling was the best chance a working stiff would ever get."

"How long ago was that?"

"Twenty-five years. I was nearly forty when I finally met Lee. He used to call it our red-letter day."

Ah, port wine, the Great Lubricator.

"Um . . . ," I said, truly hesitant.

"What, Mr. Thurman? What did you want to know?"

"Why did Bill leave?"

"I was a fool," she said. "My family didn't approve, and my ex-husband wanted to try again, at least that's what he said. Now that I look back on it I think my mother put him up to it. I told Bill it was over, and right after he was gone Julian left me again."

She pushed her empty glass at me and I obliged.

She downed the shot and gestured for another.

"Maybe you should slow down a little," I said.

She looked at me and smiled.

"You might not be his blood but you remind me of him," she said. "Somebody might think that you're not to be trusted, but I know better. I knew better about Lee but didn't follow my own instincts. I still play poker because of him."

"Can I see those books now, Miss Highgate?"

"I suppose. Will you leave as soon as you see them?"

"I think there's still a couple of shots left in this bottle."

She smiled merrily and rose.

The Ethics of Psychoanalysis, by Jacques Lacan; *The Descent of Man*, by Charles Darwin; *Kapital*; *Macbeth*, *Hamlet*, and *Lear*; *The Gift of Death*, by Jacques Derrida; *The Concept of Anxiety*, by Søren Kierkegaard. These were the volumes contained in an old leather satchel with double-grips for the hand and a strap for the shoulder.

"If he got very excited by something he'd scribble notes in the margins," Corinthia told me. She was nursing the glass of port I'd poured.

"This is wonderful," I said. "My sister Katrina will be very happy."

"Why didn't you bring her with you?"

"She doesn't get out of the house much."

"I understand," the septuagenarian said, nodding at her own bare cell.

"You say Bill moved to New Jersey when you two broke up?"

"Yes," she said.

"Do you remember where?"

"Hoboken. That's it, Hoboken. I used to have a number, but it got thrown out with the bathwater."

The lock in the door started making scratching noises.

A middle-aged white woman, maybe forty-five, entered, carrying a plain paper bag by its paper handles. She had a womanly figure and a handsome face. Seeing me stopped her in her tracks the way someone might freeze if they saw a huge gutter roach scaling a whitewashed wall.

"Aunt Corinthia," she said, looking at me. "Is everything all right?"

"Come in, June," my hostess said. "Come in. I want you to meet, Mr., um, Mr. Thurman."

I stood.

June stood still.

I smiled.

Whatever facial expression she made, it wasn't welcoming.

"Who are you?" she asked.

"Mr. Thurman, honey," Corinthia said. "Come on in and close the door."

June's hair was too brown and her breasts stood up like a young woman's might—the nearly magic technology of dyes and modern-day bras. Her reaction to me could have been panic or passion.

"I came to buy my uncle's books from your aunt," I said, putting a crack in the wall of fear that loomed between us.

June was one of those New Yorkers who lived in a world populated by only the people of her choosing. I was sure that she rarely, if ever, talked to strangers, or even wondered at all the brown skins and strange accents that surrounded her on every street. She had her relatives and her church, her friends, and maybe a part-time job—just like any other white Christian woman from the heart of Middle America.

"Junie," her aunt said. "Come in and meet Mr. Thurman . . . and close the door."

One of the by-products of such an insular life was an irrational obedience. June wanted to run away screaming but instead she came toward us, a lamb to the slaughter, just like her aunt had been before the application of sweet wine.

"Port?" I offered.

26

JUNE AND CORINTHIA had the same port wine gene; half an hour after her initial fright June was seated upon a third folding chair at the bare table in that unadorned room. She was laughing and free.

I remember thinking that in years gone by those women would have been afraid of me because I (or, more correctly, my dark skin) represented a fear-inducing *other*. But now they felt that they were the other and I was somehow an envoy of the dominant people. They saw my friendliness as a kindness rather than the obeisance that my father's sharecropper parents offered up with their smiles and deferential silences.

I paid one hundred dollars for the books and two hundred for the old light-brown leather satchel.

June kissed my cheek at the door.

It was a heartfelt kiss, sensual in its innocent placement.

Even though I was there under an alias, I felt I was experiencing a real connection with those women in that tomblike dwelling in the depths of the Upper East Side.

———

I CALLED MARDI and had her tell Iran to meet me at Rudy's, a small take-out restaurant on Avenue C.

"Tell him to bring me that special flashlight and the other stuff Bug gave me," I added.

I GOT THERE first. There were three tables in the place. I sat toward the back, leafing through William Williams' lost library. I hadn't read some of the books but I was acquainted with all the authors. I liked Williams' taste. He was a complex thinker who worried about a pedestrian world. He'd scribbled notes on almost every page.

Evolution makes better murderers, he jotted on the title page of *The Descent of Man.* Below that he scrawled, *Darwin meets Dante in the sentiments of this title.*

I actually grinned at some of his idiosyncratic jibes.

"Hey, boss," Iran said, pulling me from my intellectual eavesdropping.

It's funny how a phrase shines a light on what's happening and then illuminates a path just up the way. Iran worked for Gordo but had been hired by me. Now I was using him as an operative in my evolving relationship to the world.

"You bring it?" I asked.

"Right here." He placed a plain brown paper bag on the table and sat down opposite me.

"What you readin'?" he asked.

"I don't know yet. You eat?"

"Some potato chips and a soda."

I handed him a twenty and said, "Go up to the counter and order us two of the specials."

While he did this I turned a page on Darwin.

Evolution and politics are inextricably intertwined, Bill wrote. *The question is, is it a science in the strict sense of the word? And also, can biology somehow replace the domination of Capital?*

Who was this guy?

When Iran returned I put away the old hardback and turned my attention to the politics of crime.

"So explain to me this thing with Gorman," I said.

"I already told you back when you gimme the job at Gordo's."

"That was when our lawyer called me and said you were in trouble," I said. I used Breland to keep tabs on many of the people I had wronged. "He told me that you were in trouble with a man named Gorman but that was all."

Iran sucked a tooth and said, "He just stupid."

"Not so stupid he couldn't find you and kick your ass."

"Oh, man," he whined.

"Tell me the story, Iran."

"Me and Gorman's brother—"

"What's his brother's name?"

"Alvin, but everybody calls him Leech."

"Uh-huh. Go on."

"Me and Leech—"

"Hold up," I said because the cook, in his stained and, in places, singed apron was bringing our meat-loaf platters.

With no ceremony he placed the meals down in front of us, then headed back to his big grill.

"All right," I said. "Go on."

"So me an' Leech was gonna boost these crates of iPads movin' through this warehouse where a friend'a his was workin' at."

"Leech's friend?"

"Yeah. Only Leech was hittin' it with his friend's girlfriend and the mothahfuckah told us where to get in but then he turnt around an' called the cops."

"Then why aren't you in jail right now?"

The look on Iran's face was perfect, a kind of nonchalant intensity that said, *I will do anything to stay out of jail.*

"We run, man. Shit. I jumped ovah a barbed-wire fence an' almost ran up a wall. Them cops didn't want any part'a that. You know, I was movin' like I was in some kinda comic book."

"Leech, too?"

"We both got away," he said, "but Leech wouldn't own up to what he did. He just told his brother that the cops come and he didn't know why. Gorman blamed me and said I owed him six thousand dollars. Six thousand dollars."

"Why would you owe him anything?"

"He was the fence and he fronted his brother some money. Now he blames me. Stupid, that's what it is."

"Did you know that Gorman was stupid before you took this job?" I asked.

"Yeah. Yeah, I knew."

"So what does that say about you?"

Sometimes a good question from the right source is all one needs. Iran sat back on his bench and looked at me. I could see where he, for the second time in a long time, blamed himself for the trouble he was in.

———

WE WERE JUST finishing our mince pie and French vanilla ice cream when I decided it was time for action. I took the paper bag and placed the leather satchel on the table.

"What's this?" Iran asked.

"Sit here and have some coffee," I said. "Watch my bag and I'll be back in a bit."

I stood up and he said, "I want tea."

"Then have tea."

THE PEOPLE'S GARDEN behind St. Matthew's Church was only three blocks away. The property took up most of the block, and a good portion of it was hidden by a high wooden fence and deep foliage around a lovely, community vegetable garden.

I had been a regular visitor, when I was kid hiding from the juvenile authorities. The front door had always been open. It still was. I walked in, hoping to go unnoticed, and moved quickly to the front of the congregation hall and then through a door behind the pulpit.

The gardens were dark so I took the goggles and infrared flashlight from the bag Iran brought from my office. The flashlight and spectacles were a gift from a grateful Bug Bateman. Just the promise of love will turn the most irascible heart to gratitude.

The only reason the entire church wasn't covered with yellow police tape was that either there was no body or the corpse of my faux client was hidden. I was hoping for the former as I approached the eight-foot mound of compost piled at the far corner of the lot.

Donning cloth gloves, I took up a spade from a wheelbarrel and began poking around the compost heap—looking for the give of fresh-turned soil. I worked my way up to the very top before coming across soft earth.

There I dug down until I came to an obstruction. Then I took a penlight from my pocket and pointed it at the satiny pink fabric. Under the makeshift shroud was Shawna Chambers' dark, lovely, lying face. Maybe if she had told me the truth I could have saved her. Maybe.

Her hair was combed and her face composed. I couldn't tell how she'd died, only that she was dead and that her undertakers had tried to make her look as good as a corpse can manage.

Somewhat contradictorily, death is the cause of anxiety. Hurriedly, I pulled the pink fabric over her face and then re-shifted the leaves and soil to hide her. I climbed down the huge pile and made my way quickly back to the street.

Two blocks away I made a pay-phone 911 call.

"Nine-one-one emergency."

"There's a dead body buried in the compost heap behind St. Matthew's Church in the East Village," I said in a husky voice.

"What is your—" the operator managed to get out before I hung up on him.

BACK AT THE DINER I found Iran reading a *New York Post*.

"You read the papers every day?" I asked.

"No, not really."

"If you gonna come work in my office you got to read the paper, at least one paper, every morning."

"Okay," he said and the temporary deal was struck.

I sat down heavily and probably sighed.

"What's wrong?" Iran asked.

"What you should ask me is, what's right?"

"Okay. What's right?"

"Nothing. Not one damn thing."

27

"WHERE TO NOW?" Iran asked when we were on the street.

I held up a finger, took out my cell phone, hit a few letters, and sent the call.

"Hello?"

"MD, this is LT."

Silence was my answer.

"I got somebody for you," I said. "Is it too late?"

"Not until the last hour of the last day," she replied.

"Thirty minutes. Maybe less."

"I'll be here."

When her side of the connection broke off I folded my phone and raised that hand in the air.

"Taxi!"

THE YELLOW CAR moved like a fish up toward the Thirties. Our driver had a Spanish name and dark skin. He said not one word from the pickup to the drop-off.

That was in front of a small residential building on East Thirty-third.

I pressed the buzzer and waited.

"Where's this?" Iran asked.

On the ride he'd asked me where we were going.

To the first question and its iteration I answered, "You'll see."

A minute and a half later the dirty white door swung inward. Standing in a light shining from above was Mary Deharain. Mary was tall, thin, and white. She looked to be over fifty but not yet retirement age.

I met her when I was still working the wrong side of the street.

Unknown to her she had been married to a serial killer named Bob Deharain. Mary was no saint but when she discovered her husband's predilections she contacted me through a mutual acquaintance in the secret world of stolen properties. I gathered evidence against Bob for a murder he committed in Flushing: a housewife whom he'd done terrible things to. This information I made available to the police through a third party.

It was one of the few cases I ever undertook, back then, without asking for a fee.

The next time I met Mary she was dressed as she was the night I brought Iran Shelfly to her understated boardinghouse. She had on a long velvet dress that had at least a hundred coin-shaped mirrors sewn into it. She had many dresses, all of the same style. That night it was a royal-blue costume, its hem touching the floor. She had various versions of the same dress in black, red, yellow, and deep green. I never asked her but I imagined that the mirrors were there to remember all the innocent lives her husband had taken. He was a prolific killer but had only been convicted of the one crime.

"Mr. McGill," she said and then she turned her intense gaze on Iran.

"Iran," I said, "this is Mrs. Mary Deharain."

"Ma'am," my protégé said. He even ducked his shaved head an inch or so.

"Mrs. Deharain has six rooms on the fifth floor and another six on the sixth floor of this building," I told Iran. "For a hundred and fifty dollars a week she and the girl working for her serve meals and wash bedclothes."

"I don't have no money, man. You know that."

"Room and board is on me," I said. "On top of that I'll give you a stipend for doing work in my office."

"How much is a stipend?"

"We'll start it at two hundred a week and see how it goes."

"Breakfast is served at seven," the severe landlady said. "Lunch at eleven forty-five, and dinner at six-fifteen. No loud music or TV in the rooms. No food, either. No guests."

"No guests?" Iran said.

"You can be friendly with the other boarders," I added, "but no personal questions, understand?"

"Yeah," he said, nodding. "I get it."

I turned to Mary. She nodded. Her face was oval-shaped and lovely but sad, like some long-suffering character from a Dickens novel. She had loved Bob. She still visited him at Attica every third week. He never found out about her betrayal. He didn't know that she knew about the full range of his crimes.

"I'll see you at the office in the morning," I said to Iran.

"What time?"

"Let's say nine-fifteen."

I left him at the threshold of the unexceptional building, to make my way into the night.

I LIKE WALKING the nighttime streets of Manhattan. Ever since I was an adolescent on the run from the juvenile and foster-care bureaucracies, I found the darkness and electric light soothing. I feel in control when I see bright neon and deep shadows. This relaxation allows me to think more deeply about the twisted nature of other men and myself.

No one knew where Chrystal was; not her husband, her living sibling, or her parents. She was, most probably, in trouble— big trouble. And the only facts I had to go on were lies: Shawna pretending to be Chrystal, some drawling cowboy acting as if he were a nerdy billionaire; the rich man giving me money and then crying extortion.

There were three dead women: two married to Cyril Tyler and one who had merely pretended to be his wife. I had been paid twenty-two thousand dollars so far and had yet to figure out what task it was I was supposed to accomplish.

I grinned a dark smile on a darker street and once again took out my cell phone to make a call.

"Hello?"

"Hey, baby, what's up?"

"I came home to a house full of children who say that they're brothers and sisters but look like a family of cousins," Aura said.

"I guess you could say that their mother got around."

"I see."

"Somebody murdered her, and in the same room where the children were sleeping."

"My God."

"I'm sorry to put them with you but I didn't know what else to do."

"That's because you did the right thing," she said kindly. "They can stay here as long as you need."

"Can I do the same?"

"No."

28

IN THE MORNING I awoke next to Katrina. She was sleeping peacefully. Looking at her, I knew that she was deep into her affair, and having such a good time that her usual restlessness was quelled. This didn't bother me. Katrina and I were connected in ways that I couldn't explain if I wanted to. We didn't love each other, not in the marital sense. Our proximity and the children made us family. I wasn't her brass ring, but the ride was over and I was the best bet on a field of nags.

I dressed quickly and was almost out the door when she said, "Leonid?"

"Yeah?"

"I haven't seen much of you lately." She sat up in the bed and stretched languorously.

I met Katrina in her springtime. She was beautiful in a way that only Scandinavians can be. She had hair of blond fire and skin the color of the milk that gods drank before shaking mountains. That was a long time ago, and though she was no longer that stunning youth, her beauty was experiencing a kind of Indian summer, a resurgence that even I could see—and feel.

"You been goin' out with your friends," I said.

"I miss you."

"I'm right here."

"Can we have a special dinner tonight?"

"Sure. That'd be great. I'm in the middle of a case, but I'll try my best to get a few hours for dinner."

She took a deep breath and sighed, lay back in the bed, and closed her eyes.

I liked her very much right then. Live long enough and you can learn to appreciate just about anything.

MARDI WAS ALREADY at her desk at 8:09, when I got in. She wore a medium-gray cotton dress that, I knew from previous days, came down to the middle of her calves. There was a blue stone depending from a silver chain around her neck.

She was organizing and reorganizing her desk, and my life.

"Good morning, Mr. McGill," she said, standing up.

Her pale blue eyes scoped out my mood. It was hard for her that morning because what I mostly felt was confused resignation.

I walked up to the desk and looked at her papers. Mardi wrote in purple ink. It was one of the few ways she held on to a decimated childhood and so I didn't complain.

"You want me to run down and get you some coffee?" she asked.

"How's Marly?" I asked. That was the receptionist's younger sister, the reason she and Twill had planned to murder her father.

"Fine," Mardi said with a smile. "She's going into sixth grade in September. She wants new clothes."

"We could all go shopping together one Saturday if you want."

"You'll spoil her," the nineteen-year-old woman said.

"That's what girl children are for."

"Should I go get you that coffee?"

"No. Sit down. I need to talk to you."

She lowered into her office chair, the same chair I once used to lay low the man-monster Willie Sanderson. I took her visitor's seat, hunching forward to put my elbows on my knees.

"What do you think about Iran?" I asked.

"He's nice."

"You know that's not what I'm askin' you. And even if he was nice, that's probably the least important thing about him."

"Are you going to hire him?" she asked.

"What makes you think that?"

"You never let anybody else sit at one of our desks before."

Our.

"He's had a hard life, M. Maybe harder than he deserves."

The last few words registered in her pale eyes.

"You're a good man, Mr. McGill," she said and I couldn't help feeling that she had seen inside my head and understood that I had been a party to Iran's downfall.

"It's not about me," I said. "I like the kid. I think he's got potential."

"Yeah," she said. "He's loyal and knows more than people might think. He'd probably be pretty brave but not like you or Twill. Not many people can be like that."

She wasn't looking for a raise or job security. I had stepped in and kept her and my son from becoming murderers. I'd given her a job when she didn't know what else to do . . . And, of course, I made certain that her rapist father was in prison and would never harm another child.

I shook my head and grinned, stood up, and said, "Here I am the man of secrets and I got Dodona answering my phones."

"Who's that?"

"Look her up."

IT WAS TIME to get down to business.

As soon as I was behind my desk I picked up the phone and dialed a newly memorized phone number.

"Mr. Tyler's line," Phil, the pastel aide, said.

"Leonid McGill for Mr. Tyler."

"He's not in."

"Find him and get him on a phone, wherever he is."

"I'm sorry, sir. I can't do that."

"I have important information that he hired me to find."

"Hold on."

In the silence I wondered if I should just take the money and forget about artists and billionaires. But then I remembered those children. I'd made them a promise.

"Mr. McGill," Phil said. "You're on the line with Mr. Pelham."

"Hello," the white-on-white man said over a line strained with crackling electric static.

"I asked to speak with Mr. Tyler," I said.

"He's indisposed."

"I can wait until he gets out of the john."

"Mr. McGill," Pelham, the soul of patience, said. "Cyril is out of the country and I am at a meeting of one of his boards in Denver. Neither of us can do much for you at the moment. So . . . if you have information, please pass it along."

"My business is with your boss. It would be unprofessional to pass along private communications."

"Have you heard from Chrystal?"

"I can only tell Mr. Tyler that."

"He has given me the authority to debrief you."

"First I heard of it."

"I am his lawyer."

"And I'm his investigator. So if he wants what I got to give he will have to call me."

I hung up the phone, wondering at Tyler's lines of communication. Pelham most likely knew about the complaint lodged against me with the NYPD. He was almost certainly the one who filed the grievance. But he gave no inkling of their ploy.

What were they up to?

The intercom buzzed then.

"Yes, Mardi?"

"There's a Patrick O'Hearn here to see you, sir."

In the background I could hear a man's voice mumbling.

Then Mardi added, "He says to tell you that it's Old Sham."

I took a deep breath filled with pedestrian uncertainty. I had no desire to speak with Old Sham.

Then I exhaled the words "Send him down."

29

SHAM O'HEARN was on the short side, only five seven, but still he was taller than I. Originally his nickname probably came from the Irish good-luck flora, the shamrock, but as time went on the word reverted to its true meaning: deception, fraud. Patrick O'Hearn—a living, walking lie.

Sham was thin with hazel eyes and lusterless white skin. He usually wore clothes of gray and yellow with a touch of brown thrown in. That day he had on a checkered brown-and-tan suit that was both new and cheap, a shirt that hinted at gold, and a dark-brown hat with a short brim and a green feather in its band. He was carrying a briefcase that looked as if it were woven from freshly cut hay.

He also wore green-and-yellow tennis shoes. Sham was always ready to run.

"Mr. McGill," he said upon entering.

I nodded from my chair. No reason to stand up when Sham walked into the room. I had no respect for the man, even when I was a crook.

O'Hearn took any slimy job that slithered up to his door. Worse, he'd go out and find dirt on spouses and business partners and then offer to sell what he knew to the injured parties.

He reveled in seducing the wives of cheating husbands and switching sides in the middle of a case if that betrayal increased his bottom line.

I couldn't believe that anyone liked Sham O'Hearn; not even his mother, or his reflection in the glass.

"What's up?" I asked.

"Can I sit down?"

"Are you gonna be here that long?"

He lowered onto the chair nearest the door, perching at the edge. There was an apology in his eyes, a squinty twitch, too.

"I'm sorry about this, Mr. McGill," he said.

"Sorry about what?"

"I took a job and, and if I want to get paid I had to . . . you know."

"No," I said. "I don't know why you're here, Sham. And if you don't start making sense I'm gonna put you out."

"Times have been very hard," the fifty-something Irishman said. "I wouldn't have taken the job if I knew."

"I'm in the middle of a case, man. You got something to do with that?"

"I, I don't think so."

"Then say what you got to say and get outta here."

The straw briefcase was on his lap. He opened it and took out a nine-by-twelve manila folder.

"I could have sent this," he said. "But I didn't want you searching me down. It wasn't my idea to bring them here, and if it wasn't for the cash, the money I need for my rent . . . You, you know I gave up my office and I'm working out of my apartment now. I can hardly afford that."

I put out my hand. He could live in the street for all I cared.

Screwing up his courage, my so-called peer handed the folder across the table. He had to leave his chair for a moment to accomplish the transfer but he did so from a squat, not standing up straight.

The folder contained nine glossy photographs. They were all of Katrina and a much younger man having what I can only call enthusiastic sex. There was fellatio and doggie-style, sixty-nine and what was most likely anal. There were fingers and tongues, thighs and acrobatics—sex as I have never had it with anyone.

As I sifted through the photographs, my mind was dominated by two thoughts. First I wondered how Sham got such great shots. Katrina and her boyfriend were obviously in a private suite somewhere. The photos were taken from a variety of angles, and with a telephoto lens.

My second thought was actually a surprise. Katrina's lover wasn't Dimitri's older schoolmate, Bertrand Arnold. It was a dark-skinned Negro, possibly an African, with a jagged Y-shaped scar on his powerful left buttock. He wore a light-blue condom and she a pair of red high-heeled shoes.

I stood up from my desk.

"I didn't know it was your wife when I took the job," Sham said all in a rush. "You know what it's like. You do this kind of work."

"How much did he pay for these?" I asked.

"Six, six thousand. A thousand up front and the rest after I make the delivery."

"How will he know you did that?"

"He said that he would know."

"Get outta here, Sham," I said.

"Listen, man—"

"I said, get out."

That was all he needed. Sham rose, turned, and fled from the room in one fluid dancelike motion.

I put the pictures back in the folder and that in the top drawer of my desk. Mardi never went through my drawers. I waited a few minutes for Sham to have vacated the floor. Then I left for a place I knew in Greenwich Village.

THE BROWN BAG BAKERY had taken over a space that had once been an antique toy store on Bleecker Street. It was all glass and chrome, making it seem more like twenty-first-century robotics than a comfortable shopping bag.

Two young women with a variety of piercings and multicolor hairdos smiled as they sold cream puffs, cupcakes, and the occasional loaf of bread to the throng of customers. At the far end of the counter, standing toward the back, was Bertrand Arnold in white pants and a black T-shirt, covered by a denim blue apron. He had brown skin, straight black hair, and a boy's face, though I knew he was in his mid-thirties.

I walked straight up to Mr. Arnold and looked him in the eye.

His face went through its paces quickly. At first he was surprised to see me, and then, almost immediately, he remembered that I was a private detective and would have found him out. He had tried to hide his identity by having Sham get the photos to me but somehow that hadn't worked. He resigned himself to my presence there and gestured toward a door that led into the back. I held out my hand for him to go first.

He led me past a huge refrigeration unit into a big kitchen where other brown-skinned, straight-haired men were preparing the breads and pastries for a wall of ovens. From there we went into a small hallway lined with lockers. This hallway ended at his office door.

He sat behind the desk. I sat on top of it.

"You know why I'm here?" I asked.

"I'm not going to pay that detective," he said.

"I don't know why not. He didn't give up your name."

"He didn't?"

"The minute I saw those pictures I knew you paid for them."

"How?"

"Because you been wettin' yo' beak in Katrina's fountain for six months and more," I said. "You went to Atlantic City together in March and then turned around the next month and met her in Chicago when she lied and said that she was at a family reunion."

"You knew?"

"Listen, kid, when you meet a woman willin' to betray one man to be with you, then you can bet dollars to doughnuts that she will do the same goddamned thing to you."

"If you knew, then why didn't you say something? Why didn't you do something?"

I took out my .41 magnum and placed it on the desk between us.

Bertrand was transfixed by the weapon.

"Is this what you want?" I asked him.

All the love and betrayal and jealousy flowed away in the face of that ugly black gun.

"No," Bertrand said clearly, without a falter or hesitation.

"If you do one more thing to try an' mess with my wife I will be back. Do you understand me?"

"You're, you're here to protect her?"

"She ain't much, I'll give you that, but she's Dimitri's mother, and I will not stand for you to try and bring her down."

"But she was with me," the baker said, "for months. Aren't you mad about that? Aren't you angry about D'Walle?"

"There's only two things I need to know," I said.

"What?"

"Did Dimitri know about you and his mother?"

"No. He's been distracted ever since he met Tatyana."

"Do you know where Dimitri is?"

"He borrowed some money from me and flew to Paris. He said that Tatyana was going to meet him there."

"Then there's nuthin' else between you and me, Bert," I said. "But if you do anything else to mess with Katrina, if you just go yell at her in my house, I will destroy you—completely."

I let those words hang in the air a moment and then retrieved my pistol.

30

BACK OUT ON Bleecker Street—with its tourist shops and old-time Italian specialty markets, its storefront fortune-tellers and overpriced clothes designers—I wondered about time and the people who wasted it. Almost every hour of every day was a wasteland of TVs, radios, lying newspapers, and people like Bertrand Arnold railing against his predestined fate. It wouldn't matter so much if the malingerers of the world didn't want to drag me into their ditherings. What did I care about the newest reality show about truckers or bail bondsmen? What did it matter to me if a cow in New Zealand gave birth to the world's first three-headed calf or who my wife cuckolded me with?

Why would a man having an affair with someone's wife reveal her infidelity to him? Could revenge heal his broken heart or mend Katrina's errant ways? If I shot D'Walle, whoever he was, would Bertrand have gotten what he wanted?

It was like blasting a cloud of butterflies with a shotgun because you were earthbound and jealous—it made no sense and was a waste of the little time we had to make sense in.

Thinking these thoughts, feeling the weight of the pistol in my jacket pocket, I found that I had walked across town to Broadway and was on my way north. My thoughts were fragmented and weightless. It was the state of mind a boxer is put in by a solid right hand to the side of his head. Things are a-jumble but he knows that there's one important fact that needs immediate attention. Maybe there was a three-headed calf somewhere, but that knowledge won't help the situation.

Keep your gloves up, Gordo shouted at every arrogant young boxer who thought he was too fast, too slick to get hit. But even the thought of Gordo sent me veering off course. The man who took the place of my father . . . dying in the same room where I had planned the demolition of many an innocent, and not so innocent, life.

This last thought arrived with me at the front door of Aura Ullman's apartment building. Instinct and a sense of duty had brought me there. The children were my clients now and their mother's death was my job.

"Yes?" came the answer to my ring.

"Aura?"

"Leonid," she said as the buzzer sounded.

She was at the open door when I got there, the sun flooding into the hallway from behind her. She smiled and held out both hands to me. I took them, pulled ever so slightly, and felt her ambivalent resistance.

"Come in," she said.

The living room was a mess. Children's clothes and toys, coloring books and storybooks strewn here and there. There were smudges on the TV screen and a half-eaten peanut butter and jelly sandwich on a paper plate set on a chair that belonged in the dining room.

Aura smiled and I learned something about her: she loved the disarray of children.

"I had to buy clothes for all of them," she said proudly. "They said that you took them away without time to pack."

"Where are they?" I asked.

She smiled and gestured toward the wall-sized window that looked down on the private park.

In a small clearing Theda and Fatima were leading the brood in a lopsided circle dance. Theda held the littlest boy, Uriah, and Boaz carried his smallest sister. They were laughing and singing.

Aura smiled down on them.

"Thank you, Leonid," she said.

"I love you," I replied.

"Let's sit down."

I SAT IN a blue cushioned chair and she on the off-white sofa that had suffered some stains in the last twenty-four hours.

Noticing me notice the spots, she said, "I can get the furniture reupholstered after you've found their aunt."

I wanted to ask her what she'd found out from Fatima and her little clan but there was a question on the table.

"There's no time for us, Leonid," she said.

"I can make time."

"No," she said, "you can't. You've got too much to do, too many irons in the fire."

"We could leave New York. I'd do that for you."

"I can't allow myself to go there," she said. "Please . . . be my friend for the time being."

"For how long?"

"I don't know," she said. "Maybe forever."

I had killed men with my bare hands, taken enough punishment to have died many times over myself. I had enemies and a special policeman assigned to bring me down and send me to prison. There were people suffering at that very moment because I had framed them. And yet there I was—a teenager with a gaping heart.

I took in a deep breath and then exhaled, remembering what was important and why I was there.

"Have the children told you anything?" I asked.

"Only that they want to go live with their Aunt Chris in a house on top of a big building."

"Did they talk about what happened to their mother?"

"I think she was murdered, Leonid."

I didn't want to say what I knew right then. She loved having those children in her house and there didn't seem to be any reason to corroborate her fearful empathy.

Luckily the front door flew open, spilling in children along with their laughter and thumping grace.

"Hello," Aura said, rising for her daughter and the small mob.

They laughed and greeted and talked about needing water and bathrooms and a DVD.

Theda and Aura started to work on these needs while the oldest sister stood to the side, arching her body in an odd, mature way.

"Fatima," I said.

The girl widened her eyes and walked toward me. She held out her hand and I led her out onto the tiny balcony.

Pulling the glass door shut, I sat on one of the two pink cast-iron chairs out there. Fatima climbed into my lap as if we had known each other for her entire life.

"I like you, Fatima," I said.

"Uh-huh," she agreed.

"And I'm going to be honest with you because that's the only way we'll be able to help each other."

"All right."

"You know your mother's gone, right?"

"Yes."

"And so we have two things that we have to do," I said.

Fatima put her right hand against my chin and rubbed the stubbly hair there. Through my peripheral vision I could see Aura watching us from inside the apartment.

"What two things?" Fatima asked.

"I have to find your aunt so that I can get the man who made your mom go away and so that you can go live with Chrystal."

"We want to be with our Aunt Chris," Fatima said with emphasis.

"So we want the same thing."

"Uh-huh."

"Tell me what you know about Aunt Chris," I said.

"She's beautiful and brave and never lies about anything she says she'll do," Fatima said in one breath. "And one time when Mama Shawna was sick she promised to take all of us to live with her if anything ever happened to Mama."

"That's very nice of her," I said.

"Yes."

"Do you have any idea where Auntie Chris might go if she wanted to get away for a while?"

"It's a secret."

"Really?"

"Uh-huh. Aunt Chris told me that I shouldn't never tell anybody, not even Mama."

"And have you ever told anyone?"

"Only Boaz, and he didn't say anything."

"Well, Fatima," I said, "I know all about secrets. I have so many of them that I forget what they are sometimes. And I don't want to make you tell something you promised not to, but I have to find Chrystal and you have to decide if finding her is worth telling her secret. I mean, do you think that she'd want you to tell me?"

Her serious face enchanted me: a child making her mind work in ways that felt impossible but must be done.

"I think she wants us to find her," she said at last.

"Where can we do that?"

"Maybe at her getaway house in Saltmore, Altmore, something. It's a place that she bought a long time ago when she sold her first painting. It's a big secret, so you can't tell anybody else. It's a little white house with a yellow one on the right and a gray one on the left. And you have to take a train ride to get there."

"Thank you, Fatima," I said. "You can count on me, I will find Chrystal."

———

A FEW BLOCKS away from Aura's I made a call on my cell phone.

"Hello?" a pleasant voice answered on the seventh ring.

"Tam? It's LT."

"Mr. McGill," she said.

"That open offer for dinner good for tonight?"

"Absolutely. We're eating at about six-thirty. Timothy will be in maybe an hour before that."

"I'll get there as close to six-thirty as I can."

I got off the phone and shivered like a wet dog.

31

Wasting time is a big problem in the world we live in, that's for sure. But it doesn't mean that we necessarily have to know what the goal is for every step we take. Sometimes we do things that are not directly connected and yet are still significant.

These activities, in a life like mine, might at times be dangerous, or even foolhardy; but life, even at its best, is a sucker's enterprise. No deity would trade places with one of us fool mortals, not even for an instant.

At 6:24 I knocked at a door to a one-family home on Fifth Avenue not far north of Washington Square Park. It was a five-story pink affair with dark-green vines growing on the walls. The stairs were greenish marble and the oak door ancient. There were three hidden camera lenses watching me, two from in front and one from the branches of a tree at the sidewalk.

A man answered the door. He was not a centimeter over five nine, with a slender (but not thin) frame, combed short brown hair, and eyes the same tone. His trousers were green and his tan shirt square-cut.

He was wearing an old pair of brown, backless slippers.

"LT," he said. He even smiled.

Slippers.

I nodded and muttered something that was meant to sound like a greeting.

"Come on in," the man said, moving backward and gesturing broadly with his left arm.

The foyer, and every other room I had seen in that home, had dark hardwood floors and teal-colored walls.

"Can I take your jacket?" the man asked.

As I shook my head I could hear the thunder of little feet.

"Surprise, Uncle L!" the seven-year-old boy yelled.

From three feet away he bounded into my arms. I swung the nut-brown boy around in a circle and then held him high in the air.

"You got me, Thackery," I said. "You got me."

"I got him, Daddy," the boy, now almost upside down, shouted at the man.

Thackery's father looked worried as any man might when a brute like me manhandles his offspring.

"Leonid," a woman said from the doorway leading to the ground floor of the twelve-million-dollar home.

"Mama, I got Uncle L," Thackery said, laughing madly.

The woman was darker even than her son. She had a plain face but there was something about her that spoke of prayers and angels—an inner beauty that could not be contained.

"Tam," I said and she came forward to kiss me while her squirming son thumped down to the floor.

"You're here right on time, LT," the mild-mannered man said. "We just put dinner on the table."

His wife smiled, kissed me again, and then hugged me.

"Come on in," she said.

I smiled and she put her arm around me.

I'm proud to say that I didn't tremble at all.

A MAN WOULD have to be crazy to sit down to dinner with a contract serial killer, even if that murderer was now retired and driving a limo to keep busy.

Tamara had prepared a meatloaf of veal and lamb crusted with chunks of apples and peaches. There was also a tropical fruit salad, wild rice cooked in chicken broth, and collard greens simmered all day along with ham hocks and then finished with pearl onions.

The dining table was from a sixteenth-century French master, carved with gargoyles and saints along the apron. Each leg was a horse standing on its back legs carrying riders who were holding on for dear life.

The food, the décor, even the color of the walls made little sense outside the family's unique context, but this was the home of a man and woman, neither of whom should have been able to survive in this modern world.

"Daddy," the boy said.

"Yes, Thackery?"

"Uncle L told me that he almost fell out of the tree across the street one time."

"He did?" Hush said, smiling and looking at me.

"Uh-huh. Would you almost fall?"

"I wouldn't be silly enough to climb a tree."

"Why not? I like climbing trees."

"Maybe that's why your uncle told you that he almost fell," Hush suggested. "Maybe he was telling you that anybody can hurt themselves falling out of a tree, even him."

"Not me," Thackery said bravely. "I wouldn't ever hurt myself fallin' out of a tree, huh, Mama?"

"Not as long as your father or I am there to catch you," Tamara Cunningham, Thackery's best teacher, said.

"And Uncle L," the boy said. "Uncle L would catch me, too." It wasn't a question.

We had a very enjoyable meal. Every now and then Thackery would get loud or fidgety but all Tamara had to do was reach over to touch him and the nervous energy would drain away.

Hush told stories about a brave knight who wore black armor and a beautiful princess who loved him. The princess was kidnapped and the knight's best friend saved her and then the knight saved the best friend and they all lived in a big pink palace where the full moon shone every night and the days were all sunny.

It was another side of the assassin, a side that only the people in that room ever saw.

It gave me the feeling of being singled out—like an elk in the crosshairs of a high-powered rifle.

AFTER A SERVING of strawberry rhubarb pie and ginger ice cream Hush said, "It's time for bed, young man."

Thackery's eyes showed his disappointment, but he got up to kiss his mother and then me.

"Good night," he said and Hush led him off to bed.

When they were gone Tamara made to rise, saying, "I'll get you some more coffee."

I held out a hand, not quite reaching her.

"I don't need it," I said, and she sat back down.

We were silent a moment. She liked me. I was that knight's friend. I had saved her life, and Thackery's, too.

"Timothy loves you," she said after a deliciously enjoyable period of quiet.

"Maybe you shouldn't tell him that."

She laughed and said, "You're the closest thing he has to family outside of us."

"How are you doing, Tam?"

"I love my husband and son," she said. "They are everything to me. But . . . but I'd like to have something for myself. Maybe I could take classes or something. It's only that Timothy worries so much. Whenever I'm gone he thinks the worst. Once I went to visit my brother in Florida and when I came back he was a wreck."

I remembered that long weekend. It was the only time that I had ever seen Hush drink alcohol.

"Tell him what you need, honey," I said. "He'll just have to figure out how to deal with it. And I'll find you a babysitter, one that'll meet his high standards."

Tamara smiled. She and I were on the same page for reasons completely opaque to me.

Hush walked back into the room then.

"He wants you to come up and tell him a story," he said to his wife.

"Okay," she said. "Will you still be here when I finish, Leonid?"

"You bet."

When she was gone Hush went back to his chair.

"She likes having you here," he said.

"You wanna go take a walk with me?"

He knew what my words meant. I could see the funeral lights going up behind his eyes.

32

ON THE STREET we looked like any two working-class stiffs at the end of a too-long day. Hush wore a brown jacket over his tan shirt and I was in an iteration of the blue suit that was my uniform.

"How many of those suits do you own?" Hush asked as we walked along the pathway beside NYU's monolithic library.

"Four now," I said. "It used to be only three but I bought one to keep in the office in case Katrina puts the other three in the cleaners at the same time."

That was a lot of meaningless chatter for us and so we strolled along in silence for a few blocks.

When we were waiting for the light at Houston Street it was my turn to speak.

"Two women," I began. "Allondra North and Pinky Todd. The first was lost at sea, fell from a yacht off the Florida coast. The second was killed by a homeless man on Fifth Avenue. He hit her in the head with a stone and then escaped in broad daylight."

"I remember that," Hush said as the light turned green. "The guy just ran up behind her and whacked her where the skull meets the spine."

My heart tittered. It wasn't a real laugh but an inner revelation of anxiety. That was when I explained that both women were purported to be having problems with the same man—their husband.

"The woman who told me all this," I said, "was just pretending to be his wife. She was murdered in front of her children not two days ago."

We were walking in the touristy part of SoHo then. At one time this was a neighborhood of warehouses and small Italian shops, but now there were restaurants and hotels, and street vendors selling everything from big silver rings to paintings of naked women with fat bottoms.

Hush had his hands in his pockets and his eyes on the sidewalk until we passed Spring, headed south for Canal. Then he looked up at me.

Lower SoHo was dark and silent at that time of evening. It was a place where a man like Hush could speak freely.

"You remember what you said to me on this street five months ago?" he asked.

I nodded, admitting to the shadows that I did.

It had been a lesson that my sometimes anarchist, sometimes Communist, but always revolutionary father had drilled into me and my younger brother when I was nine and Nikita was seven.

Some people live outside the sphere of Law and Man, dear old dad used to say. *They see something off the road or follow after a tune that no one else can hear. This solitary event leads them on a journey that could be taken by no other. They're gone for years from their families and the world. They have fantastic adventures and battle for the freedom of all men.*

Then one day the same flash or color or song that led them away from everything and everybody leads them back into a life

where they don't belong. All of a sudden there are rules and cus-
toms that, if you touch any part of them, will hold you, trapped.

Tolstoy McGill meant this as a warning for the true radical or militant. You were never to abandon your goal—not even for love.

It occurred to me one day that my father's cockeyed warning contained so much truth that Hush might see it as a positive illu-mination of his transition from murderer to family man rather than a signpost cautioning him to turn back into the darker ways.

"How did you do it, LT?" Hush asked.

He stopped walking, so I did, too. Two women who were a dozen paces behind us crossed the street almost as if that was their plan all along.

I smiled at the innate intelligence of the young women in short dresses and bright colored heels. That smirk was also in recognition (for at least the hundredth time) that Hush, possibly the most dangerous individual man in the world, considered me his peer and maybe even an example of the way a man was sup-posed to live his life.

"You still going to that Buddhist monastery?" I asked.

Hush shook his head and then we were walking again.

"Now that Tamara and Thackery are here I like to spend the time with them. It was either the job or the retreat."

Hush drove a limo for an upscale New York service. I never understood why. He was a millionaire many times over but he worked four days a week driving around people who would have run screaming if they had any idea who he was.

"But you still meditate, right?"

"Yeah. I do an hour or so in the morning, and sometimes, when things get cold in my head, I hit it at night, too."

"When you were at the monastery they talked about enlight-
enment sometimes."

We were crossing Canal. The street vendors were closed by
then and it was pretty empty. Hush and I turned left, walking
over toward Broadway.

"They did," he said.

"I once heard a student of Chogyam Trungpa, the great
Tibetan master, say that meditation is a gesture toward enlight-
enment, though that was a state of knowledge that we would
never truly attain," I said. "I think he meant that we'll never be
wholly in the real world. It's like we're shadows, invisible to most
people. What we have to do is concentrate real hard just to be
seen at all. And it's that concentration that may one day normal-
ize us, make us members of the group."

"But what about our sins?" the ex-contract killer asked.

Sins?

My surprise at his word choice must have shown in my face
because Hush said, "I know that what I've done is wrong, Leonid. I feel it every time I look at my son."

I smiled. We turned left onto Broadway. When I looked up at
the sky all I could see was darkness. The words came to me from
a place I could rarely connect with.

"It's a luxury to feel guilt, Hush. Little Thackery might sneak
into the cupboard and take a cookie when his mother told him
to leave them alone. Afterwards he feels guilty. That's because
he's innocent and needs to confess because he was a bad boy but
still able to be forgiven. That's not us. There is no forgiveness
for us. For people like you and me, guilt is an indulgence. It's
meaningless, like a platter of caviar served up on the front lines

of a war. Our confession, our clemency, comes from doing what's right."

I wanted to say more but the tap shut off.

Hush stopped walking again.

The look in his eyes was angry and hurt, like a suitor who has just been snubbed.

I'm used to giving people bad news. *Your wife and your best friend* . . . Things like that. Some people get mad when they hear things they don't want to believe. That's all part of the job—but I wasn't so blasé about the impact of my words walking north on dark Broadway with Hush.

He winced and I wondered.

He looked both ways and I wondered some more.

"I can't say for sure but I think you've run across the path of a man named Bisbe," he said and I realized that I'd been holding my breath.

"Bisbe?"

"I was the last word when it came to killing," Hush continued, nodding. "Meat and potatoes. Never fancy unless I had to be. But if I had to be, I could kill a man with a hailstorm. But Bisbe's crazy. You hire him to knock off a man with a bullet behind the head and BB'd kill him with a tooth infection or a suicide. Superstitious people say he's some kind of mystic. I think he's just a madman."

"Are you sure?"

"That he's a madman?"

"That he killed these women."

"Nothing's for sure," Hush said, "but for a homeless man to hit that woman with a perfect killing blow and then to disappear in broad daylight . . . safe is better than sorry."

33

As I explained the particulars of the case, Hush and I walked back to his door. He took two steps up and stopped when he realized that I was not coming with him.

"You want some coffee?" he offered.

"No, thanks. I need to be getting along, figuring out what to do next."

"If you want my advice I'd say take a vacation. I hear Tokyo's nice."

Warnings, even from Hush, always brought a smirk to my lips.

"My client left six kids to fend for themselves."

"She lied to you."

"So? Why should she be any different?"

Hush winced. This was an expression of his concern.

"Thanks for the talk, LT. I'm not a lost cause, you know."

"Say good night to Tam and Thackery."

"We have to do this again soon," he said.

I nodded and turned away, ruminating over the little scenes of my life. I was like a bug that had learned to live close to, maybe even inside of, fire, so that the predators would be scared away—going to hell to keep the bad men off my tail.

Thinking of bugs, I pulled out my cell phone and punched a few digits.

He answered on the second ring, "Hey, LT."

"Bug."

"What can I do for you?"

"You get an answer?"

"An envelope with a MetroCard wrapped in a small sheet of lined notepaper. I took it down to the subway on my evening power-walk and ran it through the machine they got down there to show the amount. It had forty-nine dollars and fifty cents on it. The card looked a little beat up. I figure Twill has a read-write stripe machine and he gets people to pick up discarded cards in the subways. He might even be tapped into the MTA computer system. He takes the money you transfer and gives back more than four times as much."

"You sound impressed," I said.

"I am. I mean, it's a pretty simple scheme, but it took your son to implement it. He's only a kid but he's way ahead of everybody else."

"I'll call you back," I said, breaking off the connection.

"Hello?"

"Twill?"

"Hey, Pop. What's up?"

"Katrina there?"

"Mom went out with Dorrie to a movie."

It was a phrase that might as well have been code for: *She was out with a man who had a Y-shaped scar on his left buttock.*

"You hear from D?" I asked.

Twill hesitated. That was good for my purposes.

"Come on, boy, I know that Tatyana called and Dimitri borrowed money from Bertrand."

"That Bertrand's a dog, Dad," Twill replied.

"I was asking you about Dimitri."

"He's in France, man. Flew to Warsaw, met Taty at the airport, and then they both winged it down to Nice. He called me because he needed some more cash."

"He came to you because of all your savings from that box-boy job at the supermarket?"

Twill went quiet.

"Where'd you get the money, Twill?"

"I thought you wanted to find out about D."

"Where'd you get the money to send to your brother?"

"It was only a couple a hundred. I used the money I got from Uncle Gordo that time."

"You're going to be eighteen soon, son."

"Uh-huh. I know."

"They bust you again and I won't be able to get you out of it."

"I ain't doin' nuthin' to get busted for, LT. My hands are clean."

"Don't jerk me around, son."

"No sir, not me."

"Okay. The next time Dimitri calls tell him I need to hear from him. All right?"

"You got it."

After we said our goodbyes and got off I called Bug again.

"Hey, LT."

"Can you hack into Twill's account?"

"Can a hot knife cut through butter?"

"Empty it," I said, "every centavo. Put it somewhere safe."

"Okay." There was reluctance in Bug's voice.

"One day you'll have kids," I said in response to the hacker's tone, "and when you do you'll understand."

"Maybe so," he said. "I'll get on this right now."

34

I WAS ON NINTH STREET near Third Avenue. The night was electric but empty. There wasn't much traffic of foot or tire, and though I was standing still, my mind was breaking all the speed limits.

Hush was rarely wrong about contract killers. He knew his profession and I had the good sense to avoid a fight that I was bound to lose.

Twill's business had to be shut down but it wasn't just that. I had to somehow stop my favorite son from drifting into a life of corruption. There was no way that he could comprehend, in his youthful confidence, how the weight of his actions would pile on him, on his soul.

I was making progress but it was like having taken three strides into a five-hundred-yard-wide minefield. I could see the other side. I could imagine walking on ground that wouldn't blow up under my feet. But first I had to take that next step, and then the one after that.

"Excuse me, sir," a man's voice said in a tone of false deference.

A car door slammed shut.

There were footsteps of more than one man.

I smiled at the respite this minor threat offered.

"Yes, officer?" I said before turning around to meet the cops.

They were, of course, both taller than I. They were white, but that hardly mattered. Young men, they made the mistake of thinking that I was no threat because of my height and weight and obvious age.

"What's going on?" the one on my left asked.

"I'm standing here on an empty street taking stock of my life such as it is."

"You been drinking?" the other inquired. This one had a beauty mark on the left side of his face, half an inch from the nostril. Being a man, he probably called it a blemish.

"All my life," I said. "But not in the last twelve hours."

"Show us some ID," Beauty asked.

"Why?"

"Come again?"

"I'm a middle-aged man, wearing a suit, standing alone on a public sidewalk with nothing in my hands. What about that is suspicious?"

The cops moved toward me—a movable barrier against my anger.

"Show us some ID," the guy without a mole asked.

I closed my eyes, considering first the immediate response of civil disobedience. Then I gathered my intelligence, opened my eyes, and stuck two fingers into the breast pocket of my dark-blue jacket.

Coming out with two laminated cards, I handed these to Beauty.

He took them and read the contents. It was my PI's ID and

driver's license. Both of them had my real name, so the encounter was bound to continue.

"Wait here," Beauty said to his partner and me.

He went to the squad car to call in. The police were always supposed to call in when they came across my name. I was infamous.

"Would you submit to a search of your person?" the cop left with me asked.

"By Beyoncé, if she asked nicely," I replied.

The cop's eyes tightened and my phone made a sound that I recognized.

"You can answer that," my guard told me.

"And you know what you can do," I told him.

Revolution is fought on every street corner of every city, town, and hamlet in the world, my poor besotted father used to rant. *The only true power that the authorities have is the people's belief in that power.*

Beauty returned and said to his partner, "Let's go."

"What?" the cop said and I thought.

"They said to leave him be."

"But he resisted."

"The captain got on the line," Beauty explained to the both of us. "He said to let him go."

The cops gave me *the look*, the gaze that's supposed to stay with you long after they're gone. I grinned and waved at them as they folded their long bodies back into the black-and-white and then drove off to find some other suspicious loiterer.

Once they were gone I wondered about a police captain somewhere telling his minions to lay off Leonid Trotter McGill. I was

Public Enemy Number 26 or so in the city of New York. I've been rousted for vagrancy, littering, jaywalking, and public drunkenness. They could have put me in stir for seventy-two hours on a resisting-arrest beef.

I might have worried if my phone hadn't sounded again.

"Hey, Aura," I said into the cell.

"We were interrupted in our talk earlier," she said.

"Luckily for me, I'm sure."

"Where are you?"

"A twelve-minute walk from you."

"Meet me at Trey's in half an hour."

"Yes, ma'am."

TREY'S IS A SMALL BAR with a really good pianist and sometimes a singer, Yolanda Craze, who could bring tears to the eyes of the dead.

That night Yolanda had off and so the music was just deeply moving, somewhere just outside of the heart of desolation.

Aura came in fifteen minutes late. She always did that on a date. I was used to it. She wore a loose-fitting, antique-white dress that somehow showed off her fine figure anyway.

I was sitting at a small round table away from the white baby grand with a bottle of Beaujolais breathing for her.

She took her seat without stopping to kiss me and I didn't complain.

I held out a hand, palm up, and she touched it with four fingers.

"What were you doing in the neighborhood?" she asked.

"Dinner with Hush, planning an international bank heist, and then being stopped by the cops for standing still on a street corner."

"They'll kill you one day, Leonid."

"That and breathing," I said, "the only things that all human beings hold in common."

She smiled and looked down at my hand on the table.

This was the beginning of her speech, I knew. So I kept quiet, if pensive.

"When you," she said and then paused. "When you were in the hospital after being stabbed and beaten, I was there looking at you unconscious and burning with fever. At the time all I thought about was you. I used all my will to imagine you healthy and smiling again. But later, after you were out of danger, I began to realize that this was your life and even if we were together you would be in that bed again and again until finally one day you wouldn't recover."

She looked up into my eyes, maybe hoping for me to deny her claim. But I didn't have anything to say.

"Theda loves you, and I do, too, Leonid. I would die for you. I would do anything . . . but even if you left Katrina, how could I bring you completely into my life, knowing that you will be killed violently, senselessly?"

The notes of the piano made no musical sense at that moment. They were dissonant sounds coming from nowhere and flittering off into space like children jumping from a fast-moving merry-go-round.

I had no answer to her question, so I sat back and nodded.

"Will you still love me?" she asked.

"Let me walk you home," I answered.

35

SOMEWHERE BETWEEN TREY'S and bed I called Zephyra, asking her to reserve a first-class seat for me on the earliest morning Acela train down to Baltimore. I left a text with Mardi to look up real estate sales in and around the Maryland city for transactions by Chrystal Chambers for a year or so after the time of her first successes as a painter.

The talk with Aura, in spite of the bottle of wine, had left me quite sober. She saw my life the way it was and loved me accordingly. Who and what I was, was what she loved and, at the same time, too much for her heart to bear.

This thought trailed after me on the early-morning taxi ride to the train station, down the long concrete platform to the first-class car. It settled with me into the single seat on the right side of the upscale cabin.

"First class, sir?" a not so young white woman asked. She had pink-and-dirty-blond hair and the hint of an elaborate tattoo just above the line of her uniform collar.

"Yeah." I handed her the machine-generated ticket I got upon entering Penn Station.

She handed me a menu. I waved it away.

"Ate a bagel in the station," I explained.

She shrugged and moved on to the seat behind me.

"Good morning," she said with a note of recognition in her voice.

"Good morning," an elderly, male, German-accented voice replied.

I knew that voice—only the voice, not the man who spoke, not personally at any rate. It was the voice of a celebrity, some-one I knew about from the media.

Who was it?

"You're going down to meet the president?" she asked.

"Just a dinner," he said. "How are your children?"

Tickled, she replied, "Wonderful."

"Doing well in school?"

"The girl, Rebecca, is. Felix just wants to rip and run."

"It takes longer for boys to settle in," he said.

"I hope so."

Another man entered the car. The way he walked said that he worked for Amtrak but he wasn't an engineer or porter. Older, near about sixty, with a certain recognizable strain in eyes that looked out for trouble, he gauged me and then proceeded to the voice I recognized but had not yet identified.

"Good morning, sir," the train security man said.

"Mr. Landsdale," the voice greeted.

"Everybody treating you okay?"

"Marvelously."

"I hope you can go down there and kick some butt, sir," the slender, gray-haired troubleshooter said. "They want to turn this country into Russia down there."

The celebrity laughed softly and said, "The wheel is always

turning, Mr. Landsdale. Wait long enough and you always come back to the place you started from."

"I hope so," Landsdale said, though I wasn't sure he understood the symbolism.

While they spoke, a dozen or so first-class passengers boarded. Men and women in business attire with cell phones and briefcases, laptops and personal DVD players.

I stood up to put William Williams' satchel in the storage area above my seat. Glancing to my right, I saw that my neighbor was none other than Rainier Klaus, called by some the Architect of Death in Southeast Asia, in a war either forgotten or misunderstood by anyone under forty in contemporary America.

Mr. Landsdale looked at me and I returned to my seat, wondering again—wandering in a mind littered with details aglow with ancient passions, like long-dead stars glittering in a moonless night.

My father used to lecture me about Mr. Klaus. He worked in the State Department. There he planned the decimation of nations judged to be the enemies of democracy's master— corporate America. It was he who initiated the carpet bombing and legal torture. He was said to have such a good memory that he never wrote anything down and so neither he nor his bosses were ever held accountable for their crimes.

His assassin can use the legal stand of self-defense, my father used to say.

Hundreds of thousands of deaths were on this man's head and he was going down to advise our new liberal president.

I was armed and fast. My father, in his unmarked grave somewhere south of Mexico and north of Antarctica, was hoping for an impromptu assassination. But I was no judge, much less an executioner. The wheel that Klaus talked about did its orbit, and all I could do, all he could, was to hold on.

I HAD TO do something so I stood again and took down a few of William Williams' texts on politics and philosophy. Almost every word was highlighted in either pink, yellow, or blue. Many phrases were underlined and there were cryptic notes throughout.

The unconscious is not known but ignorance gets no hearing in the court of Fate, he wrote in Lacan's *The Ethics of Psychoanalysis*. In Lear he wrote, *Yes, the stink, this odor is how you can tell what festers in the hearts of bricklayers, seamstresses, and convicts.*

Much of what he expressed was so idiosyncratic as to make its meaning indecipherable. The language was fevered, maybe not quite rational. But there was also banal information. Shopping lists, special dates (like Corinthia's birthday), and more sinister info like the shadowing of a man from one part of the city to another.

I followed him again today, Mr. Williams wrote on a flyleaf at the back of *The Gift of Death. He kissed his wife goodbye and then went to see his lover. They dallied on a park bench while the children of the people he destroyed wallowed in fear. I had a pistol in my pocket and sweat in the palms of my hands. But that man was long dead, we both were. Now we were ghosts and no action would change that.*

"I see you're reading *Kapital* by Marx," a voice said. "Are you a Communist?"

I turned to see Rainier Klaus standing next to my seat. The train was moving. He was probably headed for the john. I hadn't even noticed us leaving the station. There was a swamp outside the window. A solitary heron, standing on one leg, stood sentry over the muck.

"Not reading exactly," I said, patting the unopened tome sitting on my tray.

"No? What, then?"

"I'm a private detective and these are the books of a man who went missing a few decades ago. I've been retained to find him, and these books are the only testament."

I think it was my last word that really got the diplomat's attention.

"Maybe he doesn't want to be found," Klaus suggested.

"Since when did what we want change the acts of others?" I asked.

He smiled, shrugged, and said, "I cannot argue."

A burly-looking man at the end of the train was watching me closely.

"Tell me something, Mr. Klaus."

"Yes?"

"Do you ever feel guilty?"

He looked down into my eyes and took at least fifteen seconds to consider my question. Finally he said, "Every year I go to the countryside of northern Vietnam. There I visit the towns and provinces with a group of doctors to bring aid to those who need it. My wife used to come with me. Now my sons come along.

"But, to answer your question—no, I do not feel guilt. That would be an insult to my enemies."

Klaus moved on, and I was reminded of my conversation with Hush. Killers lived and died in their own ether.

I opened the cover of Williams' copy of *Kapital*; a folded-up and yellowed scrap of old newspaper lay there. It was a torn section of the real estate page of a Hoboken newspaper with an ad for an apartment circled.

I scribbled down the phone number on one of my false-identity business cards and tucked it neatly away in the breast pocket of my blue jacket.

36

WHEN THE TRAIN was pulling into Baltimore's Penn Station I reflected on the fact that I'd come there because of an uncorroborated hunch. Fatima just remembered the sound of the name of a place where her aunt had a secret hideaway. The child could have been confused, or repeating the name of some hamlet in Maine or South Carolina.

I left New York because I needed some time off and didn't know how to take it in a straightforward fashion. Between Hush's transformation and Aura's bright light of perception, between the deaths of three young women and the children I took, I was exhausted and, worse, a little uncertain.

Looking up, I saw Klaus returning from the head for the fourth time.

"Excuse me, sir," he said in his powerful, if elderly voice.

"Yes, Mr. Klaus."

"You never said whether you were a Communist or not."

"I was trained not as a party member but as a revolutionary," I said truthfully. The burly man in the back of the train stood up, though I was sure he couldn't have heard my words. "Somewhere on that journey I lost my way . . . or maybe found it. Anyway, the answer to your question depends more on you than it does on me."

My response seemed to amuse the mass murderer.

"May I have your card?" he said.

I gave it to him, more to bedevil the bodyguard than for any other reason. The hapless protector watched from six strides away as I got close enough to cause all kinds of permanent damage.

"Leonid?" Klaus said upon reading the card.

"Just part of my training," I told him.

THE BALTIMORE TRAIN station's waiting room was the size of a hangar for a dirigible. The Acela arrived twelve minutes early and so I decided, for no clear reason, to wait in the huge space with its long wooden benches, high ceilings, and murky windows that allowed in copious, if filtered, light.

Taking out my PDA, I found that Mardi had done her work for the week.

Using Bug's templates she found that eight years earlier Chrystal Chambers had bought a small home, comprising only nine hundred square feet of living space, on a street named Freeling Drive. The deal was brokered by Starkman Realty and the mortgage was held by a small bank in New York called Herkimer-People's Trust, a name that would have caused my father to give me a lecture on the incestuous and corrosive nature of capitalism.

"Excuse me, sir?"

She was young, poorly dressed in brown cotton pants and a

baby-blue short-sleeved blouse. Her hair was straightened in places and not in others—as if maybe in the middle of a hair-dressing session she told the stylist that she couldn't afford the appointment. Mahogany brown, twenty at the most, her shoes were pink and plastic. Her once-red nails were cut close.

"Yes?" I said.

Twenty feet away a black man, maybe forty, was watching us closely. This reminded me of Rainier Klaus and his ineffective bodyguard.

"I need some money to buy a, um, a ticket," she said.

"That guy in the black pants and gray shirt put you up to this?" I asked.

"Um . . ."

"That's all right, sugar," I said. "I'll do what you want, just tell me if that dude is running you."

"Yeah. He my boyfriend."

"Drugs?"

"Uh-huh."

"For the both'a you?"

"Just him. Just sometimes."

"What's your name?"

"Seema."

A security guard was watching the man watching us.

"So I'll tell you what, Seema. I'll give you some money if you want it. But I'll also take you out of here and drop you anyplace else you want."

Her eyes pondered over the broad field of possibility.

"Brody won't let me go."

"Brody can't stop you, baby. 'Cause you know I am both a rock and a hard place."

She must have recognized the paraphrasing from some old-time relative.

"I bettah not cause no trouble, mistah." She turned as if to leave me.

"Hold up, girl," I said. "I told you I'd give you money. How much you and Brody need?"

"Fi'ty."

I reached into a back pocket and took out my thirty-year-old red-brown wallet. I teased out a fifty-dollar bill and a business card. These I handed to Seema.

"Put the card away," I said. "If you feel sometime later that you need to get out, just call me. I will be there and I will do my best to help."

Up until that moment there was a kind of unfocused intensity to the young woman. But something about the weight of all the promises, along with the very real money and card, caused her to look directly at me.

"Thank you. Thank you very much, mistah."

She put the card in one pocket and the cash in another and then turned away. As I watched her approach Brody I began to understand that my profession had somehow changed into a calling.

IN THE PARKING LOT there was a bright-yellow Prius with the keys in a magnetized little box attached to the inner side of the back bumper. This was a benefit provided by a nationwide network of car rental services that delivered vehicles of all kinds to clients like me. Zephyra always had a car waiting for me, no matter where I needed it.

USING THE GPS system in my phone I entered the address and drove out from the train station's parking lot.

The route took me through side streets and shabby avenues where business had almost stopped, filled with pedestrians looking for a way to hang on.

Baltimore has a large black population, souls who have been there for generations, and who have not yet received the notice of a postracial America.

I passed through neighborhoods that were once fancy and now slum, and areas that had started out working class and stayed that way. The route I was traveling took me past few, if any, chain stores; no fancy coffee houses or *99 Billion Served*, no grand supermarket parking lots or warehouses that sold everything the oppressed Chinese population could produce.

There were places like *Juma's Grocery Market* and *Cosmo's Boiled Crab and Ribs*.

Freeling was a quiet street of little matchbox houses. Most looked kept-up. My GPS told me that I had arrived at my destination so I pulled up to the curb between a lime-green pickup truck and a purple 1969 Cadillac.

The house I was aimed at was number 47. The whitewashed wooden structure was boxy, with a lawn fourteen feet wide and two feet deep. To the right there was a yellow house, to the left a gray. The front door had no porch or pathway, not even a step up.

I stopped there for a moment, William Williams' satchel in hand, gathering my wits. My clients were a bunch of kids whose dead mother had hired me under the pretext of being the owner of this small home.

If running a fool's errand were the key, then I had access to the kingdom.

"Excuse me," came a man's voice that was totally devoid of deference.

There were four of them, three men and a woman, all black, all very serious, if not angry. One of the men was carrying a small gardening spade in his left hand. I wondered if he had just stood up from landscaping or if he'd picked up that tool specifically for my detriment. I also wondered if he was left-handed.

"Yes?" I said to the mob.

"What you doin' here?" a fortyish dark-skinned man in a loose-fitting yellow T-shirt and black trousers asked. Five eight, short by most standards.

I held up the briefcase and said, "My business."

"What you want wit' Miss Murphy?" the woman asked. She was taller and heavier than the first speaker. Her color was that of maple syrup in a glass jar, but in shadow.

My response was to set my satchel down on the sidewalk.

"What?" a very tall, gray-brown man said. He wore a buttoned-up, short-sleeved red shirt.

"Whatever you want," I replied.

Threats always make me a little crazy. It's my childhood code of survival kicking my ass—and everyone else's in close proximity.

"Hey, man," said a fellow who was both tall and heavy.

My smile was irrepressible.

"Excuse me." The words this time were friendly and feminine.

A glance to my right revealed Shawna's face—if that visage had been scrubbed of makeup and resentment in the guise of sneering sexuality. She was wearing a faded baby-blue T-shirt and loose blue exercise shorts.

"You know this man, Miss Murphy?" the woman member of the vigilantes asked.

"He's not Melvin," Chrystal Chambers-Tyler said.

"Ms. Murphy?" I said. "My name is Clayton Adams, from Child Services in New York. I've come about your sister's— Shawna's—children."

This pronouncement left her no choice. She took in a breath that was half a gasp and then said, "Come in . . . come in, Mr. Adams."

37

THE LIVING ROOM was small and filled with sunlight that fell on a pine floor and furniture that was mostly antique white. The sofa and chair were upholstered in pale ivory, and the low coffee table and bookcase, with only seven books on it, were made from unfinished ash. A real cork-stoppered bottle of red wine stood on the table, accompanied by an elegant, unused, glass.

"Have a seat, Mr. Adams," Chrystal Chambers-Tyler, known in that neighborhood as Miss Murphy, said.

I was tired, tired of false names, of lies, of hiding in general.

I sat on the cushioned chair, placing the satchel next to my right ankle on the pine floor. Then I held up my hands, fingers splayed wide.

"My name is Leonid McGill, Mrs. Tyler," I said, "and I'm telling you right now that I'm sick of lying and being lied to."

Hearing her name brought on a shock of fear that quickly gave way to resignation. The look said, *If he wants to kill me, then I'm dead.*

"A woman came to my office claiming to be you," I continued. "She looked a lot like you. She told me that her husband wanted to kill her. I guess she meant that your husband wanted to kill you. Anyway . . . I went to him and he acted surprised, but not before he tried to fool me into thinking that another guy, who looked a lot like him, was the real Cyril Tyler."

Chrystal sat with excellent posture on the white sofa. Her face had stopped communicating.

"Was there really something about Fatima and them?" she asked. "Or was that another lie?"

As she spoke these words, a solitary tremor went up her neck, moving her head just slightly.

"I went to a commune on Avenue D where Shawna, your sister, was supposed to be living. She wasn't there, but the children were being held against their will. I got them out of there and they said something about a man putting their mother to sleep and then this guy Beria and his friends burying her."

"She's dead?" Chrystal could have been Fatima right then. The question was that innocent. There was the potential for pain, but she held that down, admirably.

"I don't know for sure," I said, "but I decided to take the kids someplace safe. I asked them what they wanted and they said that they wanted to be with you."

I was trying very hard to stay within the realm of truth, as far as I knew it, but admitting to direct knowledge of a murder was further than I wanted to go.

"Do you think that Shawna is dead?"

"Like I said—I don't know. But there isn't any sign of her, and her children were alone in the commune."

Passing sadness showed on her face like a ghost drifting between us.

"Are the . . ." she said and hesitated. "Are the police involved?"

"I thought it would be better to come to you first."

"Why?"

"Your sister gave me a twelve-thousand-dollar retainer," I said. "I know that your husband's two previous wives either died or disappeared under questionable circumstances, and the kids are just kids. That's a straight path here to you."

"And what do you want?"

"This is as far as I could get on my own. I put the children someplace safe and came to you. The question is—what do *you* want?"

There are moments when the emotional red tape between strangers gets cut—immediately. Usually it takes many hours, lots and lots of conversation, and the presentation of indisputable proofs before people, intelligent ones at any rate, can even begin to trust each other. After all, most of what people say is lies; in church, in court, even under the threat of death. People lie when they think they're telling the truth. It is one of the most universal human traits.

But every once in a while the need to trust causes us to ignore the implacable crush of lies. I could see in Chrystal's eyes that she needed to trust me.

"I could call the kids for you right now," I offered. "You could talk to Fatima on the phone."

She didn't say the word but everything about her demeanor said *yes*.

I entered Aura's number and on the fourth ring Theda answered.

"Hello?"

"Hey, girl."

"Uncle L, hi."

"How's it goin'?"

"We're building a fort out of cardboard boxes. Fatima and Boaz are the Indian scouts and the rest of us are waiting for the attack."

"Put Big Chief Fatima on, will ya?"

The phone made some muffled noises and then a timid voice said, "Yes?"

"I got somebody here wants to talk to you, Fatima," I said before handing the little cell over to the real Chrystal.

"Fatima?"

The smile that blossomed across Chrystal's face was something I had hankered for in a long life of solitude. It was the love of a relative who felt a connection with a child who needed that emotional touch.

I wanted that contact more than anything.

They talked about Fatima's brothers and sisters, about the house they were staying in and what the child thought about me. There was no mention, at least on Chrystal's part, of Shawna's possible death.

"Of course you can all come live with me," the grateful woman said. "But we have to make sure that it's okay with your mom."

This last phrase was very important. The children, the older ones at least, were pretty sure that their mother was dead. But knowledge for children is a different thing than it is for adults. Finality is slow in coming for those whose bones have not yet stopped growing. Shawna would be with them for a very long time. She'd be with Chrystal forever.

They talked for at least fifteen minutes before the child was drawn back into the immediacy of her life.

When Chrystal handed the phone back to me there was a shy look in her eyes. I had seen something of her that very few ever had. She was open and vulnerable and fully expressive of love.

Our fingers touched when I took the phone.

"Satisfied?" I asked.

"If that's what you call it," she said. "Thank you for taking care of the kids. I'm always worried about them. Shawna lives such a dangerous life."

"Did you sell a necklace called Indian Christmas to a woman named Nunn?"

"Yes," she said, a little startled.

"And did you give some of that money to your sister?"

"For her and my brother."

"Are you afraid that Cyril is planning to have you murdered?"

There's a limit to honesty with strangers. I had come right up to that border.

Chrystal turned her head away from me. She crossed her bare legs, and I experienced a moment of excitation that passed quickly.

"I know a guy," I said, "a driver for a limo company, who'd be happy to drive the kids down here. Getting custody might be difficult if you're not in state, and I don't think you want them in the foster-care system."

"No," she said.

It was like we were old friends or family. I wanted to press her, to find out about her domestic situation, which was so vague. But there was an unspoken prohibition that kept me silent.

I stood up.

"I'll get back to New York and have the kids brought down here. If you need anything, here's my card."

She stood to take the card but caressed my fingers instead.

"Would you like to stay for some wine?" she asked.

She brought out another glass and poured more than one round.

I remember the first kiss.

38

THERE WAS THE SMELL of French roast coffee in the air.

Sunlight gathered in the chiffon-yellow curtains, spraying its cool brilliance on the white bed. There were no paintings on the walls anywhere in the artist's home. My watch, the only thing I wore, said 7:17.

I tapped the crystal face and smiled.

When I sat up I remembered the first bottle of wine. It was very good stuff.

My clothes were neatly folded on a straight-back ash chair two paces away. I stood up, fell back on the bed, stood up again, conquering the dizziness, and then got my pants and shirt on with hardly a wobble.

CHRYSTAL'S KITCHEN WAS predominantly yellow. The sink was paved with slightly uneven lemon tiles and the floors were grapefruit linoleum with a smudge of green here and there. The walls and cabinets, the ceiling and table and chairs, were all painted the color of deep-yellow roses. The old-fashioned stove was yellow enamel with little blue gas jets cooking our breakfast.

All she wore was an oversized violet T-shirt.

I reached down through the neck, cupping her breast, as I kissed her neck. She returned the passion by pressing back against me.

"What's for breakfast?" I whispered into her nimbus of hair.

"If you don't move your hand it's gonna be you in that chair over there."

I kissed her again and moved back six inches or so.

She looked me up and down, took a deep breath through generous nostrils, and smiled.

"That was very nice last night," she said. "Sometimes you need something and you don't even know what it is."

I sighed and nodded.

She gestured toward the chair that she'd recently threatened me with.

My eyes asked a question.

"Don't worry," she replied. "I'll feed you first."

I went quickly to the chair and she laughed.

"Whole wheat waffles, shirred eggs, and hickory-smoked bacon," she said, and then went about making those words into reality.

She served me black coffee and offered hot milk, which I declined.

Watching her cook, I was silent. She didn't hum, but that was about the only thing missing. I realized that I had fallen for my reluctant client when she smiled upon hearing Fatima's voice. I was enamored by the love she felt for another.

"What?" she asked when I smiled at my flittery, yellow butterfly of a heart.

"Come sit," I said.

She brought the breakfast on a butter-colored tray and served me.

I was experiencing the unfamiliar sensation of embarrassment.

After a few minutes of awkward silence she said, "Talk to me, Leonid McGill."

"At first," I said and then swallowed to get some moisture in my voice. "At first I was thinking that you should have some of your steel canvases on the walls. Then I saw that the rooms, the way they're laid out and painted, are pieces of art in themselves."

Chrystal smiled and I felt like a child who'd given his mother the right answer.

"I always knew that I was going to be an artist," she said, reaching across the table to touch my hand. "And not any water-colorist or etcher, either. I was going to work hard, and with dangerous materials. I was going to make what was hard soft and what was soft impenetrable."

"You thought these things when you were a kid?"

"I didn't have the words back then but the ideas haven't changed since I was four years old.

"I didn't marry Cyril because he was rich," she said. "It was because when I came to his house the first time I saw the long hall that led to his office and told him I wanted to paint it hot pink. I said that if he let me do that to his house, then he could do whatever he wanted with me."

"That's why you married him? Because he let you paint two walls?"

"After we finished fucking, we talked . . . for hours. I didn't like the sex, but he was able to talk without competition, and to love without lust or dominance."

Our eyes met with these last words and I wavered. This also was a new feeling. It made me wonder at something I might have missed, some kind of violation and settlement in a relationship that I had not previously experienced.

"Cyril told me that he believes that he has a power, a cursing power that operates without his volition," she said. "His psychic, a man named Marlowe, had apparently confirmed this as a fact, and even though I don't believe in that stuff—his wives are still dead."

My mind was wandering down that long pink hallway. I wanted to linger there for a while to comprehend the meaning she imparted.

But I had a job to do.

"So you think he killed them?" I asked.

"I think he thinks he did, and I'm an artist—my whole life is imagination."

"Shawna told me that Cyril has moved to another bedroom and talks all night to a woman on the phone."

"He's always had his own bedroom," she said. "Our sex life was never the center of the relationship. But he has been distant, and he did talk on the phone late at night. He lost weight and some-times went away for weeks at a time."

"And is that why you came here?"

"I sold the necklace and went away. I told Cyril that I thought he was turning sour on me and that I didn't want to go the ways of his previous wives."

"What he say to that?"

"He swore that he wasn't upset with me and he just wanted a

few months to get his mind straight. I told him fine, and that I'd call him in the fall."

"Was he okay with that?"

She hunched her shoulders and came over to straddle my lap.

I kissed her and asked, "But then why did you send Shawna to me?"

"I didn't." She shook her head and I kissed her.

"What sense does it make for her to come to me on her own? And who would kill her?"

"Maybe she went directly to Cyril," Chrystal speculated.

"And you think that he's capable of murdering her?"

She stood up and went back to her chair, making me want to stop talking about the case at all.

"I don't know," she said after a long, thoughtful pause. "I've never been afraid of Cyril. I feel the violence that formed him, but it never seemed to have motility."

Her use of this last word shocked me. I was made suddenly aware of the complexity of Chrystal. She was the odd combination of the hood and a postdoctoral student, of a merchant marine and a woman who lives in perfect equanimity as long as no one brings a hot color into her line of sight.

"You say 'the violence that formed him'?"

"His father was a brute," Chrystal said. "He beat him and his brothers, and his mother, too. The only way that Cy could get back at his father was to pretend, in his mind, to have killed him."

"How does the inheritance play out?" I asked.

"I made him do a prenuptial agreement separating our monies before we were married, but on our fourth anniversary he tore up his copy of the agreement. He said that he loved me and trusted me."

"Seven years, right?" I said, referring to the length of their marriage.

She nodded.

"He hired me to give you a message," I said.

"What?"

" *'I love you and would never be upset about anything having to do with your actions or oversights.'* "

The inept wording brought an ever-so-slight smile to Chrystal's lips.

"I have to ask you something," I said.

"Will it keep me from climbing up on you again?"

"Probably."

"That's a talent," she said. "It's harder to turn a woman off, you know."

"You don't seem shocked about the possibility of Shawna's death."

"You're a talented man, Mr. McGill."

"What was it about Shawna?" I asked.

"Is she really dead?"

"I think so."

Chrystal took a moment to ponder the lifelong relationship between herself and the woman her mother called a wild creature.

"Instead of working with steel, my sister wrought art on her own body and mind," the postdoctoral ghetto sailor proclaimed. "She made babies and enemies and never took the easy way, not once in her life. I loved her but I'm not surprised if she's dead."

I nodded because there was nothing to say about the artist's sober view of life, love, and death.

"I'll take the train back this morning," I said. "The kids will be with you by tonight."

"No," she said. "If Shawnie's dead, then I need to find her and bury her and take Fatima and them someplace safe."

"You're probably safer away from New York."

"Maybe, but I'm not worried about that," she said.

"Why not?"

"I have you, don't I?"

39

WE WERE ON the road in the yellow Prius, well on our way to the train station, when my phone made the sound of a growling bear. The Bluetooth was already in my ear because I had called to get my messages. So all I had to do was reach into my pocket and press a button to make the connection.

"Hello," I said.

Chrystal touched my shoulder.

"Mr. Mack-gill?" a woman said.

"Yeah?"

"This Seema."

"Why . . . hello, Seema," I said with forced sangfroid. "What can I do for you?"

"Did you mean what you said yesterday?"

"Every word."

"Can you come get me right now?"

"It might take an hour or so, but I'll get there sooner if I can. Where are you?"

"I stoled his money," she replied, giving me a way out, I supposed.

"You mean the money you collected by asking strangers for a train ticket to nowhere?"

"I guess."

"Then it's really your money."

"I'm at a laundromat on Phillips called Dusty's."

"That's an odd name for a place to clean clothes."

"That's the name of the woman that owns it," Seema said with no humor whatsoever. "She was a friend'a my mother's."

"Does Brody know where you are?" I asked.

"You remebah his name?"

"Does he know where you are?"

"He thinks I'm out shoppin' fo' food, but if he looks in his money draw he gonna know what I did."

"Give me the address and I'll get there as soon as I can."

I disconnected the call when I had what I needed, handed the phone to Chrystal, and asked her to enter the address in my GPS.

"Where we going?" she asked with no distrust that I could glean.

I explained about Seema and Brody.

"Hm," she grunted.

"What?"

"Most people would have just waved that girl on and gone about their business."

"Turn left in fifty yards," commanded a woman's voice from my phone.

"Yeah. Yeah, you're right about that," I said, to Chrystal, not the phone.

"Is it some kind of sickness with you?" She might have been serious.

"Can I drop you somewhere while I take care of this?" I replied.

"No."

"No?"

"I wouldn't miss it."

"It might be a little risky."

Her grin might have been mine in the mirror.

DUSTY'S COIN-OP LAUNDROMAT was a dingy little place with a big exhaust pipe over the front door letting out great gouts of steam.

"You have arrived at your destination," the GPS woman said.

When I drove past the establishment, Chrystal said, "It's right there."

"We'll go around the block."

Everything looked all right. Brody was nowhere to be seen and there weren't any lookouts waiting in the recesses or doorways on Phillips Avenue.

There was an alleyway behind the little laundry. A pass through there showed me a back door.

I drove around the block again, finally parking across the street and at the far end from Dusty's.

"Got anything that needs cleaning?" I asked Chrystal.

"Just my mind."

"Well, come on, then."

"You're not going to ask me to stay in the car?"

"You're safer with me."

DUSTY'S COLORING MATCHED her name. Her skin was grayish brown, like some mouse fur, and her eyes glinted an unhealthy yellow hue. Seated behind an old teacher's desk, she was my age but looked older.

The establishment was a long, slender aisleway with double-stacked washing machines and solitary dryers down the right side and wooden benches on the left. There were no customers in sight, but five or more of the machines were running.

I supposed people dropped their clothes off with Dusty and she washed them, charging by the pound.

"You got laundry?" she blurted.

"It'll just take a minute," I said.

"No funny business in here, mistah."

"Just lookin' for a friend."

"This ain't no bar," she said, "ain't no ho' house."

"It's okay, DD," a voice called from behind a big chrome washing machine that stood like a sentry guarding the rest of its machine brothers and sisters. The huge unit had a round glass door throwing up flashes of red and orange inside the frothing of dirty suds.

Seema poked her head around the side of the vibrating chrome-and-glass monster. Her eyes fixed instantly on Chrystal.

"Who's that?" she asked.

"The friend I came down here to visit," I said simply. Every word was true, even if there were some temporal disconnections.

Seema was suspicious, still wearing the dowdy clothes she'd had on the day before. The only additions to her ensemble were a little red cloth bag, clutched in both hands, and a swollen, discolored left eye.

"So?" she said.

"That's what I should be asking you, girl. Here we are. What do you want?"

"I need to get outta here," she said. "I need to get away from him."

Saying this, she glanced at Chrystal, and I realized that she was thinking that I had been offering to take her on in some romantic or maybe business capacity. This was a revelation, because I was distracted by the ill-advised dalliance with my client.

"You got family?" I asked.

"Not that I wanna see. An' anyway, Brody know all my people."

"You ever been to Eastern Light?" Chrystal asked.

"You mean the church ovah past the seaport?"

"It's a retreat," Chrystal said to the both of us. "The people who run it are Hindu, but they don't practice or proselytize."

"Huh?" Seema said.

"Brody out there," Dusty warned.

There was a sea-green '80s Chevrolet driving past the front door of the store. I reached into my pocket laying my hand on a gun I had no license to carry in Maryland. I could feel my back muscles bulging and had to take a deep breath to ease my natural impulses.

"Let's go out the back," I said to my charges.

They knew to take direction at a moment like that.

THE BACK DOOR of Dusty's led into an alley that smelled of maggots and human feces. The lane was wide enough for a small car, and there were various denizens reclining in doorways, crevices, and other nooks and niches. I kept my hand on the pistol as I led the women.

We came out on Allen Street and walked the half block to Phillips. As we crossed the avenue toward my sunny little car, I saw Brody, followed by two other men, walking into Dusty's. At that moment he glanced in my direction, looked right at me. Seema was on the other side, hidden by my bulk. Brody didn't recognize my suit or frame.

Lucky for him and his friends.

EASTERN LIGHT was a temple of ancient East Asian design located in a nicer part of town. On the way over, Chrystal explained the place to both of us.

"They offer shelter for people, body and mind," Chrystal said. "They teach classes, serve meals, and have small rooms with cots for special cases."

"And how come you know so much about them?" I asked.

"I volunteer, and I also contribute money."

"Brody gonna find me here," Seema said.

"I doubt it," Chrystal assured her. "They're under everybody's radar, and they don't take many residents. For the first little while, at least, you will be in the inner circle and even the day visitors won't see you."

"I'm not givin' 'em my money," Seema said.

"They have their own resources," my client replied. "If you want to hold on to that little bag, that's fine, no one will try and take it from you."

"So you just gonna leave me here?" Seema directed this question to me.

"For the time being, sugar. You need a place to get centered."

"I thought you wanted me to be with you."

"I never said that. I said I'd get you away from Brody. That meant I'd get you someplace safe, but I'm not a pimp or a gangster. I'm a detective, like the card says."

"What if I don't like it here?"

We were parked at the ornate gate of the temple grounds. Chrystal was sitting next to me, while Seema sat in the center of the backseat. I turned around to look her in the face.

"If you don't like it, you can just leave, or call me and I'll either come down myself or send somebody I trust to get you."

"How'm I gonna call? Do they even have a phone in there?"

I reached into William Williams' satchel and came out with a small black phone wrapped in a power cord, one of the throwaways that Bug kept me supplied with. This I handed to the girl.

"You still have my card?" I asked.

She nodded.

"Did Brody give you that black eye?"

Another nod.

"Then let Chrystal take you in there, and give it three days before you make up your mind what to do."

It wasn't what she wanted. It wasn't what she expected. But Seema didn't have much choice.

"Okay," she said.

I waited in the car while my client escorted the girl through the gate and gardens and into the lavish domed building. I sat there for a quarter of an hour wondering at the odd connection between me and the solid-steel artist.

ON THE TRAIN, Chrystal and I sit side by side, mainly in silence. I used the time to consider the murder of my initial client; also Dimitri and Twill; also Gordo on his deathbed; and, to a lesser degree, the man William Williams.

An hour into the ride I called Seema.

"Hello?" she said after the sixth ring.

"Seema."

"Mr. Mack-gill?"

"How are you?"

"Okay, I guess. They food taste funny but they nice."

"You feel safe?"

"I guess. They give me this tiny little room and told me that I could work anywhere I want to for my rent—the kitchen or the laundry, whatevah."

"I'll call you at the end of the week to see how you're doing."

"If I get cleaned up, can I come down to you?"

"It's not about that, girl. I'm just helping you."

"Okay. But you gonna call, right?"

"Definitely."

If Chrystal heard this conversation she gave no sign of it. She just stared out the window, blinking now and then like a camera on a very slow shutter release.

40

As we were pulling into the Newark train station I turned to gaze at her profile.

The train was pulling out again before she asked, "What?"

"You say that you and Cyril don't have a very powerful erotic connection."

I didn't need to say anymore. She understood the implications.

"I know a man," she said. "His name is Lod, he lives in Astoria. We . . . we get together sometimes."

"Cyril know about him?"

"Maybe not his name, but he knows."

"How about a big guy, dressed all in brown, maybe pretends that he's Cyril sometimes."

"Him and me? I don't think so."

"What's his name?"

"That's Cyril's bastard stepbrother—Ira Lamont."

There was a full stop at the end of her answers. I needed more information, but her tone told me to slow it down. I didn't mind. I was just another lemming—standing on line.

———

"Aunt Chris!" a child yelled when we came into the door.

Then all the children mobbed the woman their mother had pretended to be. They hugged and kissed and finally got down on the floor, the whole gang of them.

The four-year-old, Dorian, moved away after a while. The copper-colored boy picked up a stuffed tiger and started a conversation with it.

"Dorian," Chrystal said playfully.

"Yes?" he said in the same tone and timbre.

"Don't you love me anymore?"

"Yes, I do," he said, still looking at his doll.

"Then come here and give me some sugar."

The boy laughed and ran back into the brood.

AFTER A GOOD WHILE of playing and reconnecting, Theda took the kids to her room for the castle game that everyone liked to play. Aura, Chrystal, and I sat at an oval table that looked down on Gramercy Park, there to sip wine and discuss murder.

"So you don't know what your sister was talking about when she came to my office?" I asked Chrystal.

"No," she said, "not at all. I mean, I *did* feel pushed out by Cyril, and I was worried about his history with wives ending up dead, but he didn't want to kill me. And even if he did I wouldn't go to Shawnie about that. She could hardly hold her own life together."

"But you gave her the money she paid me with."

"I gave her fifty thousand dollars. Some of it was for her and some to give to Tally if he needed it. She said that she wanted to get out of that commune and get a job in a beauty shop."

"And you just gave her that much money?" I asked.

"Yeah. Why?"

"That's a lot of money."

"So? My husband owns a farm in Brazil that would take you three weeks to hike across. My room in his house is worth a million dollars on the open market. And, anyway, I don't really care about money."

Aura was silent, listening to a conversation both spoken and unspoken.

"Fatima told me that they buried her mother in a garden near where they lived," Chrystal said.

"I called the police. If they found her it should have been in the papers."

"It was," Aura said. "This morning. The police found her yesterday."

Without being asked, Aura went into the kitchen and came back with the *Post*. The story was pushed to page eight because of a drug overdose in Hollywood, a has-been star who made the headlines one last time.

We were silent while Chrystal read her sister's pop obituary.

The children's laughter wafted in from down a hallway and through a door.

Chrystal put the paper down and looked at me.

"I have no idea what's going on here," she said. "But I want you to find out who did this."

"She hired me to protect you," I said.

"She can stay here, Leonid," Aura said. "No one knows, and the children need her."

"Thank you," Chrystal said and the deal was sealed.

"I'm not the police," I said to anyone who wanted to listen. "I don't arrest people, or solve crimes for that matter. I will look into this deeply enough to make sure you and Shawna's kids are safe. But when I get anywhere near the truth I'll turn it over to the cops. Arresting people and bringing them to trial is what you pay your taxes for."

"Okay. I just need to know."

That was the end of our little tête-à-tête-à-tête. It was time for me to get out there and make the streets safe for artists and orphans. But sitting at that table, between those two women (either one of whom I loved more than my wife of twenty-odd years), I was frozen.

That's when Chrystal reached across the table and touched my left wrist.

"Thank you."

Aura took in this intimacy. I noticed her and she saw this regard in my eyes. It was the way Escher probably saw the world: an endless reflection of awareness advancing and receding.

"Aura," I said.

"Yes, Leonid?"

"I might need a space to work this thing."

"Office or apartment?"

"An apartment would do fine."

Without a word she stood up and went to her bedroom door.

When she was gone, Chrystal said, "Don't worry. I won't cause a problem."

Yet another point of view in the endless knot of desire.

Aura came back with two key chains that each held three keys.

"The place is on East Thirty-first, over near Madison," she said. "Address and apartment numbers are on the tags."

"Keep this and leave it downstairs at the Tesla," I said, handing back one of the key chains. "Tell them that someone coming from me will pick them up. And can you make sure that there's a live telephone jack?"

"Yes."

"And one more thing."

"What's that?"

"Get somebody to go to Mardi and ask her for the special black phone. Get them to connect it at the apartment."

She nodded, not quite looking me in the eye.

There was nothing else to say, and so I left the apartment, made my way down the stairs to the front door, and walked outside—where I could start breathing again.

41

Son—my father rarely called me son—*you have to remember that when it comes to love, men are less experienced than women—much less. If a woman falls in love she knows just where she is. Her mind as well as her body comes into bloom. When a woman feels love it's like a great mind opening, like Karl Marx when he first understood capital. When men fall in love, we just turn stupid. A man in love is a man operating without the benefit of history. He thinks that today is different from every other day, that the woman he's lookin' at is different, fundamentally, from all other women.*

Love will beat you down worse than any bull or truncheon. Love will rob you of your reflexes and everything you know. And because of all that, it will be the greatest challenge you ever meet.

That speech came back to me as whole cloth in the backseat of the taxi I hailed in front of Aura's building. I'd been thinking about Tolstoy a lot in the previous days. He was a philosopher in reverse; a man who had encountered the truth at an early age and then spent the rest of his life trying to get away from it. I understood, with little rancor, that my old man's truths were the opposite of themselves, so much so that they appeared workable.

A feeling of filial ardor came over me. I heard my father's voice again and loved him the way I had as a child. This feeling was like a parasite moving under the skin, that at first fascinates— before the terror sets in . . .

"Here you go," the gray-headed white cabbie said.

We were in front of Cyril Tyler's building.

I'd spent the whole time unaware of its passage.

. . . *a man in love is a man operating without the benefit of history* . . .

THE LIGHT-COLORED DOORMAN with the beautiful voice recognized me. He didn't like me any more than the last time we met but posed no challenge to my entry.

I took the first elevator, negotiated the doorless hallway, and entered the second lift. This took me to the suburban New Jersey mansion on the top of the building.

There was an Olympian feel to the open space.

Phil, the whitest black man in America, was approaching from across the lawn. I waited for him to arrive, wondering what it felt like to work in a place like that.

"Mr. McGill," Phil said when he reached me.

It might have been a greeting, but it lacked sincerity. His tone and the look in his eye said, *Why are you here?*

He was wearing a peach suit and a sweet, citrusy cologne.

"Phil."

"What do you want?"

"Common courtesy would be nice."

Phil had no response to that, so I said, "I'd like to talk to Mr. Tyler again. The real Mr. Tyler. Not his lawyer or his bastard brother—the man himself."

"No."

"No?"

"You can't come up here making demands, Mr. McGill. You're forgetting your place."

My *place*. For a moment I was flummoxed by the young man's words. This tickled me. I couldn't remember how long it had been since I was actually surprised by something someone said.

Phil believed that he'd gotten the upper hand due to my silence. He said, "So if you don't mind . . ."

"You know, Phil, you're right."

"What?"

"Well," I added, "not right exactly, but accurate—about place, I mean. You and I are in different places. You up here on the mountaintop, with blue sky and bright sun no matter what time of day it is. There's never a shadow over you, and even on a cloudy day the light gathers in the clouds above your head."

This high-toned language silenced the biracial aide.

"And me," I said, "I'm from another plane completely. I live in a shithole where the gasses rise up to block the sun. Down where I am there's serious global warming. Up here it's cool and breezy, so much so that you might think you're removed from the shit. You might make a mistake and think that you were born up here and not down in the muck where I live. But I'm here to tell you that I am the man that will drag your ass back down to where it came from."

It was a muscular monologue, enough so that Phil became circumspect, both physically and verbally.

His stillness and silence were a balm to my rising anger.

"Now let's try this again," I said. "Leonid McGill here to speak to Cyril Tyler."

"He's not here," Phil said, his face and voice devoid of animation.

"Where is he?"

"I don't know."

"You wouldn't lie to me now, would you, Phil?"

He had no reply to my question.

I believed the young assistant but still had the urge to grab him and hold him over the side of the building just to hear him yelp and beg. This desire caused me, not for the first time, to wonder at my own motivations of late.

Quashing these violent feelings, I said, in a very mild tone, "Tell him that I have accomplished the task for which I was hired and that I have his answer."

AFTER THAT I followed the rabbit warren down to the street, an insane reinterpretation of Alice in pursuit of the ever-elusive hare.

42

BACK ON THE STREET, a few blocks from Cyril Tyler's building, I experienced the momentary prickling of impotence across my forehead. It's the sensation that a true athlete-boxer feels when there's a punch coming that he hasn't seen, a real hammer blow that will end the bout forthwith.

I turned to my left—just to see if there was someone standing there, watching me. There wasn't, and so I took out my cell phone and a note I had scribbled down and shoved in the breast pocket of my blue suit. I entered the number and pressed send.

"Fawn David," she said, answering the phone after only one ring.

Her voice was certain and crisp, businesslike. I was thrown off, mostly because I was used to preparing my lies while the phone rang in my ear.

"Hello, Ms. David," I said out of reflex. "My name is McGill and I'm looking for Bill Williams."

"Excuse me?" It was her turn to feel lost in the exchange. "Did you say Bill Williams?"

"Yes."

"Do you, do you mean William Williams?"

"Yes."

"Oh my God. I haven't heard from Mr. Williams in almost fifteen years. Maybe more. How did you even know to call here?"

"I'm a private detective," I said, feeling a bit vulnerable with
the honesty. "I was hired by a man named Vartan, Harris Vartan, to locate this Mr. Williams. Vartan had the number of a
woman who had known Bill and who was in possession of some
of his books. There was a real estate ad that he'd circled pressed
into the pages of *Kapital*, by Karl Marx. This number was in
that ad."

"Yes," Fawn David said, "yes. Mr. Williams lived in the room
out back for seven years. Wow. I haven't even thought about him
in such a long time. He was a very nice man—exceptional."

"In what way?" I asked, standing on the sidewalk of what
passes for a side street on Manhattan's Upper West Side.

"He was . . . such a nice man. Very interested in what people
had to say, and very well read. It was really because of him that I
started my business."

"What business is that, Ms. David?"

"Middleman Enterprises. I research all kinds of products
and, for a percentage or a fee, depending on price, I help people acquire special items for business, personal use, or just a
present."

"So if I wanted a special breed of dog . . ."

"I'd research the breed and give you a list of prices, breeders,
and anything else you might need."

"And how did Mr. Williams get you on this path?"

"He told me that I could do what I wanted to, exactly what I
wanted. He said that I didn't have to settle for less."

I suspected that there was something important missing

from the information she gave, but that was more about her than the absent, probably dead, Mr. Williams.

"I'd love to come by and see where it was that he lived," I said. "I doubt if I'll find him, but I'd like to try my best."

"That would be wonderful," Fawn David said. "You can drop by any time. I'm always home. When you work for yourself the day never seems to be over."

"I know what you mean. I'm working a couple of more active cases at the moment. I don't know when I can come exactly but I'll call you in a day or two to see when is best for you."

"Anytime, Mr. McGill, anytime at all."

I was a little surprised about the welcome the young woman expressed. At the time I supposed that it was because she lived in Hoboken; maybe people were more hospitable there.

"HEY, LT," BUG said, also answering on the first ring.

"You sound tired."

"I'm always tired. Iran works me until I'm almost dead. And he puts me on the scale every morning. If I weigh just a pound more he doubles the exercises. So I can't even eat. I'm hungry all the time, man."

"You asked for it, right?"

"Fuck you."

"Hey," I said, grinning at no one. "You see? It's working. Iran's got your testosterone up high enough that you wanna curse a light-heavy like me."

"I transferred the cash," he said. "It's in a special account that Twill started just today."

"Twill?"

"He started the account, but he doesn't know it."

"Oh. Okay. That's great. Thanks a lot, Tiny. You're a real talent."

I ALWAYS CARRIED throw-away phones that Bug kept me supplied with. This one had a tortoiseshell body and a Utah area code. I used it to compose the following text to my son's phone: *I got your money, boy. If you want some of it back you'll meet me @ the Harvell Club on 9th Ave and 14th St @ 3:45 this Friday. Beat Murdoch.*

I smiled to myself, thinking of the mental anguish I would be causing my delinquent and nearly perfect son. I had met killers and thieves, drug dealers and pimps, billionaires and extortionists, zealots of all kinds, and still Twill remained unique. He was a bright spot on the face of the sun, a shadow in the depths of space.

My real phone made the sound of a loon at sunset.

"Hey, Luke," I said.

"You bettah get ovah here, LT. Your boy's got trouble."

"Right away, brother."

43

THE FOUR-STORY VICTORIAN house was painted white with blue-and-green trim and had a slanting roof of layered tar paper coated with dark-red sand. The windows sparkled and the shades and curtains were all purchased at the same time, making the uniformity picture-perfect. Down the concrete pathway that led to the entrance a little boy was pulling a blue wagon that contained an even littler girl, while two young brown women watched them and chatted from the porch.

The boy was making the sounds of a great engine.

The girl alternately giggled and screamed.

The women were speaking in Spanish.

They were all happy and at home.

Less than a year ago the nineteenth-century home-turned-apartment-building had been a self-contained slum. The paint was peeled away and most of the windows had been broken. Crackheads and other druggies crawled into the empty rooms to nurse their highs or service their johns. Once a week the deadly handsome, black-as-tar Johnny Nightly would come up from the illegal pool hall basement and chase away the riffraff.

Then one evening I was visiting with Johnny's boss, Luke Nye. For some reason, probably the bourbon, I told Luke about the recurring dream I had of escaping from a burning skyscraper by busting out a window and jumping from the highest floor.

"What that feel like?" the man who most resembled a moray eel asked.

"You'd think it would be quiet and peaceful," I said, feeling a shudder, "like a baseball sailing out of the park. But it was loud, like a battlefield soldiered by screamin' monkeys fightin' through a hurricane."

That very night Luke dreamed that some junkie had set fire to his building, causing the whole structure to cave in on his exclusive club. He sent Johnny out to hire a team of *illegal* laborers and they refurbished the building in four months' time. Now working families live over the pool hall and Johnny comes up to collect rent and to make sure there are no fire hazards.

I walked up the steps past the women.

"Good afternoon," I said politely.

"*Hola,*" one of them replied, while the other gave me a smile laced with concern.

I'm a scary-looking guy, especially if you know what to look for. From the width of my shoulders to the scars on my knuckles, anyone who lived in a part of town where people worked with their bodies knew that I dealt in trouble.

So, not allowing the women's unease to upset me, I passed on to the front door and pressed the button for 4A.

"Yeah," a voice rasped.

"It's me, Luke."

"Come on up, LT."

The door buzzed and I pushed my way in.

I TOOK THE stairs three at a time because when you're not a professional athlete you have to pick up your workouts where you
can.

The first three floors of the building were single units designed
for larger families, but the top level was divided into studio apartments that Luke's friends and guests occupied from time to time;
4A was the unit that Theodore "Tally" Chambers was given.

The door was ajar so I didn't knock.

It was a sunny room painted mostly white. There were four
occupants. Tall and slender Johnny Nightly, whose glistening
blackness was a thing of art; Luke, who was of medium height with
brown skin that seemed to be seen through a blue-green filter; an
old woman the color of a pecan shell; and Tally, who must have lost
a dozen pounds since I'd seen him last, only a few days before. The
boy's skin looked like it had a layer of yellow webbing laid over it.

The men were standing around the bed where Tally lay. The
woman was seated beside that bed, applying a compress to the
ailing youth's forehead.

"Luke," I said.

The serpentine face regarded me and nodded to Johnny.

"LT," Johnny said. "This here is Juanita Horn. She's—"

"How are you, Juanita?" I asked to show that the introduction
was unnecessary.

"Mr. McGill," she said, not turning away from her charge.

Juanita Horn had been a nurse in Trinidad. She had been young
and quite beautiful. Her man, Bell, was a rough-and-tumble sort of

guy who had trouble with the law and so came to New York. Juan-ita followed and they partied until Bell was stabbed in the back by a woman who didn't want him going back home to Juanita.

Nurse Horn attended to him as she had all of his friends when they had wounds, bruises, and breaks. Bell died from his injury and Juanita stayed on, the visiting nurse to those who couldn't afford the exposure of an emergency room. She was as good as most general practitioners, and better because she knew when the wounds and maladies were beyond her abilities.

"The kid uses needles," Nightly said in a subdued tone. "Got hep and who knows what else? Fever's bad. We were going to take him to the doctor but Juanita said that he won't die right away, and he's been saying things that you might want to know."

I bobbed my head to show that I understood and moved next to Sister Juanita. She understood the gesture and stood so that I could hunker down next the boy.

"Tally," I said as if calling into anther room.

When he opened his eyes I recoiled at the bright yellow beam-ing from them.

"She sent me to meet with him," Tally said, almost out of his mind with fever. "Sent me to tell them that Chrystal needs money, lotsa money if they want her to let up on her share of the inheritance, if they didn't want her to go to the cops."

"Chrystal said that?" I asked.

"What?" Tally was looking in my direction, but it was a toss-up whether he saw me or not. "What you say?"

"Chrystal said to ask for the money?"

"No, man. Chrystal loves that murderin' fool. Chrystal's crazy. Don't even know what's good for her."

"Shawna?" I asked.

"I'm sick," Tally said, looking into my eyes with sudden aware-ness. "Am I dyin'?"

"Did Shawna ask you to ask for money for Chrystal?"

When the boy exhaled it sounded like a last breath. It stank, too. The disease was deep in his blood and lungs, skin and eyes. He passed out and Juanita shouldered me aside. She poured alcohol on a white towel and dabbed it on his face.

"He's a sick puppy," Luke Nye said. "I'm scared just to look at him."

"Rich man killed his sister, and if he's saying what I think, he might be next on the list."

"If somebody wants to kill him," Johnny said, "he better hurry up before the kid does it himself."

"Did he mention any names?" I asked Luke.

"No, just said a guy killed his sister. Said it was in the paper. I thought you might wanna know."

"Thanks."

"Let's go across the hall," Luke said.

Johnny and I followed him out.

Room 4C DOUBLED as an office. There was a cedar desk and chair next to the window and a round maple table with five chairs in the middle of the room. Carpeting was burgundy and the walls champagne. Luke and I sat while Johnny brought out glasses and a crystal decanter filled with fifty-year-old bourbon.

"What you want me to do, LT?" Luke asked.

This was one of those rooms scattered around New York and

the world where anything could be decided. If I wanted them to let Tally die and then to be buried somewhere where he'd never be found, that would be it.

"I'd like to talk to him but I'm afraid it'd kill him," I said.

"Juanita probably could do somethin' bring him around long enough to get some answers," Johnny said before sipping at his glass.

"No," I said. "No. Call an ambulance and say you found him at the door. Say he came to the place and collapsed or something. Take his ID if he has any and let a doctor see to him. By the time he wakes up, if he ever does, the whole thing'll be over."

"So that's it?" Luke said, straightening his shoulders to get up and go.

"One more thing."

"What's that?"

"Johnny works for you, right?"

"Uh-huh."

"So what do I have to do to ask him to come do a job for me?" It was a difficult question. People like us had certain protocols when it came to business relationships. Betrayal was the worst sin anyone could commit, and so I asked the question with both Luke and Johnny at the table.

"Johnny's a free agent," Luke said, giving me that prehistoric smile he has.

"What you need, LT?" Johnny Nightly, a killer almost as dangerous as Hush, asked me.

"It might be a little risky."

"And here I thought you wanted a babysitter."

All three of us grinned and Johnny poured another round.

44

JOHNNY AND I exchanged numbers before he accompanied Luke down to the basement where the men spent most of their time. Luke's pool hall was one of the most exclusive on the Eastern Seaboard—intended for a rarefied clientele. The greatest hustlers in the world came to play on his perfectly balanced tables. Millions of dollars changed hands in that room each year, and seven percent of that went to the house.

Before leaving, I went back to the sick room to see what shape Tally was in. He looked dead but I knew he wasn't because Sister Juanita was still dabbing his forehead with alcohol.

I made a sound and Juanita looked up and over, pinning me in place with eyes that had seen more death and suffering than many a mercenary. She was still beautiful in spite of the sixty-some years spread across acres of death.

"Did he say any other names?" I asked.

"Only the ones you already heard."

"What're his chances?"

"I seen worse. Much worse. But you know, Leonid, some people die from a cold, others lived through Hiroshima."

I smiled, and she did, too—for a brief instant.

"I hear you got Gordo up at your place," she said.

"Yeah."

"How is he?"

"Stomach cancer. Doctor doesn't see much hope."

"What about Gordo?"

"You mean, how does he see his chances?"

She nodded.

"You know ole Gord, he believe in fightin' till the last round."

She smiled and said, "He would have survived that A-bomb, unless they dropped it right on his head."

GOING DOWN THE STAIRS, it came back to me, the year-long affair between Gordo Tallman and Juanita Horn. She'd been called to the gym one day because a Dominican boxer with questionable documentation had fallen badly while sparring. He refused to go to the hospital and Juanita was brought in to set the broken ankle.

For the next twelve months Gordo and Juanita were just about inseparable. And then Gordo shut her out. I was working the heavy bag the day she'd come crying from his office. The gossip was that Juanita had spent a weekend with an old friend of Bell's, that Gordo found out and cut her off. I never knew for a fact. I didn't want to know.

ANGELIQUE ARABESQUE'S white Cadillac stood in front of Luke's place. She was Luke's driver on the rare occasions he left the pool hall.

A black woman with short bleached white hair and eyes that

were gray, naturally, Angelique owned her own limo company and served almost every important personage in the Bronx.

She was leaning against the back door in her white pants suit, watching me. Angelique has a handsome face and a sleek figure, a nasty scar on her right cheek and inelegant hands. Seeing her, you got the feeling she could take care of herself. I've heard that she married an accountant but still kept her own books.

"Mr. McGill," she said as I approached.

"Ms. Arabesque."

"Mr. Nye asked me to take you wherever you needed to go."

I'd ridden the subway out there; probably would have taken it back. Angelique was a gesture on the part of Luke. He was saying that he was my friend and he could see by my situation that I needed help.

THE DRIVE BACK to Manhattan didn't take long. Angelique knew every shortcut. While she drove, I closed my eyes, counting breaths from one to ten and back again, attaining a fragment of bliss by the time the car stopped in front of the Tesla Building.

I'd breezed past the front desk and was halfway to the seventy-second floor when I finally looked at my cell phone. There was a text message from Mardi. *cio* it said. Client in office.

The peacefulness from the meditation was gone in an instant. My heart was thumping while my conscience kicked me in the butt.

For years I wanted a receptionist. I felt that if some innocent young woman was sitting at the front desk, greeting my clients, that I would no longer be a criminal but an upstanding citizen providing a service for John Q. Public. That fantasy was dashed by three simple letters—*cio*.

I banged my fist against the elevator doors, multiple times. When they finally slid open I ran down the hall, keys in hand.

I blundered into the room like a bison crashing a garden party only to find Mardi sitting behind her desk, tapping away at her keyboard. He was sitting on the wooden bench set there for clients, hands clasping a crossed knee.

I was nearly panting, wild-eyed.

"Hi, Mr. McGill," Mardi said. "Mr. Peters has been waiting patiently."

The last word was to tell me that everything was all right and I needn't be worried about her safety. She could read me like a book—a very long tome containing a thousand and one trage-dies penned in the blood of as many victims.

Mardi was wearing a simple dress made from a material the color of goldenrod. It might have been hand sewn—she was that kind of girl.

My hand was on the pistol in my pocket, there was a high whining sound in my ear, the room felt as if it were hurtling through space, and I stood there unable for the moment to move either forward or back. I was the condemned man waking from a dream in which he'd forgotten his death sentence, a fireman jarred to consciousness by a five-bell alarm.

Mr. *Peters* was wearing cowboy boots, brown jeans, a gaudy caballero shirt that wanted to be violet but settled back into tan, and a straw hat that seemed to be lacquered.

I hate cowboys, hate them.

"Mr. McGill?" Mardi asked when I refused to act like a normal human being.

I took in a deep breath through my nose.

"Huh?"

"Is anything wrong?"

I exhaled and took in another deep breath.

"Um," I said on the long journey back to sanity.

I released the pistol and withdrew the hand from my pocket.

I blew out the last breath and said, "Isn't it time for you to go on home, Mardi?"

She didn't answer the question. I knew this was because I didn't sound like myself yet. I had decided to bring my agitation into the conversation.

"Good afternoon, Mr. Lamont," I said. "Follow me."

45

I LED THE WAY to the inner sanctum, toward my office. Lamont followed silently. After I'd seated him in a blue visitors' chair, I settled behind the ebony desk and smiled. The blood in my brain was still thrumming.

"How you know my name?" he asked, the drawl a bit more evident than in our last conversation.

"Trade secret," I said, hunching my shoulders and at the same time leaning back in the reclining office chair. "What can I do for the bastard half brother of Mr. Cyril Tyler?"

"I was born in Cincinnati," he said, as if I had asked about his origins. "Moved to Texas when I was a kid, though. I worked as a cowboy outside'a Dallas, but I gave that up eight years ago to come to New York. Lookin' for the easy life, I guess. You know, if you can make it in the rodeo, you can make it anywhere."

There was an aspect of violence in Lamont's words. I guess he expected me to be insulted by his putdown of my city, and afraid of his obvious physical superiority. You could see by the way he held himself that it was a foregone conclusion that I'd be intimidated by his natural force.

I wondered if his assumptions were based on anything other than bucking broncos.

"Why are you here?" I asked.

"You told the faggot that you had information about Chrystal," he said, another scattershot attempt to rile me. "Cyril sent me over to find out what you know."

"Like they say in Hollywood," I said, "I only speak to the talent."

It took a moment for the meaning of my words to filter through to the cowboy's understanding. I watched as his bland visage turned to something a bit more sour. He sneered, glanced at the door behind and to his right, and then turned back to me.

"You'll talk to me," he promised.

It was an admirable thing, the sinister turn Lamont was able to get into his words. I almost wanted to be scared. He was used to having the upper hand in situations like this, but I didn't have time to dance with him.

The case was getting away from me. Every step I took toward conclusion got me further away from solution. The only thing I knew for certain was that three women were dead, that these women were either married to Cyril or pretending to be. I was pretty sure that Cyril hadn't committed the killings himself, at least not all of them, and so there was a man out there who might have accomplished the assassinations—possibly a man named Bisbe.

"I don't think so, Mr. Lamont," I said. "Cyril Tyler has not told me that I should report to you."

"You don't have a choice, Mr. McGill."

That was when my thoughts took what might have been considered a non sequitur detour. When I first moved into that suite I had my office completely soundproofed by a music studio professional. Walls, door, ceiling, and floor—even the windows were specialized two-ply for sound reduction.

"We always have a choice," I said.

On top of the noise-reducing insulation, I had a dozen extra-large, extra-thick plastic bags in the small supply alcove to my right.

"So you tellin' me that I have to climb over this here desk and beat the answer outta you?" the cowboy asked.

"I'm tellin' you to cool your horseshoes and chill, my brother. All Cyril has to do is call me and I will tell him what I know."

Boxing is a wonderful art. It teaches you to move inside of violence while keeping your wits about you and ignoring the potential for harm. You learn to love your enemy more than you would from any Christian sermon, because in the ring your enemy is always a clear reflection of yourself. Ira Lamont's threat was no more than an opponent in the opposite corner, waiting for the bell. There I was, on my side, anticipating his attack, loving him.

I wanted a fight, but that wasn't going to solve anything. I wasn't a boxer but a detective. This wasn't my battle, it was my dead client's last request.

"I ain't your nigger brother." Ira Lamont was filled with epithets. He came from a place where language was an invitation to violence.

Not so me.

My problem was much more complex than some contest between combatants. What Ira desired was simple, straightforward. He wanted me to kneel before him, to declare him master, and give him the words I kept close. But my needs were convoluted. I had to have Ira go back to where he came from with his dignity intact but still wary of my power. That way he would feel that he could come at me with a chance of victory.

He was to me no more than a ball in play.

"Heavens," I said, feeling that this was an appropriate response to his insult.

"Are you gonna talk to me?" he said with a note of finality to the twang.

"I don't think so."

Ira half-rose from his chair.

I took the pistol from my pocket.

Ira smiled and rose to his full height.

I pointed the gun and he was forced to put another log on the fire of that grin.

I pulled back the hammer.

A thin sheet of worry barely diffused his confidence.

The gun made the sound of a cannon blast when I fired it.

To Ira's lifelong shame, I'm sure, he flinched and jumped half a step backward. The shot had missed him completely, putting a neat little hole in the wall behind him. He was unharmed but still couldn't stop the sweat from appearing on his forehead.

I aimed the pistol at his chest.

Our eyes met.

Dimly I realized that I had lost control again. But I felt justified. Lamont had threatened me, called me names, and tried to force information out of me that would put my new client in jeopardy. I had to shoot at him—didn't I?

I pressed the intercom buzzer four times. This was to tell Mardi to clear out of the office—immediately. We'd set up that signal the first week she came to work for me. And she knew not to come back until I called her on her cell phone.

"One step forward," I said to Ira Lamont, "and it will be your last."

The cowboy had his chance. I didn't know what I'd do if he called me on the threat. He didn't, either. He actually took a half step backward.

"If Cyril wants what I have to say, tell him to come to me. Not on the phone, but in person. Man to man."

I stood up suddenly and Ira girded himself so as not to cower.

"Let's you and me walk to the front door," I said.

He considered resisting but then realized the futility of such an action. Without a word he turned and opened the door. I followed him down the long aisle of empty cubicles and through to Mardi's desk. I saw him out the front of the office, knowing that Mardi would have taken the service elevator down and out.

After Ira was gone I put the pistol back in my pocket and went to the larger utility closet that was at the far end of the hall from my office. There I pulled out a framed print of a long-necked Modigliani nude. I carried this down to the soundproofed room and used a hammer and nail to affix it to the wall, over the bullet hole.

46

I'D JUST STOOD back to appreciate the yellow-and-tan woman with the long neck and almond eyes when the office phone rang. I let the bell make its six cycles before coming to rest at the answering machine up at Mardi's desk. The painted lady seemed to be winking at me from her paper canvas.

My heart was still throbbing with vehement anticipation.

The cell phone on my desk made the sound of a harp being strummed by Harpo Marx—the savant, comedian, and maybe patriotic American spy.

"Hey, Mardi."

"Are you okay, Mr. McGill?"

"Peachy."

"Did Mr. Peters, I mean, Mr. Lamont give you any trouble?"

"He tried but I dissuaded him."

"Are you okay?"

"You already asked that."

"Can I come back to work?"

"It's late. Go on home."

"But—"

"Go home, Mardi. I'm fine. Really."

"Okay."

"Tell me something before we get off."

"Yeah?"

"Was Iran in today?"

"He was in at eight and there was nothing to do so I sent him home at four. He said that he was going to a downtown gym to work out with Bug."

I TOOK the next forty-five minutes to shepherd myself back to normalcy, or at least what passed for being normal in a life like mine.

I had a job to do, a few jobs, and I still wasn't making any solid headway. Humiliating a cowboy in an eastern high-rise wasn't going to help. Having sex with a client while investigating her husband wasn't doing much for me, either.

Cyril Tyler was a billionaire. He had a full-time, six-hundred-dollar-an-hour lawyer sitting on collapsible furniture on his front porch. I couldn't get at him the way I took on petty criminals and thieves. His brand of crime came with city, state, and federal seals of approval. He could shoot me between the eyes at midday in Times Square and never see one minute of jail time.

The cell phone growled. Not a bear but a suspicious pit bull.

I grinned and picked the thing up.

"Hey, D."

"Pops."

It had been years since he called me that. Twill had picked up the habit from his older brother, but Dimitri dropped the term when Oedipus took up residence in his heart and soul.

"Where are you?"

"Paris."

"That's something I never thought I'd hear you say, boy. My son in Paris. Damn."

"Twill told me that I better call you. I used the special number you said we could call to make the connection. I hope you don't mind."

"You in trouble?"

"No."

"Tatyana in trouble?"

"Not right now. Her boyfriend, Vassily, was in with these smuggler guys. They grabbed him but Tatyana got away. She called me and I met her at the airport and we flew here."

I closed my eyes and wondered. Was there a celestial bull's-eye on the top of my bald head?

"Do you speak French, son?"

"Uh-uh."

"Tatyana there?"

The phone made a rustling sound and then a lovely young voice said, "Hello?"

"Tatyana."

"Mr. McGill."

"I thought I told you that I didn't want you to get my son killed."

"I was alone and broke. I only asked him to send money."

"What was your boyfriend into?"

"Army weapons. He was selling them in North Africa."

"Were you a part of it?"

"I didn't even know about it until we moved here."

"Were you a part of it?"

"No."

"Don't lie to me now, girl."

"I was not part of it. I went out to drinks with him and his friends. I knew the men he worked with but I did not do anything about selling weapons."

Family, I once read, *the gateway to disaster.*

"I'm gonna give you a number," I told the femme fatale who had somehow become like blood to me. "The man's name is Eric Pardon. I did him a favor once. He owes me. Call him in one hour. He will do what has to be done and send you guys home when the time is right. You understand?"

"Thank you, Mr. McGill."

"Don't thank me, girl. You know I'm only doing this because of Dimitri."

"I know. You're a good man."

"I'm a fool."

ERIC PARDON WAS an old friend. One of the few I had from my days on the other side of the proverbial tracks. He was French but worked for the United States government for a while. He employed me more than once to plant false information on *threats to U.S. security.* When he was compromised I helped him restructure the evidence so that he was deported rather than shot and planted in an unmarked grave.

I LEFT ERIC a voicemail and trusted that he'd do right by me.

TALKING TO DIMITRI, and helping him somewhat, lightened my heart a little. He was in too deep with Tatyana, but there was nothing I could do about that. Hell, I couldn't even solve my own lady problems.

This last thought made me laugh. At the same moment the office buzzer sounded. Something about the synchronicity of the chuckle and the electric hum made me wary. I waited until the buzzer sounded again before opening the drawer in my desk that contained the monitors for the various cameras in and around my office.

Pale as ever, and even shorter than I, Lieutenant Carson Kitteridge stood looking up at the one camera watching him that he knew about. He was wearing a dark-gray suit that he bought in the late eighties.

He pressed the button again.

I got up from my desk and made it all the way to the front before he troubled the buzzer a fourth time.

"Hey, Lieutenant," I said upon opening the door.

"LT."

"You comin' in or am I under arrest?"

"Somebody heard something," he said. "They thought that it might have been a shot."

"Yeah," I said speculatively, "I heard something myself about an hour or so ago."

"Can I come in?"

"Why? I already implied that I have no firsthand knowledge of a firearm being discharged."

"Business."

I shrugged and stepped to the side.

Kit walked in and we took that long familiar walk.

———

"Smells a little like gunpowder in here," he said when he was seated in the chair next to the one Ira Lamont had inhabited.

"I don't smell anything."

The good policeman was looking around the floor, for blood spatter no doubt. Then he raised his gaze.

"Is that painting new?"

"Mardi made me put it up. Said that my office was too austere, something like that."

Lieutenant Kitteridge could smell a lie better than a discharged weapon but he had other business to transact—lucky for me.

He sat back and crossed his right gray leg over his left.

"There was a body found buried in the compost heap in the People's Garden behind St. Matthew's Church," he said, looking into my eyes.

"Down in the East Village?"

"Alphabet City."

"So?"

"It was Shawna Chambers-Campbell," he said, "the sister-in-law of Cyril Tyler, the man who sent the police after you on that extortion charge."

"Whatever happened to that investigation?"

"I'm it."

As a rule I don't share information with the police. Cops have an unerring tendency to turn whatever you say against you. Silence is always the best defense. Kit was a good cop and therefore my enemy despite any comfort we had with each other. No matter how much I helped him, no matter what he might have owed me, Carson Kitteridge would see me in prison if he could.

Regardless of this, I had a case to solve and did not believe I could do it on my own.

"Do you have a picture of the deceased?" I asked.

He took a morgue photo from his pocket and handed it across the desk.

I noted once again how much more natural she looked in death.

"Someone looking very much like this woman came to my office a few days ago and said that she was Chrystal Chambers-Tyler. She wanted to hire me."

"For what?"

"She said that her husband wanted to kill her, that he'd probably murdered his previous wives."

"Her or her sister?"

"If this is who you say it is she was using her sister's name."

"Did she have proof?"

"No."

"Why did she think he wanted to kill her . . . or her sister?"

"I don't know. Believing her story, or at least the money she paid me to believe her story, I went to her husband and asked why she'd be afraid of him."

"What did he say?"

"That he wanted to hire me to find her for him."

"Did you?"

"No. She didn't tell me where she was staying, and I wouldn't have done that anyway. So instead I agreed to tell her that he said he loved her and would never hurt her."

"Did you deliver that message?"

"No. I never saw her again."

"Where's the real Chrystal Tyler?" the cop asked.

"Obviously she left Cyril. That's why he wanted me to find her."

"You think she's dead?"

"Possibly somebody wants her that way. Maybe they've succeeded. I don't know."

"So what do you know?"

"I just told you. The woman you call Shawna most likely came to me saying that she was Cyril's wife. She said that somebody wanted her dead. And now you tell me that she is."

"I want this motherfucker, LT."

"Yeah," I said, standing up from my chair. "Good luck with that."

"Aren't you gonna help me?"

"You just informed me that my client is dead. What else can I do?"

"You can come down to the station for a debriefing."

"Tomorrow."

"Now."

"I have to do something right now, Lieutenant."

"I could arrest you."

"Go right ahead."

Kitteridge stood up.

"Are you making this hard just 'cause I'm a cop?"

"That's part of it," I said. "But the other thing is that I have things to do. You want to question me, and I'm telling you that I'll come down tomorrow."

Kitteridge shook his head and turned away from me.

I followed him toward the exit.

47

I WASN'T REALLY surprised to find Mardi working at her desk. She was devoted to me, but not particularly obedient. She smiled, and I did, too.

"Mardi," Carson Kitteridge said. "You weren't here when I came in."

"Mr. McGill sent me out for something."

"You're working late."

"He pays overtime." That was true.

"You know, if you ever want an honest job I could probably get you an assistant's position in my office. I'm due for a promotion."

"Since that last job you did with Mr. McGill," she said, oh so innocently. "Right?"

"This isn't the kind of place for you," the eternal cop said.

"It's a thousand times better than where I came from."

With a little help from me, Kitteridge had broken the case of her child-molester guardian. He knew what she was talking about. He had a whole file on the indictment, replete with home movies and firsthand journal accounts penned by Leslie Bitterman himself.

"I don't know how you dazzle them, LT," he said.

"Cult of personality," I admitted.

He shook his head and walked out of the suite. He was leaving, but as with all cops he'd be back for more.

WHEN KIT was gone I pulled a chair up to Mardi's desk and stared at her. For maybe half a minute she concentrated on the keyboard, though we both knew that she was a touch-typist.

"Can I do something for you, Mr. McGill?"

"Carson's right."

"I don't know what you mean."

"You shouldn't be working for me. The city gives benefits, and they're able to protect their employees."

"I don't need protection," she said. "I have you."

"You don't understand what I'm sayin', girl. The kind of people who come here, around me, they're dangerous. Killers, some of 'em."

"A killer isn't the worst thing out there."

"Maybe not," I agreed, "but if you got hurt on my account it would break my heart. That's a fact."

Her response was a beatific smile.

"What if I put you in a different office on another floor?" I asked.

"You need me here," she stated as an indisputable fact. "I file your papers, get your coffee."

"In a few years you could run a whole office if you went somewhere else."

"But I don't want that life. I like it here. I like it a lot."

"That guy," I said, "the one who called himself Peters. He

came in here with the intention of beating me until I gave him what he wanted."

"But you didn't let him."

"What if he overpowered me?"

"Then I'd call the police."

"What if he came after you?"

"Get me a gun and teach me how to shoot."

The first time I had ever been aware of Mardi Bitterman she'd asked Twill for a gun so that she could kill the man masquerading as her father.

"Remember the woman who came in here a few days ago?" I asked.

"The one who said she was Mrs. Tyler but was really her sister."

"She's dead."

"What?"

"Murdered."

"What happened?"

I told her everything, even Hush's suspicions about the identity of the assassin. I didn't need to ask her to keep it quiet; Mardi was a soundproof room unto herself. Her secrets were deeper and darker than anything I had ever known.

"What are you going to do?" she asked.

"I don't know. I guess I've been hoping for something to fall into place, a detail or a mistake on Cyril's part. But there's been nothing. So I think I'm going to have to try and set a trap."

"Will that be dangerous?"

"Extremely. And that's why I can't spend my time being worried about you."

"But, boss . . ." She had never called me boss before, "what you don't understand is that being in this office with you is the best thing in the world for me. It makes me feel safe."

"What does?"

"It's the way you look at me, Mr. McGill," she said. "That's the way I want to be seen."

That was the last of our discussion about Mardi leaving my employ. She was going to work for me and I was going to have to protect her. I shook my head and we both grinned.

"Okay," I said, "but will you do me a favor?"

"What's that?"

"Go home now. Go home and leave me here to think."

I TURNED OFF most of the lights in the suite and wandered around the rooms in stockinged feet—plotting. At eight-thirty the sun was still illuminating the city from the farther corner of the western sky. I felt like a foot soldier waiting for the command to go out and die for an idea that I barely comprehended.

I sat down in one of the vacant cubicles in the hallway leading from Mardi's desk to mine. I put my big feet up on the Formica desktop, wondering about toes, claws, paws, and genetic history.

I sat there, speculating, until the phone rang.

It was as if I were waiting for that call, even though I had no reason to expect it.

"Hello."

"Leonid," said my wife of too many years.

"Yeah, Katrina. Why you callin' the office at this time'a night?"

"I tried your cell phone but you didn't answer."

"Oh. Yeah. The phone's in my office and I got my big feet out here in the hall."

"What are you doing there?"

"Looking at my toes," I said. "In the dark."

"What's wrong, Leonid?"

"I don't know. Tell me why you're calling."

"Gordo."

"Something happen?" I sat up straight, suddenly unconcerned with the mystery of evolution.

"Yes and it's wonderful. He walked down the hall without his walker."

"No."

"Yes," she said through laughter. "Elsa was right behind him, but he made it on his own. It's been weeks since he's been able to do that."

"Yeah."

"Leonid."

"What, honey?"

"Come home."

"Not tonight, baby. I have a serious problem to solve. More than one."

"Does it have to do with Dimitri?"

I knew she would pick up on her baby's predicament before long.

"Actually, no," I said. "He's in Paris with Tatyana."

"Paris?"

"Our boy's growin' up."

"That Tatyana Baranovich is nothing but trouble," Katrina said.

"Just the way the McGill men like 'em, huh, baby?"

"When will he be back?"

"Few days."

"With her?"

"No doubt."

"I have to go," Katrina said.

"I'll see you tomorrow. Give Gordo my best."

"THIS IS Mr. Cyril Tyler's private line," prissy Phil said on an answering-machine recording. "No one is here right now to answer your call. If you care to leave a message, wait for the beep."

No promise to call back. No thank you for calling. I was sure that Phil's dreams were filled with the desire for unlimited power.

"This is Leonid McGill calling," I said. "I've tried to get to you every way I know, Mr. Tyler, but you've snubbed me over and over again. So let's try this: either you come to my office tomorrow morning or I go to the police tomorrow afternoon."

I felt satisfied for the first time in many days.

Going down to the utility closet, I pulled out a folding cot, set it up in the aisle and stretched out. I was asleep before my eyes were fully closed.

48

Dreaming is the true genius of man, my father told me one night after one motherfucker of a nightmare. I was six years old and the previous evening I had seen the fifties science-fiction classic *The Fifty-Foot Woman.* She was chasing me down Broadway. The streets were deserted and my breath was ragged enough that my lungs felt like tattered paper. When my father picked me up I was still screaming. I held on to him so tight that my arms and fingers ached. But I wouldn't let go. Old Tolstoy carried me to his favorite chair and cradled me, waiting for the sobs and shaking to subside. When I was a little calmer he told me about dreams and genius. He didn't try to lessen the effect of the dream itself. No. He accepted the fear, and so I did, too. He hailed my shuddering experience as brilliance.

That morning, on the cot in my office hall, I was more than half the way to consciousness but my eyes were still shut and the realm of dreams was close at hand. My thoughts were images instead of logical systems. There was a commune on an upstate farm and a cowboy hitching his palomino to a rail set out just for him. A man wearing a tuxedo but with the cowboy's face came out through the swinging doors (the commune had become a saloon). The front wall of the establishment came loose from the rest of the building and fell on the two men. The horse was crushed but the fancy gentleman was standing in the doorway, and the broncobuster happened to be situated beneath an open window. They were both standing there unharmed, with dust from the heavy impact rising around them.

"Mr. McGill."

Cowboys and communes (a word which rhymed with saloon). And then there were peas in a pod and dumb luck, two phrases somehow having the same meaning in my dream.

"Mr. McGill," a different voice said.

I realized for the first time clearly how difficult constructing a poem must be.

I opened my eyes. Iran Shelfly and Mardi Bitterman stood over me. Their proximity—and me in a bed in a perpetually empty office space—threatened to become my second first draft of a poem that morning.

"Hey," I said.

Iran had on a mustard suit and a yellow T-shirt, both close-fitting, of course. The ethereal Mardi's dress was cream and crowded with rose-colored roses. I inhaled through my nostrils, expecting the scent of those flowers to narcotize me.

"Time to get up, boss," she said.

I sat up, fully dressed except for my shoes. I was hungover but hadn't had a drink. I was an elite mercenary armed with nothing but poetry.

"What time is it?"

"Eight twenty-one," the ex-con told me.

I scanned the floor, focused on my shoes. Before I could lunge Mardi bent down and actually slipped the boatlike brogans onto my still-stockinged feet. This action soothed someplace deep inside.

"Cyril Tyler is in the outer office," she said, looking up at my satisfaction.

"What?"

"He was waiting at the door when Iran and I got here," she continued. "We told him that you weren't in yet. I didn't think you were until I realized that only one lock was on."

"Why didn't he use the ringer?"

"He was pressing it when we walked up to him."

That dream was more potent than I imagined.

"What you want us to do, Mr. McGill?" Iran asked.

I stood up, wobbled a bit, and then everything fell into place.

"You go to your desk, Eye. I'm gonna go down to the toilet and wash my face. In ten minutes you bring Mr. Tyler down to see me," I said to Mardi. "After that get me some coffee and whatever our guest wants."

The youngsters nodded, and I tried not to feel like I was somehow a fraud.

I FILLED the little bathroom sink with the coldest water I could get out of the spigot then submerged my whole head in the bowl. Fifteen seconds down and I pulled my head out. I gazed at my grizzled face in the stained mirror and dunked down again.

After the third immersion I felt almost good.

Bright-eyed, toweled, and dusted with a rolling adhesive lint remover, I was seated behind my desk, only distantly aware of just how little normalcy my life had in it.

The door swung open. Mardi came in, exhibiting perfect posture, followed by the slouching billionaire.

"Mr. Tyler," Mardi announced.

He was wearing a blue blazer, white business shirt, black-and-white tennis shoes, and blue jeans. Mr. Cyril Tyler was not designed to wear jeans, especially not blue ones. He looked like a butler dressed by his four-year-old daughter—a mishmash of good intentions and ill design.

And there I was, an unshaven, rumpled page of discarded poetry, extending a hand and smiling, no doubt wolfishly.

"Good to see you again," I said.

He nodded and mumbled something, sat in my visitor's chair and squinted at the light coming in through the windows.

Mardi backed out of the room but didn't close the door.

"Here we are," I said to the target.

"What was that message you left supposed to mean?" he asked.

Even when trying to be assertive Cyril seemed vulnerable, weak. He was like the heroic bureaucrat Grand, from Camus's great novel *The Plague*, the working-class hero.

"I needed to see you, and everything else I tried failed."

"I was out of town," he said. "I just got in last night and happened to see the blinking light on Philip's message machine."

"Well," I said in my best placating tone, "at least we're here now."

"You weren't hired by Chrystal, were you, Mr. McGill?"

"No, sir, I wasn't, but that's what she said her name was. And you sent Ira Lamont to bully me into saying that, didn't you?"

"Yes, I did, but it was his idea, not mine. And, anyway, I shouldn't have told him to come. I should have waited until I got back to the city and come myself."

"Excuse me," Iran said, coming through the open door. He was carrying a gray cardboard box that had two fancy paper cups in it. "Chai latté for Mr. Tyler and a large French roast for Mr. McGill."

He placed the cups down in front of their respective owners and left, closing the door.

"Where were we?" Tyler asked after the interruption.

"You were telling me why you shouldn't have sent the cowboy to bully me."

"I didn't send him to intimidate you."

"No? Do you know your brother?"

He threw his hands up.

"Ira said that you had come to the house and demanded to speak to me," he said. "I, I was in Europe. I wanted to come down and face you when I returned, but he said that that wasn't a good idea and that he should be the one. He said that you sounded angry and he knew how to deal with that."

"Your brother said all this?"

"Yes."

"So why are you here now?"

"Ira said that you didn't know anything. He said that he thought you were just making it all up. But after I heard that message I knew that he was hiding something from me."

"And what are you hiding, Mr. Tyler?"

He squinted again, this time not from the sunlight.

"Before I say more, Mr. McGill, I want to know why you came to my house misrepresenting yourself."

"That's easy," I said. "I didn't misrepresent myself."

"You just admitted that Chrystal didn't hire you."

"Her sister Shawna came to me and told me that she was your wife. She said that you had murdered your first two wives, that you had lost a lot of weight and were having an affair. She said that she was worried that you were going to have her offed, too. She had a picture of you two arm in arm. I did my homework. Your previous wives had died under mysterious circumstances. What was I supposed to think?"

Cyril sniffed as if I had insulted him.

"I was not having an affair," he said.

"But you did kill your wives?"

Tyler closed his eyes and sat back in the chair. He grimaced and shook his head.

"It's very hard to explain."

"I just figured out poetry this morning," I said. "Try me."

"For a long time," he began, "a very long time, I believed that I had an extra-psychic ability—the power to cause harm to people, a power I couldn't help but despise. If I wanted harm to come to someone, it did. My first wife and I had a fight on our boat. She hit me on the head with a pair of binoculars. I locked myself in the cabin, drank cognac, and nursed an evil hatred toward her. In the morning I was alone on the boat."

"What about Pinky Todd?" I asked. "You nurse a grudge against her, too?"

"She said that she had information about an investment group I belonged to, that she'd discovered certain illegal transactions we had made. For some reason she thought that she could get a better divorce settlement out of me if she held that over my head."

"Sounds like a plan," I said, "except if the victim had an extra-psychic BB gun."

"I hadn't done anything illegal, but I came to a better agreement over a settlement. I was angry. I admit it. And then she was murdered like that. What was I to think?"

"Exactly what Shawna thought—you killed your wife. All that leaves is the affair."

"I had cancer," he said.

I believe that if I had an entire lifetime to consider how he might have answered my question, cancer would never have come up.

"Say what?"

"Colon cancer," he said. "It was pretty bad. I couldn't bring myself to tell Chrystal about it. I believed that if I said it out loud to a loved one, my fate would be sealed. My doctors were in Geneva, and so I pretended to have work there."

"How does that translate into an affair?"

"In order to deal with my state of mind I entered into psychotherapy. Daily sessions. My therapist, a woman named Inola Rice, spoke with me every night on the phone. Chrystal asked if I was talking to a girlfriend, but I told her no.

"The one major thing that came out of those sessions with Dr. Rice was that I suffered from a personality disorder that caused me to believe in magical thinking."

"The belief that your rage caused the deaths of your wives," I said.

"Exactly."

"If all this is just in your head, then who killed Shawna?"

"Oh my God. Shawna's dead?" He seemed really moved, exactly the way you'd expect a man to act over the unexpected death of his sister-in-law.

"Don't you read the papers?"

"I was out of town. I told you that."

"Shawna hired me to protect Chrystal from you. Soon after, she was murdered. Do you have any idea why any of that might be?"

"No, I don't. Dead? I can't believe it."

He seemed so sincere. I wanted to believe him. It was hard to imagine him hiring an assassin. But he was rich. You didn't have to do much when you had the kind of bank book that backed him up.

"Shawna left six kids orphaned," I said.

"I know that. When I leave you, I will find them and bring them home."

"I took them to their aunt."

"Chrystal?"

"I gave her your message. She says that she wants to see you."

"When?"

"I'll tell her about this conversation," I said. "If she wants, after that, I'll call your home phone and make the connection."

"I'll be there."

"I'm sure you will be."

49

THERE WAS AN AWKWARD moment after the end of our conversation. Cyril looked as if he wanted more. I attributed this expectation to the fact that he probably always had people falling over themselves to placate his every whim.

"Is there anything else, Mr. Tyler?"

"Um, I guess not."

"Do you need me to see you out?"

A cold steeliness entered his gaze. The corners of his mouth turned down.

"Certainly not." He got up with as much decorum as he could muster and opened the door all by himself.

Through the doorway I watched him amble past Iran and on toward the exit.

I suppose that I should have been thinking about how to wrangle Tyler into a confession, or at least set a decent trap. But instead I was remembering Mardi saying, *He was waiting at the door when Iran and I got there.*

"Huh."

———

I HAD SOME time to kill, pretty much the whole day. Cyril needed to stew and maybe contact his confederates. I was sure, when not faced by the milksop, that he had caused the deaths of his wives and Shawna. His talk about extra-psychic abilities was just flummery designed to give the police and the courts excuses to forgive him.

I SHAVED and brushed my teeth in the little toilet. On the way back I noticed that Iran had earphones on and an iPod on his desk.

"The music good?" I asked.

He didn't hear the question but noticed that I'd stopped next to him and so pulled off the headset and said, "What?"

"The music. It is good?"

The young man smiled, handing me the headset. I put it on.

". . . Mr. Martins is still sitting in his chair, reading," I said in my ear. "Just like he was doing an hour ago . . ."

"Mardi's been putting your cassette notes on this iPod so that all the cases would be easy to get to," Iran said. "She told me that I should listen to a few of 'em in case I was thinking about taking a job here."

"What do you think?"

"I'm thinkin' that if I wanted to be bored to death I could go back to prison."

ON THE WAY OUT I stopped at Mardi's desk.

"I didn't know that you were moving my tapes to MP3 format."

"Should I stop?"

"You think Iran would make a good operative?"

"I'm not going out with him," she said. "You don't have to worry."

How did she do that?

I WENT OVER to the Thirty-third Street PATH Station and jumped a train to Hoboken. Chalker Road was just nine blocks from the exit. Number 243 was about five blocks on from there.

I should have called first but for some reason I wanted to get the element of surprise into our meeting.

It was a ranch-style home, smaller and yet similar to Cyril Tyler's abode, painted dark blue and bright red. There were two concrete walkways, one leading through the middle of the ragged lawn to the front door and the other at the far-right side next to a divider hedge and running down to a destination beyond the house.

I pressed the nacreous, rectangular button and waited patiently. After a while the door came open and a young woman, in her early thirties, glided up behind the screen in a sleek, brand-new, state-of-the-art wheelchair.

"Yes?"

"Leonid McGill," I said. "I called about Mr. Williams."

"Oh yes," she said happily. "Come on in. Come in."

She rolled the chair back from the doorway with obvious skill and I pulled open the screen door.

The hall would have been wider if there weren't bookshelves on either side. The lower ledges were crowded with books, knick-knacks, and papers, while the higher ones were nearly empty.

This told me that Fawn David lived alone, though this had not always been the case.

She led me down the hall, through an austere-looking living room and into a solarium where three of the walls were made from sectioned glass. The tiered metal shelving on all sides was filled with various shades of greenery. There were little flowers now and again, baby green tomatoes, and crawling vines. Two cats, one white and the other calico, stalked me from the underbrush.

"Sit down, Mr. McGill," Fawn said and gestured.

There was a small, cast-iron chair that had been painted white set next to a violet iron table. I sat, comfortably cushioned by some fat and a lot of muscle. Fawn's heart-shaped face was white like porcelain and yet seemed so soft that I had to hold myself back from reaching out and touching it.

She smiled and I felt a clutching in my chest. This disturbed me but, I reminded myself, I wasn't there for self-analysis.

"You have a beautiful house, Miss David."

"It's really all my mother's doing. She added on the sun room and paid off the mortgage. I just inherited it."

"Is your mother here?"

"She died six years ago."

"I'm sorry."

"This house is all her doing."

"Still, it's yours," I said, "and beautiful."

She smiled brighter and moved her right shoulder in my direction.

I noticed the multicolored cat gazing at me from the depths of vegetation and thought about *the artist*—Bisbe. It struck me that if I made any error, this sunny room and beautiful, crippled woman might be my last moments of sensual pleasure.

"You remind me of him," she said.

"Who?"

"Bill Williams, as you call him. He lived in a room my mother had in back. He helped to build this greenhouse."

"And how do I remind you of him?"

"You use logic to bring happiness. William always looked at the world the way it was, but he didn't let that get him down. He used to tell me that my paralysis would help me hone my attention down to the point where my life would make more sense than most other people's ever would. He was right."

"You could tell that from one thing I said?"

"You look a little like him, too," she said. "I mean, he was tall and slender and his face was long. He had a full head of hair at sixty but your skin color, it's just about the same."

"William Williams is black?"

"Didn't you know?"

"No. All I had was a name."

"You must be a very good detective."

"Either that or a really bad one."

"I don't know how much help I can be, Mr. McGill. I was just twenty the last time I saw William. He moved out and we never heard from him again. He'd be in his late seventies by now."

"I suppose you've had a lot of tenants since then."

"No. Mother got sick not long after William moved and I couldn't really manage an apartment. I suppose whatever was there when he moved out is still in there. It's not easy for me to get down there, so I don't go."

"Would you like to try now?"

"I have no idea where the key is."

"Locks are my specialty."

FIRST I CARRIED a bamboo chair down the slender tree-flanked path to the door of the small rental unit, then I went back up and cradled Fawn David in my arms. After installing her in the chair, I returned for her wheelchair. Only then did I use a special metal tool I carried around in case I encountered a simple lock.

"You're strong and innovative," Fawn said when the lock slid open.

"And I used to be young and handsome, with a full head of hair."

"You're still handsome," she said. "I like mature men."

The room was dusty—very much so. The mattress and sofa chair had been infested by mice, but the table lamp still worked and everything else was more or less unaffected by the passage of time.

Bill Williams had a very austere lifestyle. There was a small table that stood in for a desk, the stuffed chair, the bed, an empty bookcase except for a milk-colored plastic pitcher and cup, and a trunk placed at the foot of the headless bed.

"William would sit at that desk writing all night long," Fawn said. "Back then we had a ramp set up so I could come down. He always stopped working when I came. We talked for hours sometimes."

"Where was he from?"

"He never said. I asked him and sometimes I used to try and

trick him into telling me. But he'd always say that he had no history before he came here. It seemed like some kind of joke."

"Or a man who was hiding from something."

"I used to think that," Fawn agreed. "He was very secretive, but then he was generous, too."

"You mind if I crack open the trunk?"

She shook her head. I got the feeling she was just happy for the company. I was, too.

The lock on the trunk was easier than the door but at first glance it hardly seemed worth the bother. One brown shoe, a wife-beater undershirt, and a frumpy old pair of green gardener's pants was all the treasure it held.

I pulled up the desk chair and sighed.

"It was worth a try," I said.

"William used to take me down to a café not far from here sometimes," Fawn said. "He'd tell me that I could do amazing things if I put my mind to it. I'd have been happy if you found some clue that led to him."

She reached over and plucked out the solitary shoe. Shaking it, a metal locket fell out.

It was at least a hundred years old, made from bronze and silver. The girl tried to pry it open but it didn't want to come.

"Let me try," I said.

It didn't work for me, either.

"Corroded," I said sagely. "There's a Swiss locksmith in my neighborhood. Want me to take it there?"

"Does that mean you'll bring it back?"

"Yes."

"And can we go to that café and have coffee?"

50

EVEN WITH DROPPING the locket off at my neighborhood locksmith I still made it to the Harvell Club by two p.m.

"Good afternoon, Mr. McGill," the young Korean receptionist said.

She was wearing white. All the employees of the club dressed in white. The walls on each floor were a different hue. The entrance, for instance, was all red, fire-engine bright, and loud. The fourth-floor library, where they served cognac, was sky blue from the ceiling to the floor. You had to look out of the window and down on the street if you wanted variety, either that or bring in a color wheel under your coat.

"Hi, Jeanie," I said. "I have a guest coming in later on. He'll be asking for a Beat Murdoch, that's me."

Jeanie had a long face that managed to exude beauty without being pretty; the kind of face that told you to put up or shut up. She smiled briefly and nodded. Members paid a lot of money to be idiosyncratic. I was who I said I was, and that was that.

THERE WAS a phone booth on the library floor. I used it to call Aura's cell.

"Hello?"

"Hey."

"What phone is this?" she asked. "It came up all sevens."

"Harvell Club."

"Oh."

"Did you get the phone turned on in that apartment?"

"Yes."

"You didn't use your name, right?"

"As far as they know Jasper Real Estate wants that line."

"You're sure."

"Yes," she said, barely perturbed. "Do you want the number?"

"Can we get together for dinner tomorrow?" I asked, in some way hoping for another day.

"Maybe we should let things cool down for a while."

I let those words settle for a moment and then said, "Let me have the number."

I should have been happy that Aura was jealous of Chrystal. After all, that meant she wanted something, that she hadn't stopped feeling for me. But that was weak consolation. This being the case, it was hard for me to ask the next question.

"Are you at home?"

"Yes."

"May I, um, speak to Chrystal?"

There came a few seconds of muffled silence and then, "Hello? Mr. McGill?"

"Do you trust your husband?"

"I want to."

"I don't see how what happened to your sister happened

without his involvement. Shawna sent your brother to try and get money out of him, I'm pretty sure of that."

"Where's Tally? I've tried his cell phone but it just goes to voicemail."

"He's sick, jaundice. They got him in a hospital in the Bronx."

"Is he going to be all right?"

"I really don't know. I'll be happy to take you to him, but first I need you to do something for me."

"What?"

"I'm going to call you this evening . . ."

THE NEXT CALL rang once before it was answered.

"Yes?"

"Mr. Tyler."

"Mr. McGill."

"Chrystal has agreed to talk to you."

"Where is she?"

"It's not that easy. You got two dead wives and her sister was murdered. She's going to call you sometime this evening."

"When?"

"When she calls." I liked giving powerful men a hard time. But it also made sense to keep him off balance. If he was the bad man I suspected, he might make a mistake.

"Why should I trust you, Mr. McGill?"

"What does trust have to do with it? All you got to do is sit by your phone from six to midnight and wait for a call."

I hung up on him. That felt good.

———

AFTER THAT I went to a little alcove that allowed me a view of pretty much the whole library floor, including the elevator entrance, from a half-hidden vantage point behind a corner and a potted fern.

Usually I like lying in wait. That's what detectives do, they sit and watch and wait. If you spend enough time in any one spot you begin to notice patterns. After mapping out the geometrical design of the activity of any room or street you start to see where the model breaks down. It is at this point that your job begins.

But that afternoon I was nervous, antsy. Not one connection in my life felt easy. My children and wife, Gordo and Aura, even my client didn't fit in her proper place. There was a killer on the loose and I didn't know what he looked like, nor was I certain about his relationship to the crime. Rather than setting a trap, I felt as if I were in hiding, afraid of some monstrous consequence to my helplessness and stupidity.

Such were my thoughts when I noticed, out of the corner of my eye, the slender and yet elegant profile of my son.

Twill was wearing dark slacks and a light-green T-shirt. His shoes were also dark—fabric, not leather. He hadn't taken the elevator. He'd probably charmed Jeanie into showing him the stairs. This maneuver would allow him to slip into the room and look around in much the same way that I might have.

I smiled because Twill was good, very good; but I was still better.

I watched him move around the periphery trying to suss out who might be the mysterious Beat Murdoch.

After moving forward with no real plan, Twill went to one of the small round pine tables in the center of the room and sat. From there he slowly and meticulously scanned the entire room. Toward the end of this intense study he came across my smiling face.

"Pops?" he mouthed.

I got up and sauntered over to his post.

Taking a seat, I said, "Hey, Twill, what are you doing here?"

"Meetin' somebody. A friend. What about you?"

"Me too."

"Who?"

I smiled and put my left palm down on the table.

"This shit is gonna have to stop, boy."

"What?" he said, still looking for a way out.

"You know what I'm talking about. Those MetroCards."

Twill bit the right side of his lower lip, squinted with that eye, and let his head tilt to the right. It was something like the reaction I used to get from an opponent after delivering a good left hook to the body.

"Damn, Pops," he said. "How'd you get on to me?"

"Twill," I said, "I love you, son. I would do anything to protect you, even from yourself. But you got to straighten up. I'm not gonna be around forever."

Twill sat back and shook his head. I was the only person in the world who could still amaze him.

"What did you think you were doing?" I asked.

"Poor people need to ride the rails, Pop," he said. "It's not like I'm takin' all that much, and I'm providing a service for them that's under the poverty line. I see this more like a political statement than anything else."

"A political statement?"

"Yeah. Like Joe Stalin. You know, he was a bank robber before he became the king'a Russia."

The events and characters of the past are never in control of their own historical commentary, I remembered my father once saying.

I laughed—way too loudly for that particular room.

"Son," I said.

"Yeah, Pops?"

"Please."

"What?"

"I need you to take a period of four years to be guided by me. Four years where you take my lead and don't break any laws without conferring with me first. It'll be like a college education, with the exception that you'll be the only student in your class."

"How does that work?"

"I don't know. I don't, but I'll figure out something."

"Okay, Pops. I'll wait for your lead."

"You have to give up this counterfeiting business now."

"Okay," he said as easily as if I had asked him to pass the gravy.

"What about your partners?"

"I did the whole thing online. They don't know who I am—or at least they don't know that they know. I'll just say I'm turning the business over to them. I got the read/write stripe machine and Internet interface in a basement in Queens."

I ORDERED a cognac and Twill had green tea. We talked for a while longer. I promised to hold the money he'd made thus far and he accepted my custodianship. He told me again that he didn't see what was wrong with what he was doing and I told him to believe in me for the time being.

When I suggested that it was time to leave he got a little cagey and said, "Let me go out there first, Pops. Gimme five minutes and then you go."

"Why?"

"I got these four dudes out there layin' for Beat Murdoch. You know, with guns an' shit."

51

I CALLED HOME on the way over to the apartment Aura set me up with. Katrina answered after seven rings.

"Hello?"

"The old man still walkin' on his own?"

"His blood work is amazing, Leonid. The doctors have him and Elsa down there right now to redo everything."

"What's that mean?"

"Remission."

"No."

"Remission." The repetition of the word proved Katrina's deep knowledge of my soul. She understood my fears and distrust and that I hadn't traveled very far from my early adolescence when my father abandoned us and my mother died soon after. She knew that I needed her to repeat the word in the tone of the emotion it carried.

"He is very healthy, Leonid. He is strong again."

I closed my eyes and stood stock-still in the middle of the busy walkway. People bumped into me and made angry comments but I didn't care. This was the most wonderful, and therefore the most dangerous, thing that had happened in my life over the past year.

Remission. Survival when the odds are against you. Somebody you love who doesn't leave, doesn't die.

"Leonid," Katrina said through the Bluetooth in my ear.

"I have to go, Katrina."

"But—"

"I have to go."

"I want to talk to you about Dimitri."

"If you're worried you don't have to be. Between me and Twill he's fine. And if you're worried about his girlfriend . . . well, I am, too. But what you gonna do when a man falls like that?"

"He's a boy."

"Yeah, maybe. But she is most definitely a woman."

"Leonid."

"If I don't hang up this phone and get my head together I'll probably be dead before morning. Do you understand that?"

"I will talk to you at breakfast."

WHAT I SAID to Katrina was absolutely true. The elation I felt over Gordo's possible survival threw all of my natural defenses into disarray. I wanted to celebrate, to dance in the streets and drink down a whole bottle of brandy. I had mourned that boxing trainer the way the Apostles had grieved over Jesus. He might as well have been dead and buried, but here he was, maybe risen and alive.

I stopped at a little brown stoop on Eighteenth between Sixth and Seventh. There I sat, trying to remember that this was just a lull between rounds, that my opponent had been playing with me up until now and that the possibility of getting knocked out was real, and even probable.

There is no victory until the final victory, my father used to say. His words came back to me and I sighed. *Let your comrades celebrate in their foxholes and their trenches, but you remember that the war is still raging and that your enemy is sharpening his bayonets even while your friends laugh and sing.*

Those words got me on my feet. They propelled me down the street toward a resolution that was uncertain at best.

I HAD MADE it to within seven blocks of my destination when my phone sounded again. I looked at the little blue screen and hit the green button.

"Hey, Z."

"Mr. McGill."

"What you got for me?"

"Do you think I'm beautiful?"

I stopped again.

"What?" There was a smile on my face—I could feel it.

"I want to know what you think I look like."

I drew a deep breath in through my nostrils and took a step.

"Zephyra," I began, "beauty is your ugly-duckling little cousin who's been hiding in the corner ever since you walked in the room. If you were my girl I'd put shutters on the windows and break every camera in the house."

She giggled and said, "You're a fool."

I nodded.

"I'm serious," she said into the unseen silence.

"I'm right, too, girl. And I'm sure you don't need my word for it. So tell me what's wrong?"

"I kinda like Charles."

"You mean Bug?"

"Yes."

"So?"

"I always liked talking to him," she said. "From the first time you took us out to lunch. I told him to lose weight. I really shouldn't have done that, but he wanted to go out with me and I didn't know what to say."

"He's working out three hours a day. Must'a lost twenty pounds so far."

"I know. I don't want to hurt him, Leonid." That was the first time she ever called me by my first name. It was my week for firsts. "And I know if we . . . get intimate I'll probably end up dropping him."

"There's no problem there, Z."

"But he's so serious. He *wants* me."

"Just tell him you can't be like that right now. Tell him that he can go out with you on Wednesdays but don't ask about Friday nights. Tell him that you're still playing the field and that if he wants more he needs to go someplace else."

"But—"

"Tell him that and let him make up his own mind. For him it will be a mitzvah."

"What's that?"

"Something that only a woman like you can do for the man he will become someday."

———

AFTER THAT CALL with Zephyra I was calm again. I don't know what it was about her wish to keep her beauty in check that eased my own fears, but I walked a little faster—and made one last call.

There was no answer but I got a call back in less than a minute.

"Hey, LT," he said.

"You in place?"

"Uh-huh."

"Stay there till it's over, or something goes wrong, okay?"

"Whatever you say."

"Remember," I cautioned, "do not hesitate."

"Never do."

52

I WALKED INTO the fourth-floor apartment on Thirty-first Street for the first time. It was a small two-bedroom with bare, pitted oak floors and smudged, unadorned walls. I moved quickly down the tiny foyer, turning the corner into the living room. The only furniture there was a heavy walnut desk and chair set against a window. A big black phone sat on the desk, and blondish-green Venetian blinds were pulled down over the window behind it. To the left there was a closet door. I dragged the heavy desk across the floor until it was away from the window and facing the closet.

"Home again, home again, jiggety jig," I said aloud before sitting in the chair on the right side of the desk.

I took in a deep breath and entered a number on the phone.

"Hello?" Chrystal Chambers-Tyler said, answering on the second ring.

"Hold on," I said.

I pressed a button and entered another number.

I didn't even hear the ring before Cyril Tyler answered, "Chrystal?"

"Cyril?" she said.

I could hear them both without the aid of the receiver because the loudspeaker was automatically engaged.

"How are you?" the creampuff, maybe killer, asked.

"How are you?"

"I miss you, Chris."

"Mr. McGill told me that you had cancer, that that's why you were on the phone every night and why you lost weight."

"I was afraid to tell you. Even after the chemo worked, I was scared to say the words."

"I'm your wife, Cyril. We should be able to share our hard times."

"I know, honey. Can I still be your baby boy?"

Cyril and Chrystal probably expected privacy on their call, maybe even deserved it, but I wasn't going to sacrifice any opportunity to do my job for something as meaningless as civility.

I listened, without blushing, while the estranged couple talked about what they'd been going through in their solitudes. Less like lovers and more like lifelong friends, they sounded silly and childish. But for three dead women it might have seemed charming.

I was still carrying around William Williams' satchel and took out one of the largest books—Will and Ariel Durant's *The Age of Napoleon* from their eleven-volume masterpiece, *The Story of Civilization*. So while the lovers, one of whom might have been a bona fide serial killer, whispered silly nothings to each other, I read about France.

I had no idea that in 1780, France was the most populous nation in all Europe, including Russia; that Paris was the largest city, with the most-educated populace. My father had taught me a lot about the French Revolution, but he took a definite Marxist slant that left out all the romance and pedestrian contradictions.

In the background, Cyril and Chrystal chattered on about places they'd gone and things that had gone wrong. He apologized, and she held back forgiveness.

And then a chill. Not a lowering of the temperature of the room, which was pretty warm on that summer's eve, but a breeze that shouldn't have been. I cut off the loudspeaker with a finger and looked up.

Instead of green he now wore all black, and he looked all of his forty years, but this was still Fledermaus, the Artful Dodger, community friend of the East Side commune where Shawna Chambers met her end.

"Bisbe?" I said and he smiled. Grinned actually.

The gun was in my pocket and my hands were on the desk.

I wondered.

"You're like the little boy who runs after bumblebees every day for the whole summer," he said in a dreamy voice. "Finally, one day just before the fall, you catch one in your little hand, more because the bee made a mistake than you did something amazing, but now you got an angry stinger up against your flesh."

Instantaneously a knife appeared in Bisbe's hand. It was like some kind of magic trick. His speed and the fevered intensity in his eyes reminded me of a fighter I once battled, a skinny middleweight named Joe Dudd. I should have been able to beat Joe into early submission, but he was insane, living on a whole other level of violence. After only four rounds he had me on my knees, unable to rise.

I looked at a spot on the floor midway between the entrance, where Bisbe stood, and the desk where I sat. I knew that once Bisbe crossed that line I'd be either lucky or dead.

In order to get to my pistol I'd have to pull my hand back and plunge it into the pocket, pull out the gun without it snagging on the fabric, aim, and fire before my throat was cut. Either that or somehow evade his first lunge and grab him. From his speed, I doubted I could complete either maneuver.

Bisbe took a step.

I kept my eyes on his chest to keep him from guessing my real strategy.

He took another step, crossing the line of my unavoidable demise.

I made to rise.

"Stop!" Johnny Nightly, the arrogant fool, said.

Bisbe turned with amazing quickness. I grabbed at my pocket. Johnny fired his silenced gun, but not before Bisbe threw his knife. Johnny grunted and fell back into the closet from where he came. Bisbe was struck in the middle of his chest with a soft-nosed bullet. He should have been dead but wasn't.

Out of reflex I hurried to Bisbe's side. I checked him for weapons while he stared, amazed, at the ceiling. There was nothing—no gun or even a backup blade. He was as much a fool as Johnny.

The pool hall killer lay on his back, half in and half out of the closet. Luckily Bisbe missed by two or three inches and got Johnny just below the left shoulder. His lungs and heart were okay. I didn't pull the knife out but tore off Johnny's shirt to expose the wound and for him to use as a bandage.

"I told you not to give him a chance," I said.

"I never imagined anybody movin' that fast," Johnny said. "I'm sorry, LT."

"He didn't perforate *me*," I said, pressing around the wound. Bisbe moaned.

I put Johnny's hand on the makeshift bandage and said, "Can you hold on to this for a minute?"

"Do what you gotta do," he said.

Bisbe was trying to rise but the wound in his chest was final. He was never getting up again.

"Shit," he said. "Shit."

"Can I do anything?" I asked.

The question seemed to give the killer and idea.

"Forgive me."

"For what?"

"I killed people," he said. "Men and women. Kids, too. If somebody got in the way or they were too close. I, I, I see now, right now, it was all wrong. I had no right . . ."

He coughed and blood came up out of his lungs. He swallowed as if this were just some minor impediment.

He said, "I never even once worried or thought about who I killed. I just did it like Mama used to do chickens and Daddy did hogs. I never cared, but now I feel it, that it was wrong. I feel it.

"Forgive me." He grabbed my forearm with surprising strength.

"I forgive you." What else could I say? "But you know that confession frees the soul. Maybe you could help me."

"How?" he asked. His eyes were looking beyond me into an empty future.

"Who paid you to kill Chrystal?"

Bisbe chose that moment to die. His last breath butted up against my face and the aspect of life fled.

I waited a moment to give the proper gravity to his passing and then I returned to Johnny Nightly.

"Sorry about this, Johnny."

"You told me how dangerous he was and I didn't listen," Johnny said. "The more fool me."

53

I CALLED OUR special line and he answered, "LT?"

"Hey, Hush, you still know that cleaner guy—Digger?"

"Who's dead?"

"Bisbe."

"No shit?" It was the most emotion I ever heard in that ex-assassin's voice—outside his home, at any rate. "You killed him?"

"Johnny Nightly did."

"And he's still breathin'?"

"Yeah, but he got a shoulder wound."

"Gimme the address and leave the keys at the front desk of your office building. Digger'll be there in two hours. I'll cover the eighteen-grand fee. You can pay me back."

The cleaner would come within two hours of picking up the keys, and Bisbe's body would disappear—forever. Digger was one of the many specialists working the other side of the prover-bial tracks in New York. I'd never needed his services before—but there's always a first time.

———

"JUANITA HORN," she said in answer to my second call.

"Can I bring Johnny by, baby?"

"What's the injury?"

ANGELIQUE ARABESQUE picked me and Johnny up in front of the building where the artist, Bisbe, awaited his final rites. She dropped me at the Tesla Building and then proceeded to ferry Johnny up to Harlem, where Juanita would nurse him to health.

"You want me to come back for you after I drop Johnny off?" Angelique offered.

"No, baby," I said. "The business I got needs to be done alone."

She gave me a speculative look, and then snorted, just a little. There had always been electricity between me and the driver. But I was in no mood for any further human contact—unless that connection included Cyril Tyler's blood.

I WAS MAD. Not angry, but insane with rage. Cyril Tyler had fooled me just enough; he embarrassed me. And I'm not the kind of man you want to make a fool of.

I got some tools and papers from my office, dropped off the Thirty-first Street apartment keys for Digger at the front desk, and grabbed a cab up to Cyril Tyler's building.

All I had to do was flash a forged senior city inspector's ID at the beefeater on duty and take the elevator to the eighteenth floor. From there I went out to the fire escape at the end of the hall and climbed up to the vacant nineteenth floor. Using a grappling hook and a thick rope, I crawled up the wall to the roof. It took some struggle, and a couple of times I nearly lost my grip. But I had madness and rage in my sinews—that and real, honest-to-my-father's-not-God's hatred.

I MADE IT across the lawn with no challenge. The door to Arthur Pelham's porch-office was open. The door beyond that was ajar.

This was going to be easy. Digger would make $36,000 off me in one night.

"Mr. McGill," Ira Lamont said from the opening to the hot-pink hallway. "You bring that pistol?"

"I don't need it for you, son," I said.

He took off his lacquered hat and dropped it to the floor, where it clattered and wobbled.

I hate cowboys.

There was some kind of martial-arts style to his attack. It seemed like Brazilian capoeira. He came in low and tried to brush my legs out from under me with a sweep.

I took a long step backward and he tried the same maneuver again. This time I moved to the side and he put his booted foot through the glass window-door of Pelham's office. From there Lamont leapt in the air, a missile of muscle and bone. I waited for him to get airborne before throwing a straight right at the place where his jaw would soon be. When that blow connected, I bounced a left hook off his right temple.

Ira hit the ground like a big bag of sand. He might have been dead, but that didn't bother me. Someone had tried to murder my client, had nearly killed my friend. I myself was living on time borrowed from earlier that evening.

If getting my revenge meant that Ira Lamont had to die, then so be it.

I walked down the long bright hall to the brown-on-brown pulp-fiction library but there was no one there. I wandered onward into a white dining room that was populated by a big wooden table and a dozen chairs. There was a huge chandelier suspended above the dining area but the lights were off. I passed from there into another room, a pale blue and light gray living room. The colors of the room reminded me of something. It was the same color scheme that Azure Chambers had to protect her from any loud thoughts or notions.

Cyril was there, sitting on an oyster-shell-colored sofa, drinking what might very well have been a two-thousand-dollar shot of nineteenth-century cognac. The bottle on the table next to him looked that old. I brought out the gun that I hadn't needed for Ira. I was going to kill Cyril. The only reason I hesitated was that it seemed a bit irrational. But between one dead mother, six orphaned children, and the overweening privilege of the wealthy, I had come for my father's justice, for revenge on the dream that dragged him down.

Cyril was dressed in a faded blue housecoat. Staring up at his Nemesis, me, his gaze froze. I took two steps forward, brought the barrel to the side of his head and set my thumb on the hammer. Something about Cyril's passivity seemed like a confession, the acceptance of his sentence.

There came a whispery sound in my ears. I realized that this was the sound of my blood literally singing for the death of this man.

"Mr. McGill," Chrystal said softly. "Leonid."

If it was a man with a gun I'd've been dead already. I closed my eyes, inhaled deeply, and accepted this perceived death.

Then I raised my lids upon a new scene in the same setting.

Chrystal stepped into my line of sight. She was wearing a revealing negligee and no shoes or slippers. It was the bare feet that told the story.

"What are you doing here?" I asked.

"After I got off the phone I took a taxi."

"Why?"

"I was sure that what Cyril was telling me was true. I know him."

"You do. Then explain this—a man broke into the place where I connected the calls. He stabbed my friend and came within a hair of gutting me."

"Who sent him?" Cyril asked, the muzzle of my pistol still against the side of his head.

"You did."

"Did he tell you that?"

"Conversation wasn't a possibility."

Chrystal took a step toward us.

"Stay where you are," I told her.

"He hasn't tried to kill me," Chrystal stated.

"An armed assassin came to the house where they thought you were calling from. He didn't come there for me."

"What are you saying?" Cyril asked.

"That you hired a man named Bisbe to trace the call that came in here tonight. That he went to the place I'd set up—to kill Chrystal, just like he did Shawna and Pinky and, for all I know, Allondra, too."

"No," Cyril said to Chrystal. "I did not."

She was looking confused, worried.

"I can't believe it," she said to me.

"Your brother told me that he came to your husband to shake him down."

"He did not!" Cyril shouted.

"And what did Tally say was Cyril's answer?" Chrystal asked.

This question wrenched me part of the way out of my murderous haze. Her brother had not actually said Cyril's name. But who else could it have been?

"You can't just kill him," Chrystal said, fighting for her man.

"Yes I can. And it would be self-defense. A guy like this could end my existence with just a shrug."

"I don't believe he did it," the maybe-murderer's wife said.

Her conviction lowered my gun. I sat down on one side of the billionaire, his wife settled down on the other.

"Tally told me that Shawna sent him to shake down somebody for major money. He had some kind of dirt about Pinky Todd and investment fraud."

"Pinky thought that we were involved in fraud," Cyril said. "But we weren't. There was no connection between us and any insider trading."

"But if there wasn't, why would anybody want to kill Pinky or Shawna?"

"I can't tell you what I don't know, Mr. McGill. But Pinky never had a case against me. I agreed to pay her more money only because Arthur said that that would be easier than going to court."

"And you're telling me that Tally never came to you?" I asked.

"He stole silverware from us. Chrystal told Phil that he was not to be allowed in. You remember, honey?"

Chrystal nodded.

"But," Cyril added, "I do remember that Phil told me that Tally had come around a few weeks ago. He insisted that he talk to me and, and Arthur went down to send him away."

"Arthur," I said. "Not Phil."

"Yes."

"What was the basis for the insider-trading claim?" I asked.

"An investment firm named Tagmont," Cyril said. "For all I know they might have really been involved with some kind of illegal activity. I didn't trust them and so we didn't trade with them. That's how our group works. If any one of us is uneasy we don't get involved."

"Who brought this Tagmont group to you?"

"It was a man named Lesser. He was an old school buddy of Arthur's."

Cyril sat back on the sofa while Chrystal and I stared at each other.

"Your sister thought that Cyril killed Pinky," I said. "She sent Tally to shake Cyril down but really it was Pelham that was bent. She didn't know and hired me to protect you from your husband while she collected the money from the shakedown."

"Arthur's been with me for eighteen years," Cyril said.

At that moment Ira Lamont staggered into the room. I was glad he wasn't dead.

"Hey, Ira," I hailed. "Come on in and join the gang."

54

By the time I got home it was very late.

Cyril, Chrystal, and a slightly battered Ira Lamont had gone to spend the night at the Mandarin Oriental Hotel at Columbus Circle—just in case there was another Bisbe out there. They used a special account that Luke Nye maintained at the hotel for his foreign clients. I called Lieutenant Kitteridge and told him what I knew, leaving out the killing of Bisbe and the near death of Johnny Nightly.

"After talking it over with Tyler and his wife we realized that Pinky Todd really did have something, only it was on Pelham and she didn't know it. She went to Pelham to give Tyler her demands. He, Pelham, talked Tyler into paying her off. He said that it would be cheaper than a trial, but she must have come back wanting more. Same thing with Shawna. We figure that Tally told Pelham about Shawna being involved. Pelham pegged her as the brains and had her taken out."

"What about Allondra North?" the cop asked.

"That's Florida's jurisdiction," I said. "Hey—maybe she really did get blind drunk and fall off the side of the boat."

"That's pretty weak, LT."

"Not if your guys find that Pelham's been involved in insider trading with a man named Lesser representing a company named Tagmont. Not if you offer Tally immunity and he tells what he said to the lawyer."

"Who's your client, Leonid?"

"My client is dead, Carson. I'm just tryin' to do right by her."

He wasn't happy with the story; I wasn't either. But it's rare that everything is revealed in a case like this one. Even if Cyril killed Allondra, it was probably because they were fighting, and even then he honestly might not remember.

Sitting at the hickory table in the dining room, I sipped at a snifter of brandy and truly relaxed for the first time in days.

"Mr. McGill?" Elsa Koen said. She was wearing Twill's old plaid pajamas and a nightgown.

"Elsa. Where did you come from?"

"I was sleeping in Shelly's room and I heard you come in." She gave me a tentative stare and then pulled out a chair next to me. "I must ask you something."

"How's Gordo?"

"The doctor cannot find any trace of the cancer in his blood. He will not say that he is cancer-free, but . . ."

"What did you want?"

"Mr. Tallman wants to go home."

"Is he strong enough for that?"

"He still needs help, but if someone were to come by one or maybe two times a day, that might be enough."

"He'd probably get better even faster in his own home," I said. "You know, Gordo likes to be independent."

"Yes," Elsa said, "but I'm worried about him, about his mind."

"He seems to be thinkin' okay to me."

"He told me that he wanted to hire me to be his full-time nurse. He said that he would pay my fee."

"So?"

"I told him that this was three hundred dollars a day including agency fees, and he said that was fine. I know that you had to take him in when he got sick. I understand that he is a poor man. Maybe, maybe he's confused."

My lawyer and I were the only ones who knew that Gordo owned the twelve-story building that housed his boxing gym, that he was a millionaire several times over. I only took him in because he needed to be among friends.

"Don't worry about it, Elsa," I said. "If Gordo wants you, and you're willing to work for him—"

"Oh yes," she said. "He is a wonderful man. The only reason I say this is that maybe he is having trouble thinking. I would come help him for nothing."

"No need for that," I said. "We'll make sure you get paid."

"Hello, you two," Katrina said from the doorway.

She was wearing a fancy dress designed for someone twenty, or maybe thirty, years younger; still, she looked pretty good in that pink-and-red party frock. Even from a distance we could see the effects of the wine, smell the perfume, and divine the sex. Elsa couldn't hide her embarrassment for me.

But I was beyond jealousy that night. I'd solved the case, concealed a killing, saved a life, and had come within a millimeter of murder. In that dress Katrina was the sour cherry on the ice cream sundae of my week.

"Hey, babe," I hailed. "Elsa says that Gordo's goin' home."

"That's wonderful," Katrina exhaled. She seemed to ride the

current of her fragrant breath from the doorway to a seat at the far end of the table.

"It was your feeling for him that brought him back to life," she said. "Your strength, Leonid, and Elsa's passion for him. No, no, don't turn away, Elsa, I can see how you feel. I know what it's like when something crazy gets into your heart."

Silence followed my wife's keen perceptions. We were all thinking about *something crazy* that had gotten into us in spite of all intentions. We didn't look into each others' eyes because there was too much truth in that.

Finally Katrina levered herself up on her feet and said, "I really have to get to bed. The girls and I went to that wine bar on Seventy-ninth. Oh . . . too much."

She walked unsteadily out the door while Elsa and I kept vigil on the truth she'd spilled like a ruptured oil well into the Gulf of Mexico.

"There was a package for you," Elsa said after a long contemplative pause.

She got up and walked out into the hall, leaving me with thoughts that ranged down the many paths of my misspent life. I started counting breaths and reached seven before Elsa returned.

She held in her left hand a shapeless parcel of brown paper wrapped in thick packing tape. She held the thing out to me and turned to leave as soon as I took it.

It weighed no more than a few ounces, with *Leonid Trotter McGill, Apt. 11f* penned in a fanciful hand that you got the feeling would have been even lovelier writing in some other language.

I needed my penknife to rip open the tough packaging. Inside the tape and brown-paper shell was a ball of wadded-up newspaper that held the locket loaned to me by Fawn David. It had been cleaned and polished meticulously. There were a few scratches along the sides of the ornament, probably due to the jeweler's attempt at opening it. I pressed the little button on the side and the disc sprang open.

Within there were pictures pasted to either side. On one side was a photograph of me and my brother, Nikita; on the other was a smiling pair, my mother and Tolstoy—otherwise known as William Williams.

Looking at the photos, I felt numb and stupid. My father had survived years after I thought he'd died, after my mother had perished pining for him.

Maybe he was still alive.

My cell phone sounded. It was a relief to answer.

"LT."

"Yes, Lieutenant?"

"We went to St. Benedict's Hospital to talk to Theodore Chambers. He told us that his sister sent him to talk to Tyler but that he only made it to Pelham."

"And?"

"Theodore told Pelham that he was representing both sisters, that Chrystal had the damning information and that Shawna needed to get paid.

"We went to Arthur Pelham's residence and asked him to come down to the station for a little talk."

"What he have to say?"

"He said that he needed to put on some clothes."

"And?"

"He shot himself in the head in the head."

I was in an emotional state of shock. The repetition seemed mechanical, as if maybe the phone instead of a human being was doing the talking.

"He killed himself in the toilet?" I asked.

"I guess you were right about something. We'll start a full investigation tomorrow."

I tried to have some kind of feeling about the news: joy at the resolution of a case, sadness at the death of a man cornered by his own sins, relief that the trials were over. But in reality I felt nothing. My father might still be alive. Who cared about some lawyer eating a bullet?

55

It took three weeks to get a meeting set with Harris Vartan. First he was on a business trip, and then some kind of emergency arose. I spoke to his assistant, Hamish Oldhan.

"I'm sorry, Mr. McGill," the assistant to the Diplomat of Crime told me. "But Mr. Vartan wanted me to make sure and to tell you that you are uppermost in his thoughts and that he will call you at the first opportunity."

In the meantime I went out to see Fawn David, ostensibly to return her locket but actually to see if I could find out anything else about the father whom I had in turns idolized, lost, hated, and forgiven, and who I now saw in a shadowy cleft somewhere between reunion and revenge. I had the jeweler carefully and completely remove the picture of my brother and me. Fawn loved the locket and said that she would carry it always.

I scoured the room where my father had lived while I was acting out a criminal life across the river in Manhattan. There were no more clues. He wasn't anywhere on the Internet or in any of a dozen libraries I'd sifted through.

Elsa took Gordo home to his rooms atop the building no one knew he in fact owned. Katrina made sumptuous meals and smiled more brightly every day. Only the fact that she drank too much let on that there was something unresolved in her life.

The Artist, Bisbe, disappeared off the face of the earth. Chrystal and her six nieces and nephews moved into Cyril Tyler's rooftop home with little worry of him slaughtering them in their sleep. Ira Lamont called the office one afternoon and asked if I'd like to give him a rematch.

"You caught me off guard," the cowboy complained. "If I knew you was a boxer I'd have planned it different."

I just hung up on him.

Two days later Chrystal called to tell me that Cyril would be out of town for a few days.

"I hear you," I said. "But you and me both know where that'd go."

"Are you afraid?" she asked.

"Petrified."

"So is that a no?"

"Yes, it is."

AND THEN ONE EVENING, sometime after ten and before Katrina returned from her night out with *the girls*, my cell phone sounded.

"Hello?"

"Mr. McGill," a man said.

"Hamish."

"Tomorrow afternoon. Anywhere in Manhattan you want. Shall we say about two?"

"The Red Lantern on Forty-eighth," I said. "I'll be bringing two guests."

———

TWILL, IRAN, AND I arrived at the Oceanus Hotel's premiere restaurant at one. I wanted some time with the young men before
Vartan arrived. He wasn't meeting me for the meal at any rate.
The young men had hamburgers and I ordered a simple pasta
laced with butter and shavings from a black truffle.

"You should come into the gym sometimes, Twill," Iran said.
"I could put some muscles on you."

Iran was used to the pecking order of the streets. He was a
dominant character who liked to keep the younger thugs in line.

"I don't think so, Mr. Shelfly," my favorite son said.

"Why?" Iran pressed. "You like gettin' your ass kicked?"

"It's the refutation of the three ems."

"Huh?"

"I don't need money, mamasitas, or muscle to make me a
man. And if anyone wants to question that, I got a whole pocket-
ful of answers."

I didn't laugh because Iran was a good kid and deserving of
respect. But I did wonder where Twill picked up the word "refutation." He was full of surprises.

"You hear from your brother?" I asked to head off any possible confrontations.

"Him and Tatyana be home Thursday."

"Our house?"

"Naw. You know Moms wouldn't be happy with that. They
stayed longer 'cause Taty knew where her man had holed up a
little cash. They got me to get 'em a place in Prospect Park."

I was just beginning to decipher the ramifications of Twill's statement when Harris Vartan entered the dining room. His three-thousand-dollar suit was the color of raw copper, and the jade ring on the baby finger of his left hand was brighter than emerald.

As he walked up to the empty seat a waiter came out and placed a plate laid out with a broiled chicken breast, French-style green beans, and two boiled new potatoes. Another waiter waltzed over to place a goblet of blood-red wine at his right hand.

"Twill," the Diplomat greeted. "Mr. Shelfly."

No idea how he got Iran's name, but I wasn't surprised. Harris Vartan lived in Chicago but knew more about New York than Mayor Bloomberg.

After we'd all muttered our hellos, Harris took a bite of chicken and a sip of wine.

"Excuse me, Harris," I said, "but it's hard for me to tell who's working for whom. You sent me on a journey that nearly twisted my head off."

"Is he still alive?"

"He was fifteen years ago."

"Any clue as to where he is now?"

"Why do you need to know?"

Vartan placed both hands on the table and looked me directly in the eye.

"Because," he said, "Clarence taught me everything of importance that I ever learned."

I smiled, while my two young charges shifted with mild discomfort.

"You're his son and you deserve to know the truth," Vartan said. "You have been working for me because . . . this is my debt—now paid."

He ate a little more.

The young men remained silent, and so did I, for a time.

"Iran here has a problem with a stupid man," I said halfway through Vartan's meal.

"Oh?"

"If you owe me something I'd like you to solve that problem."

"Give him Hamish's number and consider it done."

After that the ice was broken and Harris engaged Twill and Iran in a conversation about basketball. I listened, mostly. The words meant nothing to any of us.

When the meal was over we all walked out onto Forty-eighth Street and Harris got into a limo sedan.

"Who was that guy?" Iran asked me.

"Nobody," I said.

"What now, Pops?" Twill asked.

"I'd like to offer both you boys jobs working for me," I said.

"Sorry, Mr. McGill," Iran said. "Gordo already said he wants me to be a part-time manager at the gym. I think I'm better suited for that kinda work. I mean, I'll be happy to help out if you need anything, but the gym's a better place for a guy like me."

"Okay. You do what you think is right."

Iran shook my hand and punched Twill's arm. He ducked his head and turned to walk away.

"You really want me to work for you, Pop?" Twill said when Iran was out of earshot.

"More than anything, son."

"Why's that?"

"Because you're the finest man I've ever met, and because I'm your father."